MW00477348

SENTENCED TO BE A HERO

I

The Prison Records of Penal Hero Unit 9004

Rocket Shokai
Illustration by MEPHISTO

YEN ON

NEW YORK

Rocket Shokai

Illustration by MEPHISTO

Translation by Matt Rutsohn
Cover art by MEPHISTO

I

This book is a work of fiction. Names, characters, places, and incidents are the product of the author's imagination or are used fictitiously. Any resemblance to actual events, locales, or persons, living or dead, is coincidental.

YUSHAKEI NI SHOSU CHOBATSU YUSHA 9004TAI KEIMU KIROKU Vol.1
©Rocket Shokai 2021
First published in Japan in 2021 by KADOKAWA CORPORATION, Tokyo.
English translation rights arranged with KADOKAWA CORPORATION, Tokyo, through TUTTLE-MORI AGENCY, INC., Tokyo.

English translation © 2023 by Yen Press, LLC

Yen Press, LLC supports the right to free expression and the value of copyright. The purpose of copyright is to encourage writers and artists to produce the creative works that enrich our culture.

The scanning, uploading, and distribution of this book without permission is a theft of the author's intellectual property. If you would like permission to use material from the book (other than for review purposes), please contact the publisher. Thank you for your support of the author's rights.

Yen On
150 West 30th Street, 19th Floor
New York, NY 10001

Visit us at yenpress.com • facebook.com/yenpress • twitter.com/yenpress
yenpress.tumblr.com • instagram.com/yenpress

First Yen On Edition: August 2023
Edited by Yen On Editorial: Emma McClain
Designed by Yen Press Design: Eddy Mingki

Yen On is an imprint of Yen Press, LLC.
The Yen On name and logo are trademarks of Yen Press, LLC.

The publisher is not responsible for websites (or their content)
that are not owned by the publisher.

Library of Congress Cataloging-in-Publication Data
Names: Shokai, Rocket, author. | MEPHISTO (Illustrator), illustrator. | Rutsohn, Matt, translator.
Title: Sentenced to be a hero / Rocket Shokai ; illustration by MEPHISTO ; translated by Matthew Rutsohn.
Description: First Yen On edition. | New York : Yen On, 2023- | Contents: v. 1. The prison records of Penal Hero Unit 9004 —
Identifiers: LCCN 2023015000 | ISBN 9781975368265 (v. 1 ; trade paperback)
Subjects: LCGFT: Light novels.
Classification: LCC PZ7.1.S517814 Se 2023 | DDC [Fic]—dc23
LC record available at https://lccn.loc.gov/2023015000

ISBNs: 978-1-9753-6826-5 (paperback)
978-1-9753-6827-2 (ebook)

10 9 8 7 6 5 4 3 2 1

LSC-C

Printed in the United States of America

CONTENTS

Being sentenced to serve as a hero was the most severe penalty one could be given. At least, that was what the Allied Administration Division had decided. Some even called it a punishment worse than death.

Heroes served on the front line of a never-ending battle against the Demon Blight. Not even death would relieve them of their duty. Their sentence had no end. Even if they fought for a hundred years, they would not be released. Only by killing every last demon lord spreading the blight would they earn amnesty.

And the thought of accomplishing such a feat was mere fantasy—an impossible dream.

"This is bad," said Dotta Luzulas gravely. "It's over. I'm done for."

Again? I thought. Dotta had a habit of getting into trouble at least once every three days. It was all because of his damn sticky fingers. How sticky, you ask? Well, so sticky he was found guilty of treason and wound up here, sentenced to be a hero. He'd apparently been involved in more than one thousand cases of burglary before he was arrested by the Holy Knights and thrown in prison. I suppose you could call him a world-class prodigy at petty theft.

Dotta Luzulas would steal anything. I still remember bursting into laughter the day I heard the story of how he stole one of the royal family's dragons. But my smile vanished as soon as I heard it had eaten his left arm. He was a crazy guy, but so were most heroes.

"Hey, Xylo," he said. "What do you think I should do? I—"

"About that." I decided to shut him up, pushing back his face as he approached. "Do you think we can talk about it tomorrow? Maybe you haven't noticed, but we're kinda busy right now. They're working us to death."

That wasn't just a metaphor. This was a battlefield. We were in a forest at the northern end of the Federated Kingdom—the last nation left to mankind. The snow was deep, and the wind was so cold that it seemed to pierce our skin.

Humanity was on the verge of losing even this place, known as

Couveunge Forest, forever. Due to various circumstances, Dotta and I had been hiding out here since morning. Night was slowly beginning to fall, and it was already obvious how goddamn cold it was going to be.

A deadly mission was waiting for us, too: the Demon Blight. It wouldn't be much longer until it arrived. And now Dotta, back from scouting, kept mumbling, "This is bad." Hearing him was giving me a headache—I just wanted him to shut up.

"Dotta, do you know what our job is here?"

"I mean...I've got a good idea."

"Then tell me."

"We're going to fight a demon lord," he muttered, face pale as he slipped a small bottle out of his pocket. It looked like a kind of alcohol from the eastern islands made from beans. Booze like that wasn't cheap.

"Exactly... By the way," I said, pointing at the bottle in his hand, "you stole that, too, didn't you? From the Verkle Development Corporation's wine cellar, I assume?"

"Heh. Nice, right? I swiped it from one of the high-ranking army guy's tents."

Dotta mirthfully took a swig of the high-end alcohol. He looked pretty happy for someone who had just committed theft.

"I snatched the most expensive-looking one. I mean, it's the owner's fault for just leaving it out in the open like that."

"Pretty sure it's the thief's fault regardless. Besides, I doubt a guy like you could even appreciate the good stuff."

I grabbed the bottle out of his hand and took a sip. The alcohol burned as it went down. I was only trying to lighten the mood. I didn't care how it tasted, and I didn't want to get drunk.

"This is some strong stuff."

"Yeah. There's no way I'd be able to do this otherwise. We're about to fight a demon lord's army... There are going to be a ton of them, aren't there?"

"It's a big one. Around five thousand faeries were affected. Makes you wanna cry, doesn't it?"

That was the number we were given anyway. There might be a few less, thanks to our nation's grand and noble Holy Knights. I didn't want

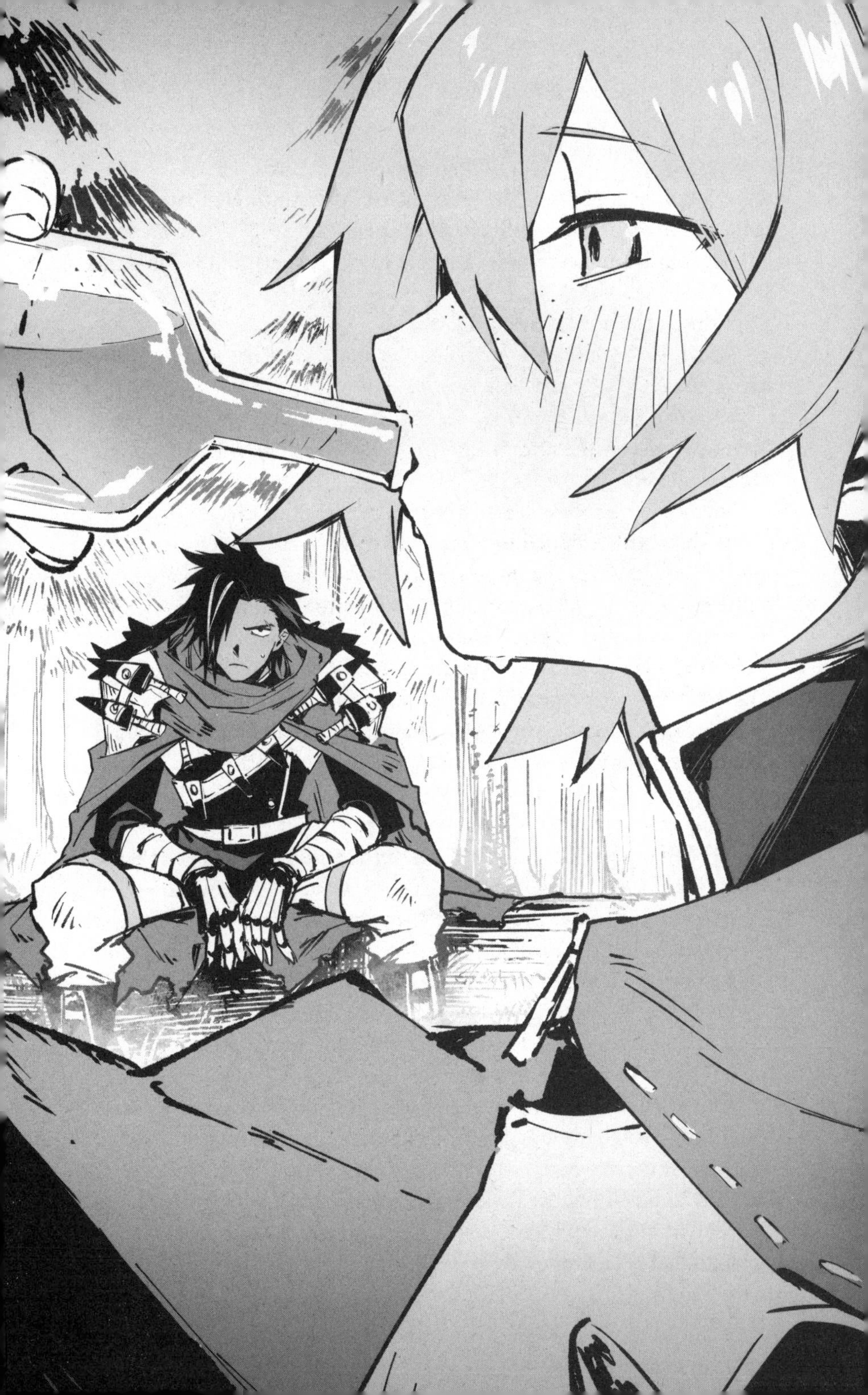

to get my hopes up, though. Even if they took out one or two thousand, it'd hardly make a difference. Because...

"It's our job to keep those faeries at bay," I reminded him. "Just the two of us."

I thrust the bottle back at Dotta.

"Yeah..." He nodded, stricken. "I know. We're heroes. We don't have a choice."

Exactly. We were criminals, serving time as heroes. We couldn't disobey our orders—the tattoos known as *sacred seals* on the back of our necks made sure of that.

Heroes like us were denied even the release of death.

If your heart stopped or your head was blown off, you would be resurrected to fight at the front lines all over again. Being brought back to life might sound like a good thing, but naturally, it had a few drawbacks. Each time you were revived, you would lose another piece of your memories or your humanity. Some had lost their sense of self completely and were now nothing more than walking corpses.

We didn't have the privilege of choice. There was nothing we could do but fulfill our mission. This time it was very straightforward, at least when you put it down in words:

Support the withdrawing troops.

We had to cover the Holy Knights' retreat until they were out of the forest. This Demon Blight outbreak had spawned around five thousand faeries and was drawing ever closer. There were no other forces covering or supporting us. The mission was to be carried out by Penal Hero Unit 9004 alone, and the only people in that unit available to fight were me—Xylo—Dotta, and a completely useless commander. Everyone else was either out for repairs after having their arms or heads or whatever blown off, or busy with another mission. They wouldn't be any help here.

Our mission would be deemed successful only if we got the majority of the Holy Knights to safety. If we failed or tried to escape, the sacred seals on our necks would torture us to death. The entire thing was utter bullshit, to put it lightly. I wanted to beat to death whoever came up with the idea. It could have been worse, though. At first, even crazier missions had been proposed, like defeating the demon lord at the heart of the Blight.

We had our commander to thank for working out our current deal. While he may have been a coward with no leadership or fighting ability, his past as a con artist and political criminal meant he was extremely skilled at deception.

"We'll make it through somehow, though…right?" Dotta glanced at me, then took another swig. "After all, we have you, Xylo—our hardest hitter. Plus, we're heroes. Worst-case scenario, we get turned into mincemeat and are resurrected later, so—"

"You don't get it," I said. Dotta needed to face the truth. "How well our resurrection goes depends on the condition of our body. If we're mincemeat or they can't recover our corpses, we'll pay the price when we're brought back to life."

Plus, we couldn't expect the Holy Knights to come back and find our dead bodies under all this snow. Not when the forest was about to become contaminated by the Demon Blight.

And if those in charge didn't have our bodies, even if they resurrected us, there would be serious side effects concerning our memories and sense of self. I'd only heard rumors, but supposedly, the way they revived heroes was by dragging our spirits out of hell and driving them back inside our flesh. The better your corpse's condition, the more precise the resurrection. But those tasked with reviving us weren't afraid to use someone else's body as long as they had all the necessary parts. However, resurrecting someone with bits and pieces taken from other people increased the chance of failure…or so I'd heard. That was how some heroes were reduced to mindless walking corpses.

"Wait! Are you serious?" Dotta seemed genuinely taken aback.

"Why would I lie?"

"I had no idea. You sure know your stuff, Xylo."

I didn't reply. Maybe that information hadn't been made public. Or maybe Dotta had simply died so many times that his memories were fuzzy.

"That's why we have to do a good job," I said. "I don't have time to listen to your nonsense."

"But—"

"And even if I did, I don't want to."

"Listen! I might've *really* messed up. What do you think of this?"

He pointed at the ground to his side. Beside him was a large object that I had been making a point of not looking at.

"...What is it?"

A coffin. That was the first thought that came to mind. It was a rectangular box with complicated designs inlaid on its surface that could fit someone of small build. If it was a coffin, it must have been for someone important.

Once again, I found myself doubting Dotta's mental state.

"Dotta... Why the heck did you steal a coffin?"

"I don't know... One moment, I'm thinking how gorgeous this box is and how I could steal it, and the next..."

I didn't comment any further, and I wasn't going to complain about his kleptomania at this point. There was no cure for his impulses. He would steal anything, and the more useless, the more he wanted it.

I was more concerned about something else.

"Hey, Dotta. About this coffin..." I placed a hand on the lid. "Could there be...someone in here?"

"Yep." He answered just like I thought he would. There was something seriously wrong with this guy. "I was wondering why it was so heavy when I was tugging it along, so I checked, and—"

"Would it have killed you to check before you snagged it?! What are you doing stealing dead bodies anyway? Makes no damn sense."

"That's what I want to know! By the time I came to my senses, I was already stealing it!"

"The hell are you getting mad at me for? Want me to kill you before the faeries have their chance?"

Now I understood why Dotta had said "This is bad."

Judging by the fancy coffin, it seemed safe to assume that the person inside was royalty—or at least a noble. Someone really, *really* important must have gone to battle with the Holy Knights and died.

The Knights would definitely panic once they realized the coffin was missing. I had only one thing to say to Dotta.

"Take it back where you got it, numbskull," I said, removing the lid to check the body.

Even I wasn't sure why I opened it.

Maybe it was morbid curiosity. If the person inside was a royal or a noble, I might know them. I had a whole list of such people I wanted to kill. I felt a wave of dark, illogical anticipation.

I didn't have any solid, specific reason for what I did, though. It was simply in my nature to be reckless.

"Dammit."

I immediately regretted removing the lid.

There *was* someone inside: a young girl—and she was frighteningly beautiful.

She was wearing the white military uniform of the Holy Knights. Her silky golden hair and snow-white skin made me think she was from the north. Her face was like a work of art, but what captivated me the most was the seal on her left cheek that stretched down to her neck. The marking likely continued all the way to her heart. I knew what it meant.

It looked similar to the sacred seals on our necks, but it was something very, very different.

"Dotta, this is bad."

"Figured. She's royalty, isn't she?"

"No. She isn't even human." I felt a stinging sensation in my head. "This kid's a goddess."

"Huh? A what?"

"A goddess. Do I have to spell it out for you?"

She was one of mankind's last hopes: a life-form created for war using the wisdom of the ancients. That was the exaggerated sales pitch anyway. But I knew the truth, and the truth was…that the sales pitch was exactly right. Goddesses were the strongest weapon we had against the demon lords.

The Holy Knights were an organization meant to protect and use these goddesses as weapons. There were only twelve goddesses in existence—well, eleven now. The fact that Dotta had managed to steal one was frankly amazing. In any other situation, he'd probably have gone down in history as the greatest thief who ever lived.

"Take it back to where you found it. Now. You've really outdone yourself this time. Even *you* know what goddesses are, right?"

"Huh? I mean…I've seen one from far away before, but…is this girl really one of them?"

I could tell from his face that he was clueless. *Right. I guess the general public has no idea what goddesses are supposed to look like.*

"She's just a little girl. I mean, the goddesses I saw were like a humongous whale or a big hunk of iron or—"

"It's hard to explain, but there are goddesses like that, too."

Goddesses were superweapons created in ancient times, now beyond our understanding. Some took bizarre forms incomprehensible to humans, while others did not. Furthermore, while they were called goddesses for the sake of convenience, not all of them had a female body, at least as far as I knew. Not that I knew all that much.

"Dotta, listen up."

It was going to be a hassle, but I decided to give him a brief explanation. That is, until I heard a roaring in the dim twilight.

It was the sound of horns and drums.

The human army—our allies. The Demon Blight Army didn't use instruments like those.

"What?" cried Dotta. "They're already here?"

I reflexively clenched my fists, then opened them again. On my palms and wrists, from my elbows to my shoulders, my skin was completely covered in sacred seals meant for battle. They had a really long-ass name—Super Multipurpose Bellecour Mobility Thunderstroke Seal Compound—and they were the only possessions that weren't stripped from me when I was sentenced.

"Sounds like there's a throng of faeries over there. Can you see them, Dotta?"

"Hold on."

Dotta opened his eyes wide and peered into the depths of the twilight. His eyes were extra sharp thanks to years of training them as a thief, so he had excellent night vision.

"…Yep, they're already on the move."

"All right, let's do this."

"H-hold on. I need to mentally prepare."

"You really think there's time for that? Try asking the sacred seal on your neck. First, we've gotta meet up with the others."

I was referring to the guys with the horns and drums. They didn't sound far, and judging by the volume, it probably wasn't the Knights' main unit of more than two thousand strong. These were most likely scouts or some other detachment.

"H-hey! Wait for me!" Dotta cried.

"Hurry. Don't forget the goddess, either. You stole her, so you carry her!"

"Huh?! Uh... Seriously? It's really heavy. Plus, I don't think taking it with us right now is the best idea, since—"

He started to argue, but I glared at him to shut him up. He loaded the coffin onto his back and followed me.

We traveled silently and at a brisk pace. I could feel the countless enemies lurking in the forest. Sounds of shouting and metal scraping filled the air as the horns and drums slowly died off. I had a bad feeling about this. We had to hurry. They shouldn't be much farther. I was sure of it.

It wasn't long until we reached an exposed slope. Then, right as I was about to slide down...

"Wait! Xylo, this is kind of b-bad!"

...Dotta suddenly grabbed me by the arm, almost sending me toppling over. I glared at him, about to yell...but stopped myself when I saw his serious expression. He was holding out a spyglass to me.

"We're already too late. Look."

"Hmph."

I crouched, spyglass in hand, peeking through the darkened trees. While I wasn't able to see clearly like Dotta, I could make out a little thanks to the lit torches scattered on the ground. That's when I realized what he meant.

The faeries beat us to them, huh?

The Knights must have been a detachment. There were only about two hundred soldiers, each one of them already dead or at death's door. There were signs they'd fought back, but the swords in the corpses' hands were broken, and giant frog-like monsters—faeries—were devouring them as we watched. I arrived just in time to see one gobble up a sword, complete with the arm holding it, chomping the limb clean off the body. These types of faeries were known as fuathan, and they were frogs transformed into monsters by the Demon Blight. They stood as tall as an adult human and had exceptional maneuverability.

Ribbit. Croak. Crrroak.

Their eerie cries could be heard coming from the darkness as their fiercely glowing eyes bounced into the air. The Knights' detachment was being trampled by them. One soldier screamed frantically as a monster bit his leg and swung him around. Another held up his shield, only for a faerie to jump onto it, crushing him as it chewed off his head. The soldiers had no chance. Blood, guts, and dirt scattered into the air.

"Th-there's nothing we can do, Xylo," cried Dotta, now white as a sheet. "Let's get out of here and hide somewhere until it's over! The faeries have already made it this far. They'll reach us any second now."

"You're right. They're moving quickly."

The detachment seemed to have been decimated mere moments after noticing the enemy, even though they were expecting an ambush. It was a testament to the faeries' superior mobility.

"But there are still survivors. Time to rescue them, Dotta."

"What?!" His eyes went wide as he stared at me, as if he thought I was a total idiot. "There's no way."

"Some of them are still hanging on."

Perhaps a little less than twenty. They were forming a circle as they tried to fight off the attacking fuathan.

"We'd be in a far better position if we helped them and had them join us."

"Yeah, if by 'better,' you mean 'dead'!"

"Listen, dum-dum. Our mission is to help at least half of the Holy Knights escape, and every person saved increases our chances of succeeding. Besides…"

"Besides…?"

"I'm in the mood to fight already, dammit." I smirked. I had more than enough reasons lined up. "Let's do this. We're saving them."

"F-fight…"

I jumped at the sound of a voice. It wasn't Dotta's. It was faltering and tinny. That was when I realized the lid to the coffin had been removed and the goddess was sitting up, emerging from the box. Her eyes flickered the color of flames as she pierced me with her glare.

"Fight… S-save… Yes," murmured the goddess as she calmly rose. "What wonderful…words. It appears…you are…my knight."

She paused here and there as she spoke, breaking up her words. Her golden hair danced in the wind, shooting out sparks, and she looked me over from head to toe with her fiery eyes. Eventually, she raised her eyebrows slightly, paused for a few seconds, and nodded.

"Very well." Her speech gradually became more fluid. "I will give you a passing grade."

"What?"

"The battle is about to begin, yes? And not just any battle—a battle to save others. As a goddess, I shall grant you victory. Therefore…" The goddess brushed back her golden hair, sending powerful sparks into the air. "When every last enemy has been defeated, you are to shower me with praise and pat my head."

There were various types of goddesses, each with their own unique personality, but they all had one trait in common: They were proud warriors with a strong desire for approval. I knew this very well because I had once been responsible for operating one.

"…Dotta." I wrapped my arm around the neck of the small man standing to my side and began to squeeze. "You were right for once. You *are* done for."

"Gaaah… You think so? Really?"

"Yeah, really."

It was all Dotta's fault. I squeezed my arm tighter around his neck.

"She's a goddess, no doubt about it. And…she's probably the *thirteenth* goddess. The one who's never been activated…until now."

The fight between mankind and the Demon Blight had been going on sporadically throughout history. If you went back to the very first war in ancient times and counted up, this would be the fourth such conflict—officially known as the Fourth War of Subjugation.

The first Demon Blight outbreak of the current wave was discovered a little over twenty years ago, deep within the mountains of a newly developing region far to the west. It was known as the Serpent.

This name stemmed from rumored sightings of a giant snake among the residents of a nearby settlement, and with the appearance of this snake, all hell broke loose. Attacks on humans weren't the only problem. The trees in the forest grew twisted and warped, small animals and insects transformed into monsters, and the land began to rot. Those bitten by the snake died, only for their corpses to rise and attack the settlement at the foot of the mountain.

But reports of these events were disregarded as tall tales and backwoods gossip. Even the Verkle Development Corporation's newspaper all but ignored them. When they heard that multiple villages had been destroyed, people dismissed it as merely an exaggeration.

The Third War of Subjugation had ended more than four hundred years ago, and many didn't even believe it was real. They thought the Demon Blight existed only in the tales of wandering minstrels and storytellers.

And so they were late to react.

Only after the mayhem really started to spread did the Holy Knights take action, forced to destroy an entire mountain with a scorched terrain seal. And even this was ultimately treated as mere rumor—or at best, something happening far away that no one needed to worry about. Some laughed it off as overblown hearsay.

By the time they discovered it was all true, it was too late. The Demon Blight had already emerged in multiple locations and begun expanding with blinding speed.

That was how humans lost half of their habitat—and how we ended up here.

I could see shadows jumping in the depths of the darkness. This was the distinctive movement of faeries known as fuathan. They were extremely vicious creatures.

Actually, that was something all faeries had in common: They would indiscriminately attack any other living thing in sight. I didn't know why, but according to Temple scholars, they were like manifestations of each creature's nightmares. I couldn't make heads or tails of that, but their appearance and ecology were certainly the stuff of bad dreams.

That's why I had to dispose of them as quickly as possible, before they slaughtered the rest of the Holy Knights clinging to life in front of us.

Yeah, forget about the goddess for now. Don't let her distract you.

Right now, I had to focus on one thing: fighting.

"Dotta!"

I pulled a knife from my belt and gripped it with my right hand. The sacred seal on my palm gradually warmed, streaming power into the blade.

"Follow my lead. Where are the faeries densest? We'll strike there to get the enemy's attention."

"Can't say I'm too excited about this..."

Dotta seemed a little frightened, but I wasn't going to let that stop me. I had already decided how we would do this. If we wanted to help the Holy Knights retreat, then we were going to have to pull off one hell of a diversion.

"Ten o'clock, one fingerbreadth toward nine." He groaned, gazing into his spyglass. "And the densest spot seems to be...around thirty-seven steps from here."

Dotta may have had good night vision, but this feat required more than just his eyesight. He had what you might call a bizarre sixth sense. His fear seemed to have made him incredibly sensitive to the presence of other living creatures, and he was unbelievably accurate in measuring the distance between himself and any such target.

"...Ah, I see."

Just when I'd finally managed to forget about her, I heard the goddess's voice.

"The scrawny man has exceptional eyesight."

What a rude thing to say about Dotta, I thought as she took a step out ahead of me.

"Now, my knight," she continued, "what is our strategy to win the battle?"

"Uh, Xylo?" said Dotta. "She's, uh..."

"Huh? Oh..."

I wasn't sure how to answer as Dotta turned a troubled gaze on me. This was bad. Really bad. A goddess was talking to me. I had to be careful about what I said.

"You mean those puny faeries...?" I began. "Well..."

We shouldn't use her powers carelessly. I was well aware of that.

"We... We couldn't possibly borrow your mighty power for such a small task. Just, uh, stand over there and watch over us."

"Oh my. Modest, aren't we?" She was clearly pleased. "But there is no need to be shy. You may depend on me. Allow me to show you my might."

"No, I'm not being shy. I—"

I began searching for the right words to turn her down, but it wouldn't be so easy.

"Xylo, we're in trouble," Dotta said, voice trembling. "One of the faeries noticed us!"

"Dammit," I cursed. *But what the hell? Bring it on.*

"What are we gonna do, Xylo?"

"We're fine."

I thrust my knife into the air, then swung my arm, launching the weapon straight forward like an arrow. It ripped through the air and struck its target like a bullet.

A brief flash of light illuminated the darkness.

Then an explosive roar.

A massive quantity of heat gushed forth, ripping apart each tree, rock, clump of soil, and fuath in the blast. I could feel the air pressure even at a distance. But this was actually a low-level blast. If necessary, I could unleash enough power to reduce a small house to ash. This time my attack had a blast radius only wide enough to take out something like a carriage.

Incidentally, the blast didn't come from the knife, but the sacred seal on my palm. It was something I'd used in my previous occupation. All but two of my sacred seals were rendered useless when I was sentenced to be a hero, and this was one of the two I had left.

This seal of heat and light's official product name was Zatte Finde, which supposedly meant "big candy" in the ancient kingdom's language. It was a cutting-edge tool used to battle the Demon Blight, and it allowed you to transmit the seal's power into an object and transform it into a powerful destructive force.

It was kind of like a flashy firecracker you could throw.

"We've got their attention now. All according to plan," I said, feigning calm. Panicking would only cause Dotta to run away.

"I-is everything really working out?"

"Damn right it is."

It was obvious that the fuathan were in chaos after the blast. In the wake of the sudden strike, they were having a hard time gauging how much of a threat we posed. They were now clearly more focused on us than the soldiers forming a circle.

I glared back at them, already sliding down the slope.

"Dotta, spray 'em with bullets! Once you're done, run in! Don't fall behind and don't forget to bring the goddess!"

Dotta took a short staff out of his belt and held it up at eye level.

"I feel like I'm gonna throw up...," he said, tightening his grip on the staff. A sacred seal was carved into the weapon.

This thunder staff, an outmoded product named Hilke, was created by the Verkle Development Corporation long ago. According to the sales pitch, its sacred seal gave it the power to unleash bolts of lightning difficult to both dodge and defend against. It took quite a bit of skill to aim, making it only a little better than a crossbow.

And Dotta was no expert.

While he had excellent eyesight and was quick to sense an enemy's presence, he lacked the talent needed to control sacred seals. But even his limited skill could be of use depending on the situation. Like when a horde of faeries all rushed in to attack at once.

A bolt of lightning flew out from the tip of the staff, accompanied by the sound of cracking metal. At the same time, one of the fuath's heads went flying, chunks of flesh going every which way and drawing even more of the enemy's attention.

"Ah! I hit one!" said Dotta, sounding pleased. "Xylo, did you see that?! I hit it!"

"With this many, I'd be more impressed if you missed. Now keep backing me up! And don't even think about hitting me, or you're dead!"

I flew through the trees, grazing them as I went, and plunged into the middle of a group of fuathan.

"Out of my way," I spat, stepping into a marsh of blood, flesh, and filth. After activating my sacred seal, I threw another knife and took out two fuathan at once—drawing their attention much more effectively than any verbal introduction. Another blinding ray of light was followed by an explosion and the grating cries of our enemies—and complaints from Dotta, of course.

"Um, sorry. It takes a ton of effort not to hit you..."

Hmph. Pretty cocky thing to say for someone with zero skill. He couldn't hit me if he tried.

"Just keep shooting and don't stop!" I yelled back. He probably heard me.

A few more bolts of lightning soared through the air as I kept running, throwing my knives. Soon we'd made quick work of every last faerie. Kicking burnt hunks of monster flesh out of my way, I called out to the surviving soldiers.

"Hey! You guys still alive?"

There were even less of them now—around ten. Barely even enough to form a circle.

"You're…"

One of them—so young he still looked like a boy—stared at me. Or rather, he stared at the sacred seal on my neck.

"…You're one of the penal heroes? What are you doing here…?!"

A mixture of relief and shock left him in a state of confusion—relief that he was safe and shock that the one who saved him was a penal hero.

We didn't have time for any of that, though. I counted the number of knives I had left. We may have stopped the first wave, but there was probably another horde of faeries on their way, and handling them all would be impossible. We had to run, but…

"…Just go away. Leave us alone," barked the young soldier. He fixed us with a resentful glare as he propped up an injured, unconscious ally against his shoulder. He was obviously exhausted himself, able to stand only by using his spear as a cane.

"What a disgrace, to be saved by penal heroes…!"

"Huh? What the hell…?" Dotta looked back at me, puzzled. "Uh, I'm pretty sure this is where they're supposed to thank us. Am I wrong?"

While I didn't agree with him completely, it did bother me.

We'd saved this punk's ass and he'd just told us to go away. Fine. Running away and leaving them behind would be much easier. We could use them as a decoy and break through the enemy lines. But…

"I understand how you feel, my knight."

Before I knew it, the goddess was standing by my side. She was a little out of breath, but it seemed she'd kept close behind us the whole time. She elegantly brushed away the hair clinging to her forehead.

"We could never run away and leave them behind. Those were your thoughts just now, yes? Allow me to handle the rest. I can take care of these weak, filthy faeries in the blink of an eye."

"No, uh… That's…"

I tried to come up with a reason to refuse, since using a goddess's powers would only make the situation worse for us. We could still fix this. We could still secretly return her to the Holy Knights before they noticed. But once she used her powers, there was no going back. I had to come up with something, even if that meant making it up on the spot.

"W-wait!"

But while I was desperately racking my brain, one of the soldiers shouted, his eyes on the goddess. He sounded panicked.

"What is the meaning of this? That blond hair, those eyes… Don't tell me…"

The cat was out of the bag now.

"Why is she with you?! What have you done?!"

"G-give it a rest already! This is no time for us to be arguing! We're on the same side! More importantly, Xylo…!" Dotta raised his voice, cutting off the soldier. He probably didn't want any of them to figure out he'd stolen the goddess. "The next wave is coming. They've already seen us. We have to do something!"

"Good point," I said.

We couldn't hold them back with Dotta's poor aim alone, and the soldiers we'd saved were all too injured or exhausted to move. We couldn't rely on their help. I was worried I didn't have enough knives left to handle the next wave, but I didn't have any other choice.

"Goddess, we have this under control, so you don't have to—"

Just then, we ran into yet another problem. I was holding the goddess at bay, unsheathing my next knife, when…

"Xylo! Dotta!"

…someone screamed right into my ear. It was the kind of piercing shriek that could blow out your eardrums. Both Dotta and I knew exactly whose voice it was, and we both covered our ears with our hands.

There was no point to the gesture, but we couldn't help it. The sacred seal on our necks was relaying this voice to us directly—yet another of the mark's special features: long-distance communication. And there was no escape from this, either.

"We're in trouble. Listen carefully! Everything's a mess. A real mess."

This was our so-called commander—the cowardly, useless con artist and political criminal Venetim Leopool. When he did bother to contact us, it was always to tell us something had gone wrong, just like Dotta. At times, it would be some dumbass order from the people in charge; other times, he was just letting us know how much worse the situation had gotten.

"It's just awful. I think we're done for. Xylo, do you have time to talk?"

"No!" I shouted, knife in hand, allowing the seal on my palm to infuse it with power before throwing it into the distance. Another explosion. Jiggly pieces of fuathan flesh flew into the air. I'd managed to take out the vanguard that saw us. That should buy us some time.

"You hear that? Does it sound like I have time to talk?"

"No. But I'm afraid you'll be angry with me later if I don't tell you this now."

"I'll be pissed either way! Now, what is it?!"

"The Holy Knights have started moving."

"Perfect! So they've already started to retreat? If that's all you have to report—"

"They're heading straight for the Demon Blight."

I couldn't believe what I was hearing. I asked him to repeat it.

"Wait. What was that?"

"The Holy Knights in the forest have regrouped and are lining up for battle against the Blight. They seem intent on stopping the enemy from advancing any farther."

"...Why?"

"You think I know?" Venetim laughed carelessly. *"The two armies are about to clash... What should we do?"*

Hell if I know, I wanted to say. Did nobody let these Holy Knights in on the plan? Or were they told and they just decided to ignore it? The Holy Knights I knew were military specialists to the bone. This kind of maneuver—sacrificing heroes as the army withdraws—should have been routine.

"Hey!" I yelled at the soldiers to our side, who were apparently so exhausted they could no longer stand. "What's that captain of yours thinking? Was this the plan from the start?"

"...Yes," replied the young soldier from before. He could barely speak. "We never believed the penal heroes would help us withdraw. Besides, Captain Kivia... No, we, the Holy Knights, value honor. We wanted to strike back at the enemy, and—"

"Are you stupid or something?"

I wanted to kick the crap out of each and every one of them, but I didn't have that kind of time right now. My entire plan had just come crashing down. I couldn't leave them sitting here in the forest while I still had orders to support their withdrawal, and there was no way in hell I was going to let them fight the Demon Blight head-on. At this rate, us heroes were going to die nasty deaths and the Holy Knights would be all but wiped out.

After all, we had their trump card, the goddess, here with us.

This is just great...

There was only one thing we could do now. If the Holy Knights weren't going to withdraw, then...

"Xylo." Dotta looked like he was about to cry. "What are we gonna do?"

I remained silent as I looked at Dotta and the ten or so soldiers behind him. Each one of them was wounded and drained. Their faces were clouded with despair. And yet they looked at us as if clinging to their last sliver of hope. *I don't like these guys. I hardly know them. I wish I'd never even come here*, I thought.

"...Goddess."

"Yes?" she replied, smiling from ear to ear. "You need my help after all, don't you, my knight? It is finally time to fight back, yes?"

"Yeah... It's...time to fight back."

She hadn't heard my conversation with Venetim. She was still misreading the situation. She didn't know who we were—who I was. In other words, I was deceiving her. But I had to do it.

"Goddess, please lend us your strength," I said, loud and clear. "Change of plans, Dotta. We're going to defeat the demon lord."

"What? Are you serious? There are five thousand monsters out there. Do you really think we can win?"

"What insolence," said the goddess. "Of course you can win. You will have my assistance, after all."

The goddess elegantly bowed.

"Now, my knight, it is time for you to make me an offering for our pact."

"...I know."

I unsheathed a knife and ran it down my right arm. I felt a sharp pain as blood began to flow.

This was how you made a pact with a goddess: The knight had to offer a part of himself as evidence of the agreement. Then you exchanged an oath. It was an arrangement between the goddess and a single knight, lasting until one of them died.

Only after forming a pact could a goddess use her powers for mankind.

"Please help us," I said.

"Then do you vow to display your greatness as my knight?"

"I do," I replied without a moment of hesitation.

Wait. That was a lie. I did hesitate, but only once the words had left my mouth. *What have I done?* I thought.

"Very well." Nevertheless, the goddess cheerfully brought her lips to my wound. "It will be my pleasure."

Judging by her doll-like features, I figured her lips would be hard as glass, but that was not the case. Her soft, smooth lips pressed against my arm, and I felt a fire ignite at the back of my mind. It was as if I'd regained a part of myself that I hadn't used for a long time, or that I'd forgotten. I could tell she was smiling. Her entire body shone even brighter than before.

Now I've done it.

For a brief moment, I closed my eyes and saw sparks on the back of my eyelids. It felt like a door had been opened in the depths of my heart. This was evidence that a connection had been made. I knew well that there was no turning back now.

You might say I had taken the first step past the point of no return. This was how I threw my life away all over again.

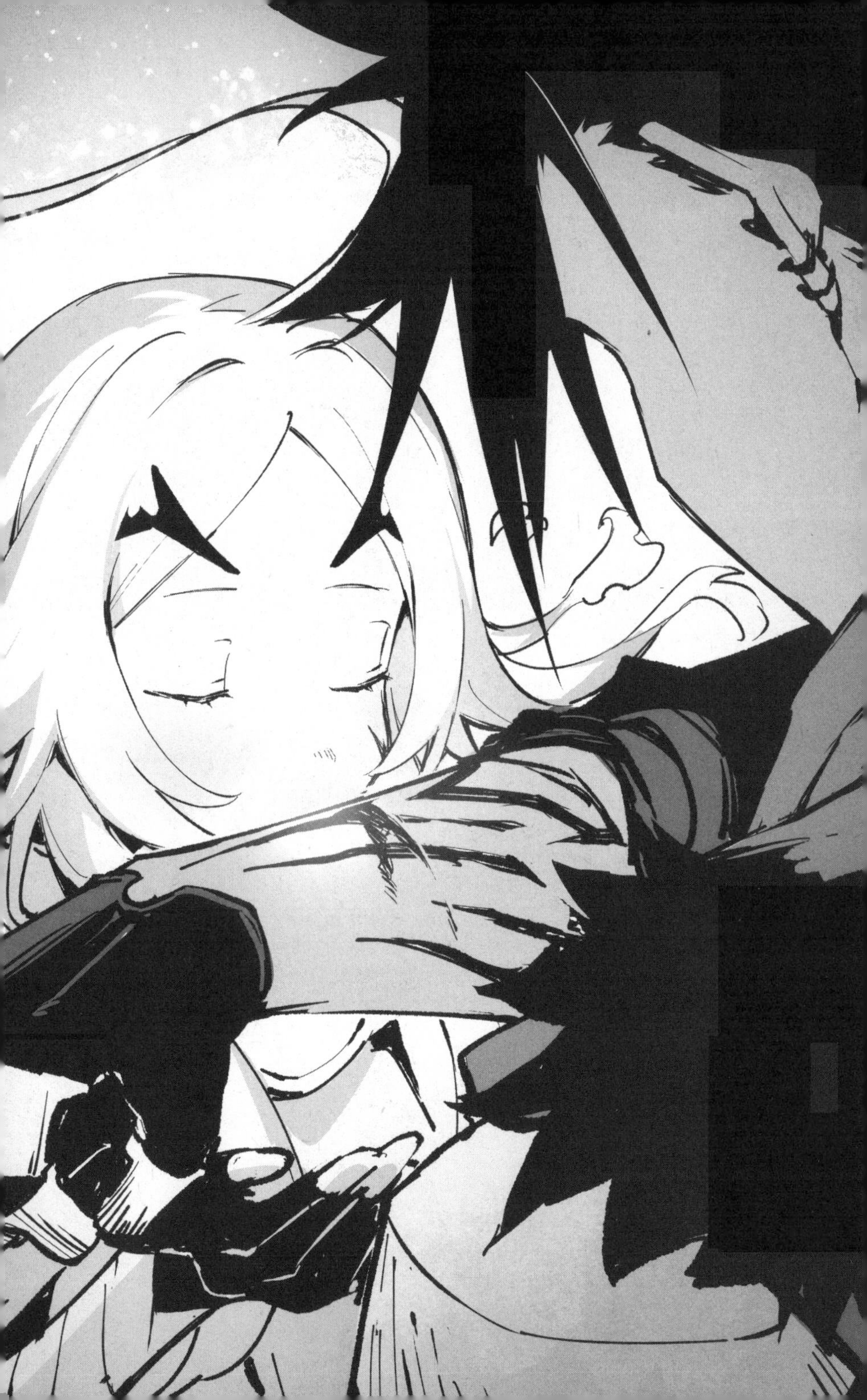

Goddesses were weapons—living weapons.

According to the history books, they appeared during the Great Civilized Era, at the time of the First War of Subjugation. For thousands of years since then, they would reawaken when the Demon Blight arose, then, their duty fulfilled, they would return to sleep in their coffins. Apparently, though it was not understood why, they lost most of their memories during this long slumber. Whatever the case, they were the guardians of this world and its inhabitants.

Each goddess had the ability to call forth something from some unknown place to fight against the Demon Blight—in other words, they had the power to summon. According to Temple scholars, goddesses were a type of gateway.

The nature of their summons was different for each goddess. Some brought forth humans, while others manifested natural phenomena such as lightning or storms. There was supposedly even a goddess who could summon visions of the future.

They required no instructions or manuals to operate them. Once a Holy Knight made a pact with a goddess, they instinctively knew what their goddess could summon and what they were capable of.

In that moment, I understood it all.

"Teoritta?"

That was the name of the young girl with golden hair who had sucked my blood.

"Yes, my knight." She brushed back her hair, causing sparks to fly.

"Xylo." She knew my name as well. "What sort of blessing do you desire?"

I saw the glitter of steel behind the flames in her eyes. Swords. Countless blades of steel: famous swords, cursed swords, treasured swords, holy swords—waiting far off in the void to be summoned.

"Go on. Pray for what you desire."

The goddess of swords, Teoritta. That was all I needed to know. I understood exactly what she could summon.

"A fence," came my brief reply.

Teoritta and I shared a basic sensation outside of intent or volition. You might call it a kind of mental picture. It allowed us to share knowledge of such things as each other's abilities or our next move in battle. I knew this feeling well. This was what made goddesses humanity's trump card.

Simply summoning something powerful wasn't enough. Sharing that ability with someone versed in war and military strategy and allowing them to operate it was what made their powers unparalleled.

"What have you done...?!"

The young soldier with the Holy Knights was furious—or perhaps it would be better to say he was in a state of grief. His face was twisted in despair. If he had the energy, he probably would have lunged at me.

"What have you done?! Forging a pact with the goddess—"

"Shut up," I shot back. "I didn't have a choice."

I'd be revived if I died, but not them. None of the surviving soldiers were capable of fighting. They were completely drained. Either way, there was no time to scrutinize the morality of my actions.

"Xylo, the n-n-next wave is coming!" shouted Dotta, his staff held aloft.

"I know."

The fuathan were almost here. Their jiggling, dark bodies ripped through the forest like a tidal wave of mud.

"Is it just me, or do they seem even more ferocious than the last batch? What are we gonna do?! We're gonna die!"

"Like hell we are, dum-dum," I replied confidently, and pointed at the incoming fuathan. "Teoritta! It's time to push back! Give 'em everything you've got!"

"'It's time to push back,' you say? I like the sound of that." She grinned happily and rubbed at the empty air with one hand. "Words fitting of my knight. Allow me to grant you a blessing."

A sound like air ripping rang out. Immediately, silver rain fell from the sky—a rain of hundreds of swords. Even in the darkness, the blades glittered brightly enough to block out everything else, searing their image into the back of my eyeballs.

With this much steel falling all at once, there would be no way to dodge. The swords mercilessly tore through the fuathan's bodies all at once. The sound of rending flesh and ear-piercing cries harmonized like a chorus of death before the blades pierced the ground, creating a barricade between the fuathan and us. It was exactly what I had ordered. We now had a fence to protect us, and more than half of the fuathan were dead.

"Whoa! Incredible...!" Dotta grimaced and grabbed his nose. The muddy fluid from the fuathan's bodies now covered the ground, letting off a terrible stench. "So this is what a goddess can do, huh? She's so strong...!"

"Yeah. But that doesn't mean we can slack off. Shoot, Dotta!" I shouted while sprinting toward the fence of swords. "Don't let them get any closer. Annihilate every last one."

I grabbed a sword stuck in the ground and raised it into the air with my right hand. My last job had beaten into me the correct techniques for throwing spears and swords.

I used my sacred seal to infuse the object with power. Just speaking for myself, there was no way I could miss from only twenty or thirty steps away. I twisted my waist and used the movement of my upper and lower body to launch the sword.

It released a flash of light at the center of the fuathan horde, then exploded. This blew up a few more, allowing us to shave off several groups of enemies in a single throw. Bits of fuathan flesh, blood, and dirt mixed together to form a terrible scene.

"Geh... I feel like I'm gonna throw up again, but for a whole different reason," Dotta said, unleashing more bolts of lightning from his staff.

His aim was total garbage, and he was doing a terrible job of slowing down the enemy. But thanks to the fence of swords, we still managed to avoid their attacks. Whenever a faerie tried to leap over the barrier, I sliced them down myself with one hand.

At that point, a few fuathan started to flee the battle. Even they seemed to understand how much more firepower we now had on our side.

"I-is it over? Can we relax?"

"Yeah. But come on, Dotta, you really have the worst aim. You didn't hit a single enemy during the second half."

"Heh-heh… Yeah, uh… To tell the truth, I don't really like hurting people."

"What are you talking about? You break into people's houses and steal from them. I know you killed people during burglaries."

"I don't like hurting people, but I put in the effort to do it anyway back then. I think I deserve some praise for my hard work…"

I didn't think hard work was the issue here, but it was probably a waste of time talking spirituality with Dotta.

The fuathan were running away, and it seemed safe to say we'd survive the second wave. Dotta dropped to the ground and desperately tried to catch his breath. He was a real chicken at heart.

"How was that, my knight?"

The goddess Teoritta stood before me, puffed up with pride. Looking at her more closely, I noticed how short she was. Her head only reached my chest.

"Were you touched by my blessing? Awed by my grand power, which annihilated the faeries and protected you? …I give you permission to praise me and worship me to your heart's content."

She spoke with extreme arrogance, but she looked almost like a child. Her eyes, the color of fire, sparkled as she thrust her head in my direction expectantly.

"Xylo, I have given you permission."

I knew what she was trying to say. I could see the image in my mind.

"Rub my head and sing my praises," she continued.

In other words, she wanted me to give her head pats and tell her what a good girl she was.

But if I do that...

I hesitated. The whole thing left a bad taste in my mouth.

Goddesses valued human praise above all else, and humans knew and took advantage of that fact. But that didn't matter to the goddesses—they needed that praise. Without it, they couldn't survive.

Was it really all right for me to go along with that? I felt like a hypocrite.

"Oh. Xylo, Dotta, you two are still alive?"

An unpleasant voice stung my ears the instant I reached out to touch her. It was our commander, Venetim.

"Why do you sound surprised?" I asked.

"Yeah, you don't even sound like you care! Why don't you spend some time on the front lines, Venetim?"

For once, I agreed with Dotta.

"Y-yes, I understand you two are working extremely hard. I will consider it." Venetim sounded a little intimidated.

"Talking outta your ass again, huh," I said. "Was that supposed to be a joke?"

"Even I could tell that was a lie," Dotta chimed in.

"Ha-ha-ha. We can continue this conversation another time. More importantly..."

He forced a laugh and changed the subject. What a worthless piece of garbage.

"Getting back to the previous topic... What are you two doing now? You still need to save the Holy Knights... If they're wiped out, we'll be in a lot of trouble, right?"

How could he be so flippant about this? He was just as involved as we were.

"Yeah, no way," Dotta groaned. "We're getting out of here. If the Holy Knights wanna fight and die, that's their problem."

"I know, I know. But aren't you forgetting something? If over half of them die, that means both of you die as well, and who knows what they'll do after they resurrect you. They might burn you alive all over again for all I know. And that would really hurt...I assume."

"Ngh..." Dotta wrapped his hands around his head and looked at me. "What should we do, Xylo?"

"Wipe that pathetic expression off your face! What is there to think about?" Teoritta scolded. She must have understood what was going on from Dotta's whining. She glared at him and stuck her finger right in his face. "There is no need to run away. We must move straight on to our next battlefield. Isn't that right, my knight?"

"All right, I heard both of your opinions, so could you be quiet for a second?"

I couldn't gather my thoughts with both of them babbling at me. I took a deep breath and decided to deal with Venetim first.

"Venetim, think you could negotiate some sort of deal for us? It's the only thing you're good at, after all."

"Very well. Give me some time, and I will see what I can do."

"Hey! Don't you lie to me. You'd never agree that easily!"

I immediately called his bluff.

This man breathed lies. I knew how he thought, and I knew the position he was in. As our commander, he directed us from outside the forest, all the while under the supervision of a royal correctional officer.

That meant he was the only person who could assess the situation on the fly and control this penal hero unit full of hardened criminals. At least, that was what he needed the royal correctional officer to believe, and he was doing a good job of that so far.

Venetim was unreliable and useless for the most part, but he was also shrewd and clever, and somehow he'd managed to earn the affection of his fellow criminals anyway.

That was the image he had to project, and he was good at it thanks to his experience as a con man. Once, he'd fooled the royal family, and he'd been in the middle of selling off their castle to a circus when he was caught. That was how good he was.

The real Venetim was indeed unreliable and useless, but none of us liked him, let alone trusted him. Even in emergencies, he was all talk. Whenever he said he would help or look into something, it was an act. He wasn't really going to do anything.

And now that the exasperatingly noble Holy Knights were rushing recklessly into battle over some stupid sense of honor, Venetim had come to the conclusion that we were all going to die.

"Allow me to handle things, Xylo. I am your commander, after all. I need to show off from time to time."

"You're only saying that 'cause you know the correctional officer can't hear us!"

"Now, if you will excuse me…"

"Trust me. You're gonna pay for this later—… Oh. Hold on."

I suddenly realized there was a way Venetim might prove halfway useful.

"Where are the Holy Knights right now? Have they made contact with the enemy?"

"Uh…"

A long pause followed. He probably hadn't bothered to check until now. Or maybe he was checking something with the correctional officer. *Stop wasting my time and have that info ready when you call, dammit.*

"They seem to be encamped a little to the north at the…uhhh…second crossing along the Purcell River. Sounds a little far, huh?"

"That's not far at all."

I rolled my eyes in renewed irritation. He didn't even know where we were. At least he'd done something for us. We were lucky the Holy Knights were so close.

In that moment, did I really have a choice?

We could have given up on saving the Holy Knights and hung ourselves. As heroes, that was always an option. We'd probably suffer an awful resurrection, but maybe we'd get lucky.

…No way. I can't do that.

This was a bad habit of mine—a part of me I couldn't change. Sighing in resignation, I glanced back over my shoulder at the beaten-down soldiers, most too exhausted to speak.

"What are you guys gonna do?"

"…We've already decided to fight and die by Captain Kivia's side," said the youngest soldier, staggering to his feet. "We have to meet up with the others."

"Don't even bother. You'll only get in the way. Your allies will die while we're protecting your wounded asses." I spoke harshly on purpose. I was used to being despised. "Head south."

We'd driven back the faeries attacking this detachment. All I had to do now was distract the enemy and meet up with the main force.

"The surveillance unit keeping an eye on us is stationed at the southern end of the forest. Once you reach them, make sure to punch a guy named Venetim for me. I'll be on my way to see your captain to air all our grievances."

"...Unbelievable." The young soldier seemed to understand what I meant by "airing our grievances." "You're really going to help us withdraw?"

"Not like I have much of a choice. I formed a pact with the goddess."

The soldiers looked conflicted, like they weren't sure how to feel about any of this. It made sense. They'd been saved, but their saviors were penal heroes. Plus, one of them had formed an unauthorized pact with a goddess. Confusion was the logical response.

To think I'd end up doing this again.

With another deep sigh, I turned around and looked at Dotta. "Nothing has changed. We're continuing the mission as planned."

"Xylo..." Dotta looked extremely uneasy. "I'll ask you one last time. Are you really planning on defeating the demon lord? Are you out of your mind?"

"I know what I'm doing. First, we're going to meet up with the Holy Knights before they get routed. That's the only thing we can do."

"Oh my!" It was Teoritta who reacted first, clapping her hands together in pure bliss. "That's my knight! It appears luck is on my side. You *are* worthy of being my disciple."

"I vote nay." Dotta raised a hand, looking less than motivated. "We might have the goddess's power, but defeating a demon lord is another story. Xylo, you don't want to die for the Holy Knights, right? They did this to themselves. After all, you—"

"That's exactly why I'm doing this."

I knew what he wanted to say. I used to be a Holy Knight myself until I was expelled and wound up here. I despised them, but I hated the foolish nobles backing them even more. They were the ones who set me up and put me here. And eventually, I planned on killing them. But for now...

"You're right—I don't like them. But you know what annoys me most? People talking shit about me, saying that's why I did what I did."

"Sounds like you're a little too self-conscious to me. If people are gonna talk, let them."

"I don't have the patience for that."

Like hell I was gonna let those scumbags think I was some petty bastard.

In the end, it came down to my old, bad habit. I knew how unhealthy it was. Put simply, I hated being underestimated. I wasn't going to let anyone look down on me, which was exactly how I wound up in this mess to begin with.

"Come on. Time to go."

After giving Dotta a good kick, I grabbed a sword stuck in the ground and pulled it out. It was a sharp silver blade, clean and glittering. As expected of a sword summoned by a goddess.

"If we don't save the Holy Knights, we're done for."

The fighting had already started by the time we arrived. The cold night wind carried countless shouts, battle cries, and the thunderous roars of lightning bolts.

"Oh no... There they go. We're too late," Dotta cried dismally. He seemed to have no desire to rescue the Holy Knights.

Smoke was rising into the evening sky from the fire at their base camp along the Purcell River. Their white armor, illuminated in the firelight, filled me with nostalgia. These were the Holy Knights, and they were using their lightning staffs and spears to attack the incoming faeries rushing across the river. Each time they received the order to fire, a flash of light emitted from their staffs, blowing the faeries' bodies to pieces.

Now and then, we heard roars even louder and more powerful than the lightning staffs. These were most likely greatstaffs installed around the base—a type of mortar enhanced with a sacred seal compound created by the Verkle Development Corporation.

These weapons were more like battering rams than staffs and needed to be assembled before they could be used. They were engraved with sacred seals and launched physical shells. They didn't have rapid-fire capability, and the seal itself had a limited supply of luminescence, meaning only so many shells could be fired before it ran out. But they were powerful enough to blow faeries apart, and they could shoot farther and were more effective than my "big candy" seal, Zatte Finde.

In other words, the Knights were still doing fine.

The faeries couldn't get past their lines of defense, and morale was high. I could see a figure in the distance giving orders to fire, carried out in perfect unison. They were even covering for areas that seemed about to succumb.

There's…no one here I know. Guess that makes sense.

I saw an unfamiliar emblem sewn into a blue flag fluttering in the wind. The emblem was a family crest of a perfectly balanced scale. Each order of Holy Knights had a different crest honoring their noble backer. There used to be twelve, and I knew each of their crests, so this group had to be newly formed, with a new backer I hadn't heard of. Teoritta, too, was the thirteenth goddess and new to the fight.

I really messed up this time, I thought, though it was obviously all Dotta's fault.

"What do you think, Xylo?" he asked casually. "The Holy Knights seem to be doing just fine without us. It probably wouldn't even make a difference if we left."

"What's wrong with you? Have you no pride?" Teoritta said harshly. "There is no greater honor than saving those in trouble, and as our squire, you should be thrilled to fight by our side! Let us share the joys of victory together!"

"I'd prefer to share something else, like delicious food…or money…"

"Heavens… I am appalled! My knight, what have you been teaching your squire? He clearly lacks education."

Dotta was breathing heavily from the trek here, but Teoritta still wore a calm, elegant expression, as if to say, *It's going to take a lot more than that to wear me down.*

I knew she was bluffing. She was far tougher than her delicate appearance implied, but goddesses still got tired. I wasn't stupid enough to point that out, though.

"I believe you should select your squires more carefully, my knight. This one lacks both motivation and spirit."

It appeared Teoritta thought Dotta was my squire. This was common among goddesses, and there was nothing I could say at this point.

My one task now was to focus on the battle at the river crossing.

The Holy Knights were doing better than expected, just like Dotta said. But that wasn't going to last forever. Even now, I saw a faerie charge forward, scoop up a few soldiers in its mouth, and swallow them as they screamed. The competition was fierce, and the spilled blood had turned the river's surface a blackish red.

"It's time to take action. This fight's been going for a while now." I was already moving, carefully silencing my footsteps. "The faeries will soon strike from a different direction."

This was an obvious strategy. The faeries were dull and acted only on instinct, but the demon lord ruling over them was different—it acted with intelligence.

And if I was on the demon lord's side...

If I was being held back at the river crossing, trying to break through the front line would result in heavy casualties. In that case, I would send a detachment to take the next crossing, either up or downstream, and go around. That seemed like the natural course of action.

The Holy Knights had already lost their own detachment and were ill-equipped to defend. The faeries we ran into earlier were probably on their way here, but the plan failed when we stepped in and destroyed them. Considering their forces still outnumbered ours, however, I figured the demon lord would send another detachment.

In conclusion, we needed to hurry and meet up with the Knights and formulate a plan to get us out of this mess.

"All right, Dotta. Time to—"

Only after I called his name did I finally notice.

Seriously? Now? I thought. *Is he really doing this now? Is he out of his mind?*

"Teoritta, where's Dotta?"

"Huh? Oh...?"

She glanced around, just as surprised as I was.

He was nowhere to be found. *Unbelievable.* How could he run away at a time like this? ...On second thought, I shouldn't have been surprised. In fact, I had to admire how quick he was.

I noticed a piece of cloth on the ground with some words written on it in black ink: *Let's split up. You do your thing while I go steal everything of value from the Holy Knights.* I was beyond exasperated. I was going to find him later and kill him. We hadn't even started here, and he'd already gone and proven that penal heroes like us were unreliable scum.

"Where did your squire go?"

"…He must have remembered some urgent business. It doesn't matter, though. He was useless to begin with. We have your powers anyway, Teoritta."

"Yes." Her fiery eyes glittered with mirth. "It appears I am truly your most dependable comrade. You are in need of a miracle, yes? You may start thanking me now."

"…I will, but can you really do it?"

There was a reason I was going out of my way to make sure.

As I said, goddesses also got tired. Their stamina wasn't unlimited, and using the miracle of summoning drained them. They couldn't keep going forever, and Teoritta should be pretty spent after summoning all those swords earlier.

"I am insulted, Knight Xylo." She pouted—a child's expression. "I am the goddess of swords, Teoritta, a guardian who creates miracles for mankind. I shall grant what you seek. That is my purpose, my meaning, my all."

Yeah, right. Whatever.

This was what I hated about goddesses. They would throw away their lives for us humans, just to earn our praise. It hurt to watch.

"Therefore, you need not hold back," she said with pride. "You can depend on me as much as you desire." I could tell she wanted me to praise her attitude as well. *Like hell I'm gonna do that*, I thought. *Never.*

"I know that even goddesses have limitations. Don't even think about fighting until you die," I spat. "I won't praise you for that."

"Excuse me?" said Teoritta with surprise.

Then, all of a sudden, the faeries overcame the Holy Knights' defenses at the river. They rushed dauntlessly through the bolts of lightning and charged right at the guard fence, destroying it. Whatever we planned to do next, first we had to stop the faeries.

"Teoritta, I need your swords. Follow me."

"Yes, my knight. I have much to say in response to your earlier remarks, but…" She elegantly brushed back her hair as I sprinted forward. "I suppose it can wait until after our victory."

Sparks flew and empty space twisted as countless swords emerged from some faraway abyss.

This time, however, they came not only from the sky but from the ground, sprouting up like plants. I pressed the ball of my foot down onto the hilt of one of the swords and used it to push off, leaping up and soaring through the air.

I could easily jump more than three times my own height, an ability granted to me by the other sacred seal I'd been allowed to keep, a product called Sakara. This flight seal supposedly got its name from a type of dragonfly in the language of the ancient kingdom. It strengthened a person's basic physical abilities—in this case, jumping power. By mitigating the laws of physics, it all but allowed someone to fly, if only for short periods of time.

Aerial battles—that was the main idea behind the Bellecour Thunderstroke Seal Compound installed in my body. It allowed me to fire explosive projectiles from the air in order to combat faeries with the ability to fly. What's more, it made mobile attacks against the Demon Blight possible.

The only drawback was that a good bit of training was necessary to master this kind of irregular hand-to-hand combat. You had to travel through the air while speedily and accurately striking your target. I was a specialist, one of only a handful in the entire Federated Kingdom.

That was why I could grab one of Teoritta's swords as I leaped into the air. I swung it over my head, imbuing it with Zatte Finde's explosive powers before I threw it.

I was aiming for the fuathan slithering through the shallow part of the riverbank, and there was no way I was going to miss.

The blast took out the center of the horde, tearing apart the faeries' flesh as fire and light illuminated the area. Water splashed wildly into the air, creating confusion among the enemy. I landed in the middle and grabbed another sword before swinging it. I never swung a sword to slash at my opponent. My aim was always to use Zatte Finde to blow them up.

There are too many. I need to start thinning them out.

I swung my blade diagonally, exploding everything the metal touched. Countless swords continued to rain mercilessly from the sky.

The fuathan charging me from the front were all skewered into the ground. Those that tried to dodge bumped into their allies and lost their balance. Sometimes they even collapsed.

I cut through the shallow water, charging into the horde while swinging my sword, exploding all enemies nearby.

"Teoritta!"

I requested another blade. The next wave would be upon me any minute. They rushed forward mindlessly, aiming at Teoritta behind me. I grabbed the summoned sword in midair and immediately threw it, blowing more enemies into pieces. Their cries filled the air as steam rose off the water.

Next enemy.

Spinning around, I found another target. I jumped and slashed at it. The spray of water mixed with its flesh and blood as it spewed into the air.

Next.

The trick here was to never stop moving.

"Hey! Is that all you've got?!" I shouted at the fuathan, showing off my confidence. I took a moment to breathe.

"You're making this too easy for me!"

As I cut another through the back, I realized all the fuathan were gone. The surviving faeries had started to retreat once their attempt to break through the Holy Knights' line of defense failed. *I guess I got a little flashy there*, I thought. Once the enemy was gone, the Holy Knights began to notice me.

Me and Teoritta, that is.

They were bewildered, of course. It didn't help that my entire body was soaked in water, blood, and guts.

I guess I should say something.

I saw someone among the Knights wearing freshly polished armor, glittering brighter than the rest. They sat on an intelligent-looking horse, holding a flag in their hand. This had to be the captain.

"Who are you?" asked an awfully wary voice—a woman's voice.

The Knight lifted her helmet's visor, revealing black hair and a sharp gaze. Perhaps it would have been a big deal back in the old days, but female soldiers were common now, especially since sacred seals could make up for any physical disadvantages. When it came to military affairs, the gap between men and women was slowly being erased thanks to the development of such products.

"Identify yourself!" said the captain. "What order do you serve?! What is your name?!" She fixed me with a piercing gaze. Soon, however, her sharp eyes drifted to Teoritta behind me. More confusion seeped into her expression.

"I-is that... Is that our goddess I see?! What is she doing awake?!"

I understood why she was yelling. I'd be just as confused if I were in her position. Unfortunately, I didn't have the time to explain, and it wouldn't change anything anyway.

Right now, everyone's lives were on the line.

"Don't worry about it," I replied, trying to end the conversation as I pulled another sword from the ground. "I get that you're confused, but this is all Dotta's fault. He's a filthy thief who's gonna go down in history, and—"

"Wait. Ahem. Hold on," the captain said, cutting me off. "What's this? Dotta? I—I have no idea what you're talking about. Explain yourself! Who are you and what is going on? Why is the goddess—?"

"We don't have time for chitchat." I pointed the tip of my sword across the riverbank. The dark of night seemed even deeper there, as if coiled, waiting to strike. "The demon lord is almost here."

"I know that! But—"

"I'm a hero, and I'm on my way to kill the demon lord."

This silenced the captain. Maybe her confusion had finally reached its maximum capacity.

"That's my job," I continued. "And it's about time I got to work, so you better lend me a hand if you don't wanna die."

Phrasing mattered in society. Or so I'd heard. I'd recently started working on it, but I never seemed to get any better.

That was probably why I always ended up drawing the short straw.

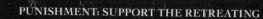

It seemed the captain's name was Kivia.

She never told me herself, but that was what the others called her. It was probably her last name, but I'd never heard it before. It sounded like something from the old northern kingdom. It was possible she wasn't born a noble.

Whatever the case, I had to hurry and improve our situation. When I'd seen the battle from afar, there seemed to be around two thousand Holy Knights. Now I counted hardly a thousand.

"Fall back. Holding the line any longer is pointless."

This was the biggest point I wanted to make.

"The detachment you sent was almost completely wiped out. I helped the survivors escape, but the next wave of enemies will be here soon. Your only chance is to flee to the east."

This should have been valuable information, but Kivia scowled at me. It was the kind of look you'd give a filthy pest. I continued, undeterred.

"The larger faeries are coming. Trolls, barghests—you know the type," I said.

These were names of convenience to differentiate the creatures.

Trolls were bipedal, while barghests walked on all fours. Both spawned from mammals, and they were both massive, with thick, armor-like skin. The rivers here weren't deep enough to slow them down. The only reason they hadn't arrived yet was because they were slow walkers.

There was no benefit to attacking them here at the river crossing. The Knights would be better off pushing back their line of defense and focusing fire on the creatures the moment they emerged from the water. Then the faeries would have to cross the river, separating them from their allies and forcing them to stand with their backs to the water.

As for *why* this would remove them from the pack—that was all up to me.

"I want you to lure the enemy over here, then hold out for a little longer," I said. "That will give me time to attack the source of the Blight. It'll be at the front lines by now." I purposely made my voice assertive.

I had gleaned all this from the speed of the faeries that had destroyed the Holy Knights' detachment. The only one that could have possibly ordered such a large group of faeries to circumnavigate the line of defense was the source itself. That meant it had to be close.

"I'll handle the demon lord."

I would travel through the air and take out the leader. That was the only way to put a stop to the incoming faeries, but I needed the Holy Knights to hold their ground until I finished. They had to lure out and destroy as many of the faeries surrounding the demon lord as they could.

"Back me up while I go in for the kill."

My request was earnest. However...

"Just who do you think is in charge here?"

...Kivia hadn't taken kindly to my advice. I didn't even need to see her face. Her tone was more than enough to convey her disgust.

"Our objective is unchanged," said Kivia with an aggravatingly serious expression. "We will prevent the enemy from crossing the river. We will guard this area with our lives. The east bank of this river belongs to the Northern Noble Alliance. It remains human territory and mustn't be tarnished by the enemy."

"Are you stupid?" I couldn't stop the words from escaping my mouth. "Haven't you got orders to withdraw? We were told to back up your retreat."

"The messenger from Galtuile told me that, as captain, I had the right to make the final call."

Galtuile was originally the name of the governing office overseeing military affairs for the Federated Kingdom. Now that office was known as Galtuile Fortress, and it served as the de facto military headquarters.

"We shall risk our lives for honor," she declared. "We are already prepared to die."

"That's the stupidest thing I've ever heard."

That was my only thought.

This was in direct conflict with our orders. It all came down to politics. Galtuile Fortress, and the military it oversaw, was funded by various nobles, such as those of the Northern Noble Alliance. Each group's motives differed, and it could lead to conflicting instructions like these.

Or maybe they just pulled our orders out of their ass. No one cared what happened to us heroes, after all. That was just as likely.

"Who gives a shit about your honor? Maybe if someone lived in those lands you're so desperate to protect, I would feel a little differently. But that area isn't even under development. Don't you care about your soldiers' lives? Or us heroes, forced to go along with you?"

"…Honor is of utmost importance. First, we were forced to withdraw from the north, and now we are given orders to retreat? I… I can take no more. Though this may be our final resting place, I will fight until the bitter end…!"

Something felt off here.

What was with this Kivia person's uncompromising attitude? It was as if she felt guilty about something, and she was trying to atone by fighting this unwinnable battle. The other soldiers were the same, with irritatingly pathetic looks on their faces. But why?

"My soldiers all agreed with my decision, and I care not what happens to the likes of you heroes," Kivia spat. "You criminals are not even worthy of death! Now explain what you are doing with the goddess."

She pointed the tip of her spear at me and Teoritta behind me.

"Why has she awakened and why did she form a pact with you?! Nothing about this makes any sense. I do not understand. I truly do not! We were prepared for anything as long as the goddess was unharmed! We were going to deliver her safely from this battle, even if every last one of us was killed!"

"Look, dammit. I don't have any excuses, okay? Someone stole her."

"Th-they did what?!" Kivia blinked in astonishment. "Someone stole the goddess? What happened to our guards? Wait. More importantly, why would anyone steal her? Are you mankind's foe? What are you scheming?"

"Enough, all right? I'd like to know why he stole her myself!"

I was starting to genuinely lose my patience. Why did I have to answer for something I didn't even do? There was no time for this.

"I'll apologize if that's what you want! But right now..."

I couldn't deny that this thing with the goddess was all our—or rather, Dotta's fault, but we had bigger fish to fry at the moment.

"We don't have time to argue. If you have a better strategy than the one I gave you, then I'm all ears...unless you still wanna defend this spot to the death, that is!"

"How dare you speak to me like that!" Kivia exclaimed. "Do you honestly believe we would follow a hero's orders?!"

"Hold your tongue, you dandiprat," Teoritta interjected, her voice cold as steel.

"A-are...?" Kivia was so flustered that I almost felt sorry for her. "A-are you speaking to me?"

"Yes. Who else? Do not question my knight's orders."

Kivia looked overwhelmed. Teoritta may be small, but she had an outsize presence. Perhaps it was due to the sparks flying from her golden hair.

"Gather your troops and make preparations to fight the demon lord this instant," Teoritta continued. "I will not allow you to waste any more time."

"...Please wait, Goddess. This has to be some sort of mistake! That man became your knight by accident! You were supposed to—"

"Goddesses do not make mistakes. This was no accident—I chose him as my knight. This is destiny."

Teoritta's words were sharp and curt. It seemed she'd mastered the overbearing attitude of a goddess. Or perhaps this was simply her true nature.

"You are far too kind, Knight Xylo." She looked back at me proudly. "Perhaps they would like to taste the greatness of my powers firsthand. Then maybe they will learn that it is my knight who gives the orders!"

She snorted arrogantly, making it clear that she expected something from me. I saw the space behind her distort. It looked like she intended to follow through on her word.

"Then you would shower me with praise, yes? ...Yes?"

"H-hold on," Kivia interrupted. "That bizarre name... 'Xylo,' you said?"

The captain seemed to recognize my name, and that was a problem. I was well-known in the kingdom, especially among the Holy Knights.

"You're... You're Xylo Forbartz! The most despicable hero of them all. What are you plotting, you goddess-murdering fiend?! You—"

But a powerful roar drowned out Kivia's words before she could finish her sentence. It was like the ear-piercing sound of countless pieces of metal being torn apart, and it was coming from the darkness on the other side of the river.

"We're too late."

I clicked my tongue. We'd wasted too much time playing question and answer, and now *it* was emerging from the depths of the rustling forest on the opposite bank.

The larger faeries were in the front of the pack: barghests (wolves the size of elephants walking on all fours) and trolls (bipedal humanoid creatures with abnormally large, apelike arms). These fur-covered beasts leaped into the river and charged at us.

Behind them was a creature as large as a house—a giant cockroach with numerous legs—clumsily lumbering across the ground. As it moved, it screeched like the scraping of metal against metal. The pitch of its call subtly raised and lowered, and a portion of the faerie throng split into two groups, left and right. Apparently, its screeches contained orders for its troops.

It was just as the reports said. That ridiculously large insect was the source of the Demon Blight. These centers of contagion were generally referred to as demon lords.

This was number forty-seven, Awd Goggie.

Each demon lord acted as a catalyst for an outbreak of Demon Blight, contaminating their surroundings as they moved. They distorted whole ecosystems, sometimes involving humans, too. There was no way to oppose one without the protection of a sacred seal, and each demon lord possessed its own unique ability.

In the case of Awd Goggie...

"Hold your fire! Don't attack the demon lord!" Kivia waved her flag, but she was too late.

A few staffs and mortars had already been fired, and for the most part, they hit their mark. That was going to be a problem. Awd Goggie lifted a few of its legs and deflected each and every projectile, launching them toward the soldiers fending off the faeries at the river. The fence on the bank burned as bodies flew into the air.

Awd Goggie didn't sustain so much as a scratch.

I didn't know the principle behind it, but this creature could deflect sacred seal attacks. At the very least, the Holy Knights' projectiles weren't working. The fact that it could strategically redirect the attacks back at us only made things worse.

These counterattacks were so aggressive and accurate that some believed it was using a sort of force field to guard against and reflect the sacred seals' power.

This meant we'd have to physically strike it with something big, but few weapons were effective against such a massive creature, and we'd still have to get close enough to attack it. You'd need something like a battering ram or a catapult. In fact, I'd heard that, at that very moment, they were preparing such relics for battle back at the First Capital.

In other words, the demon lord known as Awd Goggie was like a moving fortress with sturdy outer walls, advancing straight for us. It made perfect sense that the Holy Knights had been dealt a serious blow and forced to retreat to their current location.

"It's no use...!" Kivia's face twisted in despair. "Soldiers, prepare to use your scorched terrain seals while they're still on the other bank!"

"Stop right there. That's not something you take chances with," I interrupted. "If it doesn't work, we'll all be dead."

Scorched terrain seals were sacred seals that blew up everything in range. To use them, one had to be willing to sacrifice those bearing the seals and all the surrounding land. We couldn't afford to do that unless we knew exactly what would happen, and when you had a demon lord that could deflect sacred seals, it was anyone's guess. We had to at least take care of its reflective shell first.

I understood what Kivia was trying to do, of course. Her goal was to stop the enemy from setting foot on this side of the river. It was a show of honor, and they would use any means necessary to achieve it.

But I didn't give a shit about any of that, and I wasn't planning on dying with them, either. It seemed to me there were far too many people in this world ready to throw away their lives for some goal.

"Kivia, use your troops to back me up. I need you to distract the demon lord by taking out the little guys, and I need it done now."

"E-excuse me?" Her voice cracked, and her eyes went wide. Whatever she was feeling, it went beyond simple anger. "Why are you giving me orders? You, a penal hero, sh—"

"To survive. That's why," I declared, placing a hand on Teoritta's shoulder. "I don't plan on dying today, and I'm not interested in seeing any of you get slaughtered, either. Don't throw your life away for some stupid cause."

I wasn't speaking just to Kivia and her troops, but to Teoritta as well.

"I'll take out the demon lord. And once that's over and we're all back home alive, then…" I decided to make a promise. "Then I'll accept whatever punishment you wanna give me, Captain. And, Teoritta, I'll praise you as much as you want."

Kivia looked like she wanted to kill me, but Teoritta seemed surprised—as if she was witnessing something highly unusual. *I wish she'd stop that*, I thought.

"Come on. Let's get to it."

Across the river, the darkness squirmed. I leaped and plunged right into the middle of it. Even I knew what I was doing was irrational, but I was pissed. Maybe my anger was selfish, but I couldn't stand this bullshit everyone kept spilling about dying for honor.

Idiots.

I cursed them in my head.

I was going to show them just how pointless all that was. They would be struck dumb with astonishment. And what would surprise them most of all was that I, some random guy, would be the one to defeat the demon lord.

Just you wait.

I soared over the river. The air was cold and the wind buffeted my body. Directly below me was a horde of faeries and some Holy Knights. The ground was covered with enemies. And as for allies, I had only one: the goddess Teoritta, riding in my arms. *Hmph. Bring it on.*

"Hold on tight. I don't want you falling."

"What hubris. You have no need for worry. It is I who worries for you humans." She had the confidence of a goddess as she clung to my neck. "Now, Xylo, it is time for me to fulfill my duty, yes?"

"Not yet," I instantly replied.

I couldn't rely on her too much. A goddess's talents could only be used so many times, and there was a limit to how much they could summon. Once a goddess surpassed that limit, they would collapse like a marionette with its strings cut, ceasing to function.

In the worst-case scenario, they would die, never to return.

"You mustn't underestimate me, Xylo. I can still…"

Teoritta claimed that she was fine, but I couldn't trust her.

Goddesses had a habit of putting on a brave front. It was like they needed humans to rely on them in order to keep living. To that end, they hated showing weakness.

It still pisses me off.

I knew a way to tell how exhausted a goddess was.

You had to look at the light in their eyes and the sparks flying from their hair. These grew brighter the more a goddess pushed themselves, and the sparks flickering off Teoritta's hair hadn't stopped even while I held her. Was it because she'd just awakened? Or was this her natural limit? There was no way to tell.

"A goddess always lets their knight handle strategy, right?" I said, my voice forceful. It came out that way on reflex. "I want you to save your power for just the right moment. Let me handle the little guys," I added, purposefully casual. Yeah, this was nothing.

There were faeries everywhere I looked. A number of them flying in the air noticed me—too many. A regular person would be out of luck. Not me, though. This was going to be a piece of cake. At least, that was what I told myself.

One of the keys to mobile combat is securing a place to land.

After unsheathing a knife from my belt, I stared hard at my landing point.

A few faeries—barghests—howled into the sky, warning the others of my arrival. They were huge and unlike any wolf you'd find in nature. Their fur was thick and keratinized in places, forming quills.

All right. Just the faeries I wanted to start with.

Large faeries like these were one of the main enemies the developers of the Bellecour Thunderstroke Seal Compound had in mind. The seal allowed its user to one-sidedly annihilate the enemy without leaving room for a counterattack. But to be successful, it required both power and precision. I tightly gripped my knife, infusing it with the sacred seal's power and then throwing it like a projectile.

A brief moment passed before the explosion.

There was no way I was going to mess up the timing. It was a perfect hit. The blade skewered a single barghest, then sent out a blinding light and roared into flame. Bits of flesh flew into the air as the blast swallowed the surrounding monsters.

"Impressive, Xylo. Now allow me to—"

"Not yet."

Another key point was…

I thought back to the lessons my training had ingrained in me.

…don't stop moving. Maneuver yourself into the enemy's blind spot.

The instant I landed, I jumped again, this time a little lower. I was so low that the tips of my toes were almost touching the ground, allowing me to cover more distance.

Hovering at such a low altitude allowed me to slip between the legs of trolls and barghests while throwing knives into their bodies as I passed. The creatures exploded before they could even turn their heads.

"Xylo, surely it is now time for me to act?"

"Not yet."

I leaped high into the air once more, threw another knife, and destroyed a group of smaller faeries before kicking off a tree and passing over their heads.

It's not over. Don't stop moving… Once you stop, you'll be surrounded. Give it all you've got.

Explosions, flashes of light, more jumping.

Soon I'd caught up with the demon lord. The way I'd come was now paved with shattered earth, mud, and piles of faerie corpses. But the closer I got to Awd Goggie, the more colossal it appeared. Some mysterious power must be allowing it to maintain its absurdly massive form.

It stared at me with its big, ridiculous eyes.

"That's...the demon lord," said Teoritta.

I could tell she was nervous, and I could feel her body tense.

"I am not afraid!" she said quickly, apparently angry that I'd noticed. "Destroying demon lords is every goddess's most cherished desire. Therefore, it is time for me to fulfill my—"

"Not yet. Soon."

"Not yet? Haven't you made me wait long enough already?"

"Just a little longer. Trust me."

Awd Goggie, noticing our approach, extended a few of its seemingly infinite number of legs and tried to swat us like it would a fly.

This is exactly what I'd predicted, and I was already in the process of evading.

I can at least hit it once...hopefully.

I kicked off a tree and leaped into the air.

I dodged its scythe-like front leg, and then, as I cleared the demon lord's head, I threw one of my few remaining knives.

I was aiming for the base of one of its legs—the joint connecting to its shell. It was a midair throw requiring great precision. This was quite the trick, like threading a needle. But it was precisely this kind of ability that had earned me a spot as a captain in the Holy Knights.

"How do ya like that?!" I instinctively shouted when my knife slipped into the opening in the demon lord's shell, piercing its body.

A flash of light was followed by an explosion. It appeared to have worked, and the joint connected to the shell exploded, inflicting decisive damage. Its leg spun in a circle before tearing off. Bodily fluids gushed out of the wound, followed shortly by Awd Goggie's shrieks, like iron being ripped apart.

"Don't be so dramatic. It's just one leg."

I'd proven that it could be destroyed if one aimed for the openings in its shell. This information came at a price, though. The other faeries started to respond to Awd Goggie's cries, and it was clear they would try to catch us the moment we landed. The fuathan were already hopping on their frog-like legs. *What a pain.* I had only a few knives left, and the demon lord was now aware of what I was trying to do, so getting in another hit wouldn't be easy.

Normally, this would be the time to fall back.

But I knew I wasn't going to win if I did things the normal way, and after all, I had the goddess with me. Now it was time to try something out of the ordinary.

"Xylo, they are surrounding us. Is it my turn to fight? I feel as though I should start doing something."

"All right."

As we landed, I threw a knife into one of the fuathan trying to swallow us. The blade sunk into its skin, blowing it apart.

"It's time, Teoritta."

I jumped into a tree and pointed with open animosity at the demon lord and the faeries charging our way.

"I want you to clear a path to the demon lord. And make it big."

"...Very well! Hmph." She snorted, fire in her eyes. "Behold the power of a goddess!"

Countless swords emerged from the void, and this time their blades were bigger. They were impractical-looking claymores probably meant for use in rituals. The blades were so thick, they could stab a troll or a barghest to death with one stroke. These glittering greatswords rained down on the earth like a meteor shower, skewering each faerie into the ground while creating a path to the demon lord.

"One more time," I said, and promptly leaped into the air, tightly holding on to Teoritta while conveying to her what I wanted. "...I need a special sword. You can do that, right?"

"Do not mock me." Sparks were flying off every part of her body. It was starting to hurt to hold on to her. "I am a goddess, my knight. All I need are your devout prayers."

It wasn't long until we were closing in on the demon lord.

It rapidly moved its legs, its many eyes fixed on me. A few of its legs swung into the air, trying to catch us midflight.

This should work at least once, too.

It had already seen me attack with my knife earlier, and it knew what to watch out for. While I'd landed a powerful attack, the wound it left was far from critical. The creature probably believed it would be able to block me the second time around.

And it would have been right, if it was me alone.

"It is done."

The instant Teoritta said those words, I saw another sword emerging from the void. It was longer than any other up until now—almost a spear. Maybe it wasn't even a sword. I grabbed it, and the force almost pulled my shoulder right out of its socket. I infused the power of my sacred seal into the weapon and kicked it with everything I had.

Sakara, my flight seal, gave me extraordinary athletic abilities, allowing me to send the gigantic sword soaring through the air with the mass and speed of a bolt from a siege crossbow.

They're preparing battering rams and catapults back at the capital, after all.

The military had clearly figured out that primitive weapons like these were effective against Awd Goggie. The dirtbags back at Galtuile Fortress liked playing political games, but they weren't incompetent. Especially not when their lives were on the line.

That was why I was sure this attack would work. If it didn't, we'd be out of options.

The results were immediate.

The spear-like sword blew off a few of Awd Goggie's legs. Its blade dug in, smashing and severing them. Then its tip sailed into the creature's torso, piercing it with explosive energy. I could see its shell crack.

At the same time, there was a flash of light.

The shock wave ripped through the air as Zatte Finde activated within the monster's body. The explosion came from inside its shell, shredding its flesh while its gooey bodily fluids spewed into the air.

The results of my—of our attack were more than satisfying.

Perfect.

The strike had left a massive wound on the demon lord's body, like a crater. Fluids continued to gush out from the gash.

"All right, Teoritta. That—"

Squish.

That was when I heard it—a moist sound coming from Awd Goggie. Its ravaged body started to wriggle and squirm. Something was growing out of it with unbelievable speed. Were those new arms? Or were they like the tentacles on a jellyfish? There were two or three of them. At that moment, I had only one thought.

"Now, that's cheating."

I reacted almost unconsciously, grabbing Teoritta and promptly turning my back to the demon lord. This was ridiculous.

I was doing what I'd just warned Teoritta against. I was about to throw away my life.

After that...well, I felt a strong impact. The creature probably batted me away as if I were a fly. The world around me winked out, and all I saw was black. I could tell I'd hit something. Fortunately, it was a large tree and not a troll or a barghest.

But with that pain came despair. Maybe this was hopeless.

My attack hadn't finished off the demon lord, and I wouldn't be able to use the same move again. Fluids were still gushing from its wound, but it was gradually healing itself.

"Xylo!" shouted Teoritta.

I was in a lot of pain as I looked up at the night sky.

The demon lord shrieked in agony. *Ya like that?* I thought. As their leader temporarily ceased to give orders, the faeries were thrown into a panic like they were lost little chicks. Agitated, some even started attacking and killing one another.

"...Look at me, my knight!"

Teoritta's eyes shone brightly, almost blindingly, as she called for me. Were they really the color of flames?

I saw something else, too.

...What's this?

I hoped it was an illusion. It was too bizarre and ridiculous to be real, and it was the last thing I wanted to see.

"...Uh... Xylo...?"

And now that *thing* was peering down at me with a troubled expression.

It was history's most notorious petty thief, Dotta Luzulas. I wasn't expecting to see his dirty mug here, of all places.

"What are you doing out here?"

He was the last person I wanted to hear say those words.

It didn't help that he was carrying a barrel big enough to fit a child. When I saw what was written on it, my eyes went wide.

VERKLE CORP, HANDLE WITH CARE, LENURITZ WEAPON NO. 7... and SCORCHED TERRAIN SEAL.

"Dotta," I said.

Then I laughed. I sat up, still laughing. My entire body was in pain, but this wasn't the time to be worrying about something like that. I grabbed Dotta by the lapels of his jacket and held him down so he couldn't escape.

"You stole this, didn't you?"

"Not this time. I just happened to run into it when I was sneaking around, so—"

"Good job. I'll hold off on killing you for now."

What happened after that was nothing to write home about. Scorched terrain seals were really nothing more than a bunch of pieces of wood with sacred seals carved into them. The barrel itself was the weapon, constructed from this special wood.

Dotta had to be the stupidest person in the world for carrying it out in the open like this. The wood of the barrel contained a few pieces that functioned as a safety mechanism. Once these were removed, it would activate. The number of pieces you pulled out determined the power and blast radius. Luckily, this one was a model I was familiar with.

The demon lord's shell was already broken, so the minimum power level should be enough. There was no reason to destroy the whole forest.

I kicked the barrel as hard as I could and leaped into the air. I grabbed Dotta as well—he'd helped a little, after all. But helping wasn't all he'd done. As soon as we landed, I punched him so hard he fell on his ass.

We could hear the blast nearby as the weapon cratered a portion of the forest in a flash of light.

And that was how we managed to defeat the demon lord Awd Goggie and help the Holy Knights withdraw.

Of course, the real problems came after all that.

A brief moment of silence followed the massive explosion.

Then a roar rose up all around us.

The faeries were confused. The demon lord was dead, and they had no one left to lead them. Soon the horde would fall apart. This was the fate of faeries when their Demon Blight's core was lost.

This isn't my first.

I'd killed a few demon lords before, though this *was* the first time the ending had been so ridiculous.

I made some mistakes, too.

I wasn't all that different from these overserious numbskulls like the goddess and the Knights.

Look at Dotta.

He'd shown me a much more surprising way to defeat the demon lord. I felt like laughing. Dotta, incidentally, was unconscious on the ground with his eyes rolled back. He'd been that way ever since I broke his nose with a good punch and sent him crashing into the dirt.

I'm exhausted.

I sat on the ground where I'd been standing and took in a few deep breaths. There was someone looking down at me—someone who shone even against the darkness of the night. Sparks flew off her body, and her eyes burned as she stood there proudly.

"My knight!" Teoritta exclaimed, puffing out her chest and grinning from ear to ear, though I sensed worry in her voice. "We have defeated the demon lord… Surely you have no complaints with my divine grace, yes?"

"No complaints here." I really had nothing else to say.

"Then…" She lightly cleared her throat before sitting on her knees in front of me and adjusting her posture. It was as if she were getting ready for some sort of important ritual.

"Whenever you are ready." She ran her fingers through her golden hair. "Isn't it about time you showered me with praise?"

"Oh, right."

"Hurry. There is no need to hesitate. Come on. I am ready."

"Yeah, yeah. I hear you…"

I was dead tired, so my hand was slow as I reached out to rub her head. There was only one thing goddesses wanted in return for their services. It was extremely twisted and filled me with guilt, but if this was what they needed, then who was I to complain?

I clenched my teeth and gave her what she wanted.

"Good job."

I rubbed Teoritta's golden hair as the sparks prickled my fingers. This pain was nothing. I just had to put up with it. It was utterly inconsequential compared to what Teoritta had done for us—and especially compared to what we had done to Teoritta.

"Heh-heh." She exhaled contentedly as I patted her head. "Use more force and do not forget the praise."

"Good job surviving."

"…What a strange compliment." She looked up at me curiously. "You are praising me simply for being alive?"

"Being alive is something worth praising. Trust me. Though I know there are a bunch of idiots out there who say otherwise."

She looked like she didn't believe me. She probably didn't. That was just how goddesses were.

"Would it be acceptable for such a goddess to exist?" she asked.

"Would it be 'acceptable'? Listen here…"

She looked uneasy. Or maybe puzzled. *What is this? Why is she making this expression?* I wondered.

"No, wait. Don't ask me. Is that really something you should let others decide for you?"

"…I see." Teoritta lowered her gaze. "Then I…"

I thought I saw her face cloud over. Was she thinking about the past? What was she remembering? But I lost my chance to ask, because by the time she lifted her head again, the shadow was gone.

"Then, Xylo, if what you are saying is correct…defeating the demon lord *and* returning alive makes me even greater and more impressive, yes?!" Her smile was closer to a child's than a goddess's. "In that case, I give you permission to praise me even more."

"I appreciate it. You're a great goddess, and I am humbled to even be allowed to rub your head." I began rubbing her head even harder. What else was I going to do? "You'll probably become mankind's savior one day."

"More." Teoritta's mouth moved impatiently. She probably wouldn't stop unless I kept going.

"…You're the greatest goddess there ever was. Your greatness is so dazzling it blinds me."

"More."

"…Still not enough? You're amazing. It's hard to believe that such a grand being exists in this world—"

"Xylo Forbartz."

Teoritta still didn't seem satisfied, but I was forced to stop there.

Someone had called my name. In fact, I'd been hearing the clattering of horses' hooves for some time now. I'd just been ignoring them, since I didn't care.

"Was this your doing?"

I could see the white armor of the Holy Knights, along with a bunch of awfully serious faces. Kivia and a handful of her soldiers were looking down at me from atop their horses.

"Yeah," I said, admitting it. "I killed the demon lord."

"So I should simply accept everything that happened? Is that what you mean to say?"

The unpleasantness in her voice was crystal clear. She might kill me, depending on how I answered. And that wouldn't even come as a surprise. Killing an archvillain like one of us heroes was no different from breaking a piece of equipment. Both heroes and equipment could be repaired, after all, and a captain of the Holy Knights had that right.

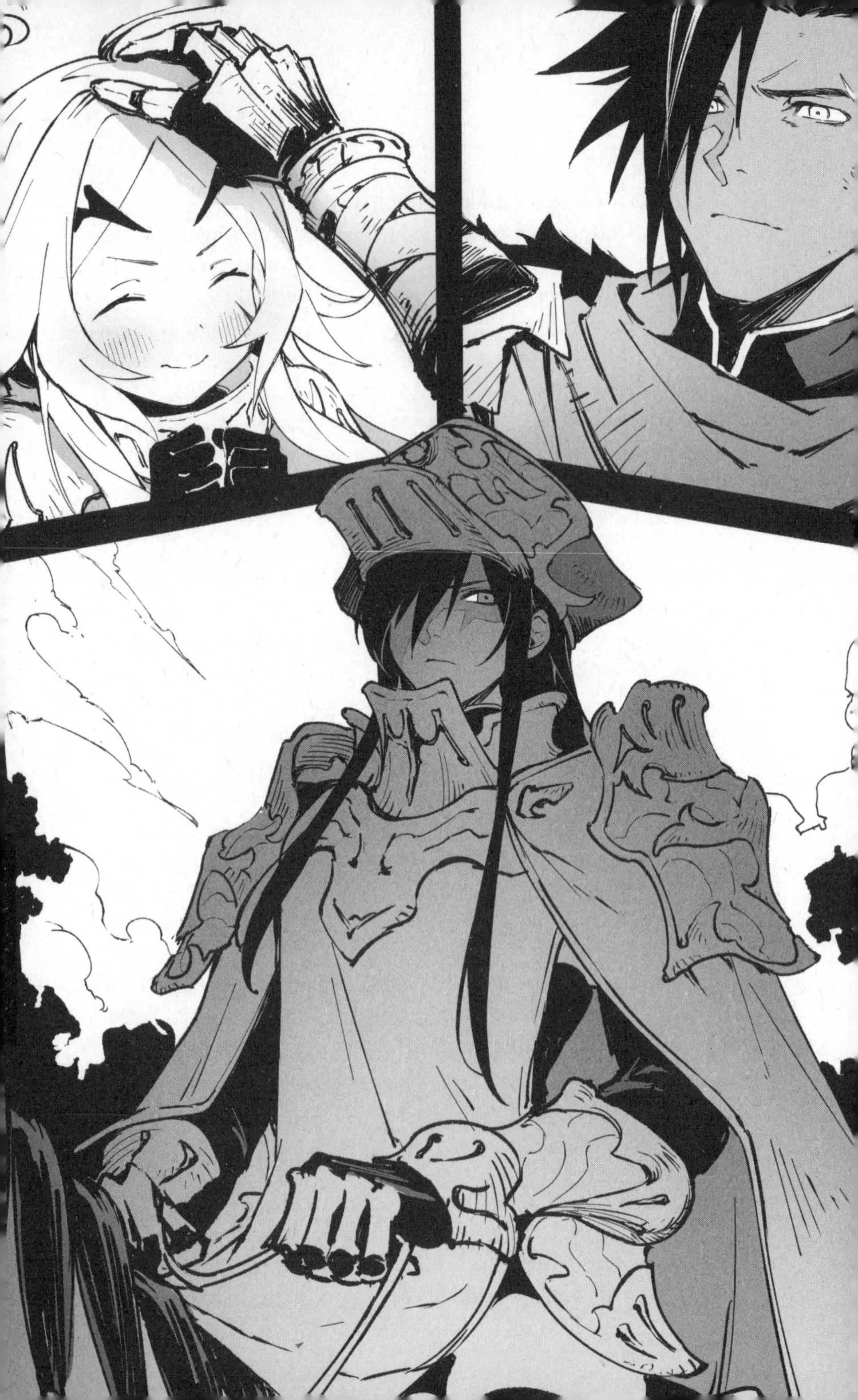

Besides, she has every reason to be angry.

This woman—Kivia—was probably the one originally meant to form a pact with the goddess. Pacts were always forged one-on-one between goddesses and knights, and there were only two ways to break them: Either both parties had to declare they were rescinding the pact, or the goddess had to die. That was it.

"You stole the goddess from us. You even stole a scorched terrain seal, and then you made the unilateral decision to use it to kill the demon lord."

"I didn't," I promptly replied. There was nothing else I could say.

"Excuse me," Teoritta chimed in sternly. "I've been wondering this for some time, but what exactly do you mean, 'he stole me'?"

"Goddess Teoritta, you were originally supposed to be…placed under our protection," Kivia said, sounding pained. "Under the protection of the Thirteenth Order of the Holy Knights."

She looked like she might cry. It was as if this was extremely difficult for her to say. Or was she lying? But why? Come to think of it, why hadn't the Knights used Teoritta—their most powerful weapon? Why had they not awakened her? Between that and their plan to fight to the death, I couldn't help thinking their behavior was bizarre.

"But this penal hero—this Xylo Forbartz—is a criminal! And he stole you and decided to forge a pact with you all by himself!"

"I see."

Teoritta's voice was extremely calm, especially compared to Kivia's. The goddess might have been putting on a bold front, but I was still surprised by how relaxed she sounded.

"Then that must have been our destiny."

She was smiling. Why? It didn't make any sense to me. Shouldn't she be a little confused? I was. Even Kivia seemed taken aback. Her mouth hung half-open.

"I believe in Xylo Forbartz as my knight," said Teoritta. "He will be the one to defeat every last demon lord, and he is worthy of my blessing."

I think that was when I started frowning. I didn't deserve this much trust. And that was beyond dispute because—

"Goddess, if I may…" Kivia glared at me with those piercing eyes, even colder than before. "Do you know this man's crime?"

"What is he guilty of?" she asked.

"Killing a goddess." Kivia spat out these words like a curse. "He is a former Holy Knight who killed the goddess he forged a pact with."

That was a fact.

That was why I didn't say anything. I remembered it all too well. The feeling of piercing her heart with a knife, the flames in her eyes when she took her last breath, the powerful sparks burning my hand—I remembered it all.

There was no way I could forget.

That was everything that happened in Couveunge Forest.

After that, my penal hero unit was given our next orders almost immediately. It was a really crappy job, intended to make up for Dotta's and my foolish actions.

We were ordered to continue supporting the Thirteenth Order of the Holy Knights while they stormed a certain underground structure contaminated by the Demon Blight. In other words, we were going to serve as human sacrifices to help them clear a dungeon.

Incidentally, I should probably mention that Dotta Luzulas was sent away for repairs after getting into a mysterious accident that broke every bone in his body.

"Xylo Forbartz, Captain of the Federated Kingdom's Fifth Order of the Holy Knights."

Someone was reading off my title.

Their voice was depressingly cold. As they droned out a long series of introductory remarks like one might chant a curse, I stopped paying attention. I had to, or I was going to beat someone to death.

"Defendant Xylo Forbartz."

Someone called my name again. It was the confessor. The confessor was the chairman and highest-ranking official at a trial, and only members of the royal family of the Federated Kingdom could hold this position. I didn't know which of the five royal families he was chosen from, but it seemed safe to assume he came from a particularly important one.

After all, this was the first trial in history for the crime of killing a goddess.

"Xylo Forbartz, you led your Holy Knights to Demon Blight Number Eleven the night before the crime took place."

I couldn't see the confessor's face, since a thin veil hung between me and the others—the confessor and the judiciary committee.

This was how trials were conducted in the Federated Kingdom.

The kingdom was made up of around five nations that decided to unite. When that happened, a combination of each nation's systems was adopted, eventually settling into the current way of doing things.

"Then, before daybreak, you engaged in battle alongside the goddess

Senerva. Does this report reasonably and accurately depict what happened?" He didn't sound like he had any doubts, but he phrased it as a question anyway.

My entire body was wrapped in chains like I was a captive beast, but they'd removed my gag to let me respond. I figured this was the last chance I was going to get to testify. What an idiot I was.

"Yeah, it does," I answered truthfully. "I fought Demon Blight Number Eleven. It was tough, especially since the promised reinforcements never came."

"Defendant, all I need from you is a yes or no." The confessor cut me off with a disagreeable tone. "Allow me to continue verifying the report. You, the defendant, unilaterally made the decision to engage in battle alongside the Holy Knights and goddess under your command, and you suffered catastrophic losses as a result. Does this report reasonably and accurately depict—?"

"No, it doesn't," I replied plainly. "I wasn't acting on my own authority. I was given orders."

"Galtuile Fortress gave no such orders. There is no record of them."

"That's a lie."

I knew that with absolute certainty. The messenger, who had arrived on the fastest horse available, had handed me an official document with our orders. The sacred seal engraved on it proved that it had come from Galtuile headquarters.

"We were told that an allied army was isolated and needed help, so I rushed to save them. The official orders stated that Infantry Division 7110 in the Uthob region was—"

"No such unit exists," roared the confessor. His tone was intimidating. "You acted hastily and without orders in pursuit of glory, forcing your men and the goddess into a reckless battle."

"No, I—"

"Your unit's arbitrary decisions have stood out for a while now. I heard that you have committed numerous offenses in an attempt to make a name for yourself and improve your status."

That was the moment I finally realized what the confessor was so upset about. Did my very existence disgust him?

"This is war," I said. "Sometimes you need to make split-second decisions in the field, and doing so was my right."

"A right granted to you by the ruling families and one you clearly misunderstand. And above all, in the end…" He paused briefly, as if even putting it into words was nauseating. "You killed Goddess Senerva. Is that true?"

"It is."

My reply instantly caused a stir on the other side of the veil. I could hear numerous members of the judiciary committee exchanging words.

"But I had no other choice," I continued. "The unit we were sent to save didn't exist, and the reinforcements that were supposed to come never showed up. We were isolated—"

"Of course no reinforcements came. There were no such orders. The entire situation was the result of your own selfish actions."

"You're lying!" I shouted, causing an even greater stir among the judiciary committee.

"Senerva—the goddess pushed herself to the limit and couldn't use her powers anymore. She fought and risked her life for the sake of our praise."

"She was your responsibility. You engaged in combat for your own benefit."

"Senerva thought she was going to be thanked profusely by the unit we were saving."

I started to ignore the confessor. I didn't care anymore. I was more concerned with conveying what happened…for Senerva's sake. I had to tell everyone what she sacrificed her life for.

"Does anyone here know what happens when a goddess loses all her power? She becomes weak and defenseless, allowing the Demon Blight to consume her."

"That has never been confirmed, and the Temple has denied there is any such possibility."

"Are you stupid? Obviously, the guys back at the Temple aren't gonna admit that."

I knew why, too. The people at the Temple had a certain doctrine.

According to that doctrine, goddesses had to be perfect. There was no way they could admit anything that contradicted this belief. But the military—the soldiers who were actually fighting against the Demon Blight—had to deal with the truth of the matter.

These people were with the military, too. I was hoping they would take into consideration just how much of a threat that truth was. This had never happened before. We weren't allowed to even mention it—this condition that affected a goddess on their deathbed.

That knowledge should have greatly affected how goddesses were used from then on.

"Just listen to me! There's no existence more dangerous than a goddess who has been consumed by the Demon Blight."

There was even a possibility that a demon lord with the powers of a goddess might be born, and that was something we had to avoid at all costs.

"And Senerva knew that. She was slowly being consumed, so I—"

"Confessor." A member of the judiciary committee spoke up. The voice was calm but resonant. I would remember it well—I could never forget it. It was seared into my eardrums.

"The defendant continues to make blasphemous remarks about our sacred goddess. We have already verified the key facts in regard to what happened... Wouldn't you agree that he should be prohibited from commenting any further?"

"I suppose you're right," agreed the confessor gravely.

I realized something when I heard this exchange. Everything happening at this trial had been decided before it even started. These people were merely putting on a performance.

"Wait! You need to hear this!" I strained my voice as the guards to my right and left seized me. "This is serious! This trial—everything—it's all a sham! I don't know what they're plotting, but there are people in the Temple and the military pulling the strings for their own self-interests."

The guards grabbed my shoulders and slammed me onto the floor so hard I almost lost consciousness.

"You don't have time to worry about me. You need to find the people behind this, and—"

Another strong impact. I almost lost consciousness once again as the guards attempted to stuff the gag back into my mouth. I tried turning my head out of the way, only to be punched some more.

"I'm gonna find you…"

Someone—a whole group of people—set us up: me, my knights, and Senerva.

"And I'm gonna kill every last one of you."

◆

"…What was that?"

"Huh?"

I suddenly heard a voice from above. Did it come from the sky? No. I was just lying down…on a crude bed made for prisoners. I blinked, then looked around. A small room, bars, stone walls with no windows. It was obviously a cell—the room I'd been allotted. For the most part, penal heroes were only allowed rooms like these.

"Oh, were you having a dream?"

A golden-haired young lady who didn't seem like she belonged here was looking down at me: Goddess Teoritta. She had her arms crossed as she proudly puffed out her chest.

"Some feeble-looking man named Venetim told me to wake you up. You may thank and praise me now."

"He did, did he? Good job. I appreciate it," I said, still lying down. "Tell him I'll be there soon."

"I cannot do that. You will most certainly fall back asleep the moment I take my eyes off of you."

"You got me there."

"Honesty is a virtue, but not all truths are virtuous! And you should praise me more for coming to wake you up!"

"Yeah, yeah." I groaned. I was not in the mood for this.

If Venetim was summoning me, that meant the next mission was about to start. And soon, too. I probably went a little too far breaking every bone in Dotta's body. Now I was going to have to team up with people I found even more aggravating.

I could already feel their presence. Actually, I could hear them shouting somewhere down the hall. Teoritta turned toward the voices and frowned.

"Xylo, who is screaming? It has been going on for a while now."

"That's His Majesty," I replied with a yawn, but Teoritta only looked confused.

"What does that mean?" she asked.

"It's not a riddle. That's just what he calls himself. He's a former terrorist convinced he's the king. And he's our unit's engineer."

"Oh...?"

She still looked bewildered, but I ignored her and sat up. There was something I had to do. *Dammit.* I felt like I was going to throw up, but this goddess would pester me all day if I didn't do this.

"Let's go... Thanks for waking me up, Goddess Teoritta."

"Heh-heh." She brushed back her golden hair, preparing herself for head pats. "Of course!"

I rubbed her head a little roughly, messing up her hair, but she grinned from ear to ear as if she couldn't be happier. Maybe it was because of the dream I'd just had, but it hurt to see that look on her face.

Order/First Solda/No. 01360019

■ ~~Addressed to: Captain Patausche Kivia of the 13th Order of the Holy Knights~~

■ ~~Orders: Continue escorting the goddess. You are to deliver Goddess XIII to Galtuile by the scheduled date and time. Avoid fighting at all costs. Moreover, you are temporarily prohibited from using any penal heroes until your troops have healed.~~

■ ~~Authorizer: Governor-General Evras Herelck of the 4th Northern District~~

Prior orders revoked.

■ Addressed to: Captain Patausche Kivia of the 13th Order of the Holy Knights

■ Orders: The goddess escort mission is suspended. You are to head to the Zewan Gan Tunnels and remove the threat. Furthermore, Goddess XIII and the penal hero unit shall be placed under the control of the 13th Order of the Holy Knights to help neutralize said threat.

■ Authorizer: Acting Governor-General Simurid Kormadino of the 4th Northern District

■ Reason for revoking previous orders: Policies are being reconsidered due to the prior authorizer's death and suspected breach of trust.

The Zewan Gan Tunnels had only been opened within the past few years.

A mineral vein had been discovered as the fight against the Demon Blight gained momentum, and those in power immediately began mining. They wanted to get their hands on minerals used in the production of catalysts for sacred seals. In the past, they built a town nearby with an iron mill and even a Temple workshop for engraving seals. Sacred seals engraved on higher quality iron could store a greater amount of luminescence and their effects were more powerful.

According to the Temple, sacred seals were a product of the wisdom bestowed onto mankind by the gods. At least, that was what they claimed.

These seals, when engraved onto an object, used sunlight as their power source and were activated by the will and life force of a human. The effects varied. Some produced heat, some unleashed bolts of lightning, and some ravaged the land. Mankind had gone on to develop this technology in pursuit of such blessings. Progress had been especially impressive when it came to military use.

Therefore, material for carving sacred seals was always in demand, and Zewan Gan helped provide it. I had heard that the Verkle Development Corporation had invested a lot of money to expand the tunnel. Excavators using sacred seals had been installed so digging could continue both day and night.

It was almost ironic that the tunnel had now transformed into a faerie.

There had been reports from early on of land being tainted by outbreaks of Demon Blight. Inorganic materials were sometimes affected just like living creatures. Similarly to Zewan Gan, the tunnels would transform, lumps of dirt would begin to move on their own, and the land would become a living, breathing faerie.

Naturally, anyone entering such a tunnel was taking a huge risk.

The change in the Zewan Gan Tunnels was first observed about a month ago. Those who went inside never came back out. Later, they were found transformed into faeries, attacking people indiscriminately. Those killed were transformed into faeries, too, creating an endless chain reaction. It became clear that the source of the Demon Blight—the demon lord itself—had settled within the tunnels.

At this point, the neighboring towns were already abandoned, and we were left with no special equipment for digging. That meant we had to dig the holes manually. We continuously pierced the ground with our shovels, scooping the dirt up and away.

We might be digging our own graves for all we know.

I decided to keep this joke to myself, however. The person I'd been teamed up with wasn't a big fan of humor.

"Hurry," he demanded from behind. He was a serious guy, but he talked a lot. "We're not going to finish on schedule with you moving so slowly! You need to start taking this more seriously!"

The man shouting at me was named Norgalle Senridge. He was a large man with a blond mustache and a permanent, pompous expression like he was a real big shot.

We referred to him as His Majesty.

He didn't really give anyone a choice in the matter. He fully believed he was the king of the Federated Kingdom—and he was serious about it.

Obviously, someone like that wasn't going to fit in with society, especially when he started committing serious terrorist attacks to retaliate against the "traitors" who "stole" his castle. But what was most unfortunate for everyone involved was that this Norgalle guy was unbelievably talented at tuning sacred seals.

For ease of understanding, I'll use construction as a metaphor.

Even a slightly crooked column can have a huge effect on the strength and stability of a house under construction. Seals were no different. One wrong curve when forming a sacred seal greatly affected its precision and output. Usually, when tuning a sacred seal to be used as a weapon, several artisans would work off a blueprint.

Norgalle, however, could do all of that by himself. To be frank, he was really something else. Thanks to his ridiculous skill, his acts of terrorism had cost the military and the royal castle untold losses. They put him on trial after that, and now here we were.

Norgalle was yet another member of Penal Hero Unit 9004.

He was currently sitting on a large wooden box like it was a throne, carving knife in hand, engraving a sacred seal onto a slender iron plate to be used for blast excavation. This was something only he could do, so there was no other way we could have split the work. That didn't make me any less pissed off, though.

"Xylo," he said sternly. "The Holy Knights are planning on storming the tunnels tomorrow morning. I'll have to order you to work through the night if necessary. I'm counting on you. I may even consider restoring your position as a Knight if you do a good job."

In his head, he was the true king. I had no idea how he could still believe it, but he seemed to think he was currently taking command on the front lines.

A king personally leading a hero into battle against a demon lord was definitely an incredible feat. It sounded like the legends of the nation's founder. At any rate, His Majesty King Norgalle was right. We had to hurry.

The Thirteenth Order of the Holy Knights meant to gain control of this tunnel.

It was a shortsighted plan, but we had to make sure it succeeded, even if it cost us our lives. Right now, we were being forced to dig a direct path to our destination. Right now, the Zewan Gan Tunnels were so twisted that old maps were completely useless.

With the land's transformation into a faerie, it had become a dangerous labyrinth. That was why we needed a shortcut. Through digging and blasting, we were creating a passage into a much deeper part of the maze.

Creating that passage was our first task, but things were a little different in King Norgalle's head. He seemed to believe that he was commanding us heroes on the front lines and that he'd given the orders for the Holy Knights to storm the tunnels.

"Put your back into it! Even the blast from my sacred seal won't break through at this rate. We might be buried alive instead."

Norgalle kept trying to motivate me like this as I dug. *Dammit.*

"Or would you rather sacrifice yourself to open up the passageway?" he continued. "I thought not! Hurry up and dig!"

"We're already going as fast as we can, Your Majesty." I started talking back to him, despite myself. "We've been digging almost nonstop since yesterday... Right, Tatsuya?" I looked to the side at my partner as I continued to shovel dirt, stone, and gravel. He didn't reply, of course.

"...Guh."

A short groan was the only noise he made.

His arms never stopped moving his shovel as he scooped out dirt like a machine. His back was hunched way over, and his expression was vacant. Resting on his head was a rusty helmet keeping his insides from slipping out through the hole in his skull.

He was a hero, too.

His actual name was unknown, but everyone called him Tatsuya. He was the longest-serving member of our unit. Nobody knew what crime he'd committed or anything else about him.

He was exactly how he looked. He'd lost both his sense of self and his ability to think. He'd died too many times—or rather, he'd been brought back too many times. Heroes had a lot to lose each time they were revived, and Tatsuya had even lost the ability to speak. He simply groaned in reaction to external stimuli.

This was also a part of our punishment.

It was just the three of us on this mission. Or to be more precise, we were the only three currently able to help. King Norgalle, Tatsuya, and me: What a team. Dotta was still out for repairs after I shattered all his bones, so at least I didn't have to worry about his sticky fingers getting us into trouble.

Our fourth and final member wasn't a hero at all.

"You appear to be having a difficult time, Xylo."

A young woman sat idly on the crate next to Norgalle.

Even this far underground, Goddess Teoritta's golden hair still shone. But despite holding a shovel in one hand, she was doing absolutely nothing. And that was probably making her miserable. She had been offering to help dig for a while now.

"Isn't it about time we traded places? I am feeling extremely energetic."

"No," I replied immediately. I wasn't going to let her waste stamina on something like this. If I requested her help, it would be in battle. While we weren't very deep yet, this was still part of the tunnel, and there was no telling when we would be attacked by faeries from the Demon Blight.

"Just lie down and rest. I need you to conserve energy."

"But you look exhausted, my knight," argued Teoritta. I'd expected this. "Those under a goddess's protection should rely on her in times of need... Besides, I have not done a single thing. How am I supposed to earn my praise?"

"I'll shower you with all the praise you want if you keep sitting there."

"I do not think that sitting is deserving of praise. I have to make myself useful."

"It's fine." I could hear my tone growing harsher. The exhaustion probably wasn't helping. "I just need you to sit still. Please."

"If you say so, my knight."

"Your Majesty, keep an eye on the goddess so she doesn't try to help."

"But of course." Norgalle nodded gravely. "The goddess is the protector of our people, and she mustn't be troubled... Please forgive me, Goddess."

Norgalle, who acted as if everyone else was below him, was very humble when it came to Teoritta. This was a new discovery. Venetim had pointed out that we could probably use Teoritta to keep the king in line in the future.

"Hmph..." Teoritta bit her lip, clearly unhappy. "Very well. I suppose I will simply watch over your human endeavors for now."

"Thanks," I replied.

Struggling to overcome my accumulated fatigue, I decided to stretch my back. I let out a deep, heavy breath and turned around. That was when I caught sight of someone I wasn't expecting.

"Xylo Forbartz."

It was Kivia, captain of the Thirteenth Order of the Holy Knights and the one originally meant to forge a pact with Goddess Teoritta.

This time she looked different—she was wearing the armor of a foot soldier, though her expression was the same: a piercing gaze like she was picking a fight. With whom or what, I wasn't sure. She had come with numerous soldiers under her command.

"It appears you are taking this work seriously."

"Of course," I said. "I mean, it's either that or die."

"...I see." She shifted her gaze to Teoritta with an unreadable expression. "Goddess, how about resting at our camp? Surely it would be far nicer than staying here."

"Your persistence is starting to irritate me, Kivia." Teoritta waved her hand pretentiously. "I told you I am fine. I must watch over my knight's hard work. It is my duty as a goddess."

"But—"

"Patausche Kivia," Norgalle loudly interrupted. "Your concern for and loyalty to the goddess is commendable!"

His booming voice was the thing that really made him seem like a big shot. More importantly, was that Kivia's first name? Norgalle had an incredibly good memory, it seemed.

"However, the goddess wishes to watch the battle on the front lines with us. We shall have divine protection." Norgalle continued despite Kivia's bewilderment. What a guy. "Therefore, as king, I must dismiss your appeal. You may go now and fulfill your duty."

"...Ahem. Xylo Forbartz. Who *is* this?"

"Just nod," I said. "You'll regret it if you try to argue. Trust me."

"Is this a side effect of his resurrection? Are his memories muddled? Or perhaps—"

"He's always been like this."

"I see..."

Kivia seemed even more surprised, but it appeared she'd made up her mind not to concern herself over it. She then cleared her throat and glared at me.

"At any rate, it appears work is going according to schedule… I am honestly surprised. I had heard this unit could be unpredictable without proper supervision."

"Well, Dotta, who you met the other day, sure knows how to be unpredictable. What a clown."

"About that…"

Kivia paused midsentence, as if she were having trouble finishing what she wanted to say.

"What?" I asked. "If you want to complain, I'm all ears. Can't do anything about it, though."

"No, it isn't that." Her eyes wandered before returning to glare at me. "I apologize."

"Huh? For what?"

"…I learned that you were not to blame. Not only was stealing the goddess Dotta Luzulas's doing, but I heard that you had no choice but to forge a pact with the goddess in order to save my detachment."

"Oh, right."

Something felt strange about her apologizing to me.

It wasn't like Kivia did anything wrong. She had made a clear mistake from a strategic perspective, but that wasn't a crime. Besides, it was the court's job to judge people.

And I was fine with Dotta and me being the villains.

"I felt I must apologize after the truth came to light. You exerted your fullest efforts to defeat the demon lord with minimal casualties. At the time, I did not understand."

"Because you were pissed. I get it, though."

"Let's pretend that anger was directed toward Dotta Luzulas. More importantly, why didn't you try to explain yourself that day?"

"Would you have believed me? We didn't have time for that anyway. And I figured having you a little mad would be perfect, since we were about to go into battle."

Kivia pressed her lips together with clear dissatisfaction.

"…I expect you to clearly explain yourself next time, since we will be fighting together as allies going forward."

"Calling a penal hero an ally now, huh? So there's a heart in that chest, after all. Think you could do a little something about this grueling mission while you're at it?"

"Don't push your luck."

"Get us some booze with our rations next time."

"Now you're making demands? You—… Never mind. Get back to work. We do not have time to chitchat. I came here to explain your next task. After digging straight down, I want you to follow this map."

Kivia unrolled a large sheet of paper before my eyes, and I unconsciously blinked at it for a few moments. The map was full of advanced, abstract designs, and its lines curved like a drunk snake dancing. Could you really call something like this a map?

"I want you to connect the path to the north. Once you reach the mine cart tracks, you can use the military post here as a landmark."

"Wait. Hold up. Is this…supposed to be a room? …Then that'd make this a door, which means…"

"Yes, and?" Kivia knitted her brow. "Is there a problem?"

I could see the soldiers behind her shaking their heads and shrugging their shoulders, and I immediately understood what they meant. Their captain hadn't yet noticed the catastrophic flaw with her map.

"What's this dog in the corner here?"

"That isn't a dog. It is a mining cart, obviously."

"…Uh-huh."

I turned back toward Norgalle, thinking maybe I was the weird one, but he had the same look on his face as I did.

"Your Majesty, what do you think of this map?"

"Hmm… I thought it was a classical abstract painting by an artist of the Venque Meyer School of Aesthetics, but it appears I was wrong."

"This is a person, right?" I said. "Halfway buried in the wall and screaming in agony."

"It looks like a horse being eaten by a snake to me," he replied. "The mystery is why there are so many."

"…That's the planned frontline base! This is a tent, these are floor-mounted lanterns, this is a pot, this is the storage area, this is a door with a lock, and these are mice—a little extra I added for fun! What is wrong with you imbeciles? This is no time to be joking around."

Unfairly enraged by our honest opinions, Kivia turned to Teoritta and held out the map. She was looking for an ally.

"Goddess Teoritta, would you reprimand these two for joking about my map? You understand what I've drawn, don't you?"

"Uh…" Teoritta paused, unsure what to say. "Um… Don't you think that this ancient mural—? Ahem. No, this is a map, right? …Don't you think it's a little too complicated?"

"See?" I said. "Nobody knows what any of this is."

Norgalle cut in next. "Wait. Why are the mice an added bonus? The curiosity is killing me, and I demand an explanation."

"…Heh. Heh-heh."

Kivia's face twisted. It almost looked like she was smiling. She was really holding it together.

"Goddess Teoritta may be unaware, but this is no work of art. Yes, this is a military document, so all you need to understand is the bare minimum. The details are not necessary."

"Oh, I see…," said Teoritta.

"The bare minimum? I can't make out a single thing on that damn map… You knights over there: Stop indulging her just because she's your captain. You're going to run into some serious problems one day if this keeps up."

"Excuse me?" Kivia's gaze sharpened, and the Knights at her side promptly came to her aid.

"C-Captain Kivia, please do not listen to the utter nonsense this penal hero is spewing."

"Exactly! We have finished what we came to do! Let's return to camp!"

"But as your captain and representative, I must maintain my dignity—"

Kivia looked like she still wanted to say something, but her soldiers continued to pacify her until she eventually agreed to go back to camp. The daggers in her eyes concerned me, but I was hopeful she would reflect and reassess her drawing abilities. We still had a lot of work ahead of us, but for now, we'd have to pray she'd at least bring us a more legible map.

"Ready to get back to work?"

"Mmph! Yes, work! We do not have time for rest!" replied Norgalle. "Resume digging. You must make up for lost time. Xylo, you could learn a thing or two from Tatsuya. Less moving your lips and more moving your arms!"

He was back to being the mine's supervisor, it seemed. I heaved a deep sigh and got back to work.

This is such a bizarre mission, I thought.

Yes, I was unhappy about the heavy labor, but that wasn't all. There was something strange about how the authorities were handling this tunnel.

If the mine had transformed into a faerie and had to be abandoned, then why didn't we just ignore it?

Outbreaks of Demon Blight that transformed land into a dungeon had a tendency to stay put. If we were going on the offensive, we might have to deal with it as an enemy stronghold. But we'd just abandoned Couveunge Forest and were about to hole up for the winter and focus on defense. So why do this now?

I could think of only one possibility.

This must have been the work of the people who set me up and made me kill Senerva. I didn't know if it was the nobles, the military, or the Temple, but there were forces plotting against me. There was no other way to explain that ridiculous trial or the fake infantry division.

But what was their goal?

If they weren't out merely to harass me, did that mean they were trying to kill Teoritta?

This whole thing smells fishy.

In the end, we worked late into the night, somehow managing to finish on time.

Tatsuya dashed forward with his rugged battle-ax and swung ferociously. He was moving incredibly fast, and the force of his blows was especially impressive considering the massive size of his weapon and all the equipment he was carrying.

"Guuuh."

Tatsuya groaned from the back of his throat. The next instant his ax spun, and the sound of flesh and bone being pulverized rang out in the darkness. A faerie was raging about.

"Guah."

Tatsuya leaped like a wild beast and swung his large battle-ax with both hands as effortlessly as if it were a carving knife. The blade's grim glow illuminated the darkness as it eviscerated the beast.

As for me, all I did was stand back and throw one of my knives. That was enough. I used a small explosion to take out a faerie about to attack Tatsuya from his blind spot. I had to be careful using sacred seal explosions like Zatte Finde in confined spaces like this. If I made a mistake and the explosion was even a little too big, it would put every one of us at risk.

Lurking in the darkness were a total of six faeries—well, seven, if you included the one I killed.

These massive centipede monsters were a common sight. Faeries such as these, with lots of legs and that lived underground, were called boggarts. Creatures that resembled spiders and insects were all lumped

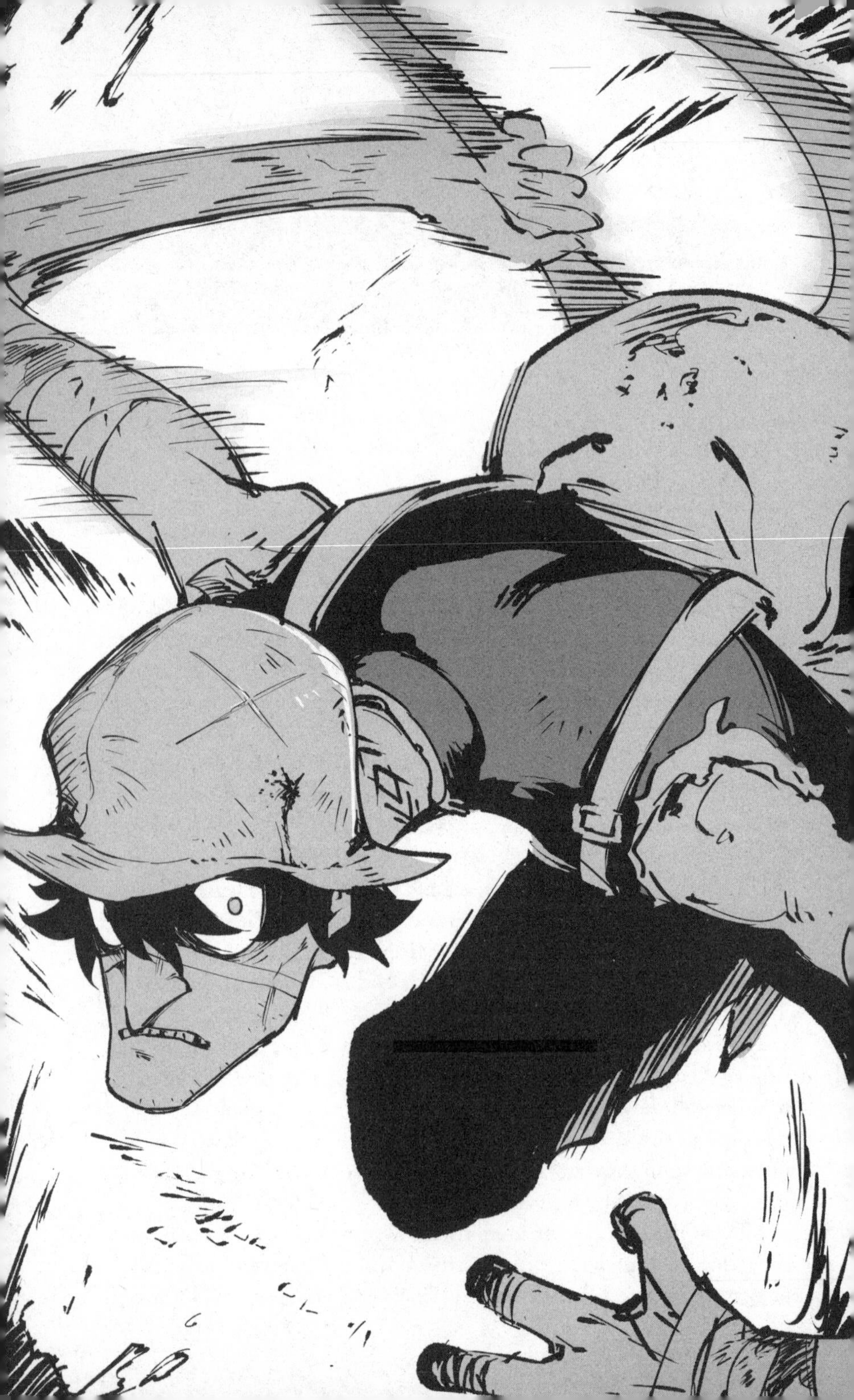
[redacted]

together into the same category. And Tatsuya was currently smashing them without a shred of mercy. Once every last moving creature was gone, he stopped and stood in a daze.

"He clearly doesn't need me backing him up," I said, staring at his now still form. "Did you see that, Your Majesty? He smashed the boggart's shell wide-open with only his elbow."

As always, Tatsuya's skill in close-quarter combat was superhuman. I could probably do just as well with my sacred seals, but I'd need to get a little creative in a confined space with a low ceiling like this.

"Impressive as always. I'd expect no less from my elite forces." Norgalle nodded with satisfaction. With one finger, he touched the lantern in his other hand and traced the sacred seal engraved there, increasing the light's power and illuminating our surroundings.

The lantern was powered by a sacred seal, and Norgalle's tuning had equipped it with several useful functions. It could serve as both a means of communication and a tool for cooking. Devices like this usually required multiple people working together to design and engrave them, but Norgalle could do it all by himself. He was not your average guy.

"What an impressive performance. He must be rewarded."

"He's been working nonstop, too," I said. "Probably about time we let him rest. Don'cha think?"

There was one thing I knew about Tatsuya. He could keep going as if *exhaustion* wasn't in his dictionary, but that was only because he lacked a sense of self and the ability to think. If you worked him too hard, he'd eventually reach his limit and collapse.

"Yes, you are correct. And this is a good spot for it as well."

King Norgalle looked up above our heads.

We had reached a relatively open area, at least compared to the passage we had been traveling down so far. From what I could tell, this chamber was big enough for around thirty people to rest.

I wondered what it was originally used for. There was still equipment here for excavating, but it was so twisted and warped that it was hard to tell what it was supposed to look like. Maybe the Demon Blight had expanded and distorted the space itself.

"This shall be our frontline base! Xylo, begin setting up camp!"

"...Yes, Your Majesty."

I nodded and began unloading equipment from the sled I had been dragging along.

It was a military-grade sled, so it was pretty heavy, but it had allowed us to bring various equipment engraved with Norgalle's seals.

Set up the frontline base: That was the penal hero unit's second task.

The Thirteenth Order of the Holy Knights was traveling deep into the labyrinth hunting faeries, and they would need a safe place to rest.

That said, Tatsuya was not good at this kind of work, and Norgalle was clearly not planning to do any physical labor. I had never seen a military engineer quite like him before, but there was nothing I could do about it. You couldn't scare him with threats, and he'd choose death before giving in.

Ultimately, I had no choice but to do things myself. I started to pull out stakes to use as posts and positioned them at roughly equal distances. These were engraved with sacred seals as well, and once you tied the ropes around them, they formed a barrier to keep faeries from approaching.

"Xylo!" came a lively shout from our band's final member. Teoritta already had a post in hand.

"It is finally time for me to work, yes? Yes? Leave it to me! Where do you want me to put this? I can shove as many of these into the ground as you want!"

"Relax."

I skewered the ground with another stake, holding Teoritta back. I shouldn't ask her to help here. It would be ridiculous to waste a goddess's energy on something so trivial.

But Teoritta couldn't take it anymore. She couldn't sit still.

"Line them up about this far apart." I took three long strides and stuck another stake into the ground. "Can you do it?"

"Hmph! What a foolish thing to ask a goddess!"

She snorted happily and skipped three steps away from my stake, counting aloud. Then she skewered her stake into the ground with great force.

"...Like this! Yes? You can leave the rest to me, my knight. Please get some rest. But do not forget to reward me handsomely once I finish, all right?"

"All right." I nodded as I installed one last post. This was only some light exercise. *I'll let Teoritta handle the posts while I take care of the other odd jobs*, I thought, already lowering a tank of luminescence, filled with the power of the sun, to the ground.

"I'm counting on you, Goddess."

"Of course!"

Her reply was incredibly cheerful and bright. She sounded just like a child. A lot of kids would do anything if it was under the guise of "helping."

And that was why it pissed me off so much to see her like this. I wasn't angry with her. I was angry at whoever made her.

…To be honest…

Holding back my irritation, I thought things over.

…I should let Teoritta help until she's satisfied. That's the correct way to operate a goddess.

That was what they were made to do, after all. They were here to be praised by humans, or so they believed. And if that's how they felt, shouldn't I respect those feelings? That was one common argument, and I didn't necessarily disagree.

I just got helplessly annoyed whenever I saw goddesses act that way.

Teoritta could probably sense this, but that didn't stop her. She kept working as if her existence would be meaningless otherwise.

Whatever. Knock yourself out.

I knew I had to just let it be. This wasn't the time or place to make decisions out of anger. All I needed to do was move my hands and legs. If I did, we'd get through this eventually. I was sure of it.

Plus, I had a lot to take care of. We needed to set up two frontline bases that day, not to mention prepare extra supplies. Battle would wear down weapons and armor alike, and consumables like food and medical supplies would run low, so units like ours were deployed ahead of time to leave supply chests along the main force's route so they could stock back up.

What soldiers wanted when it came to supply chests were two things and two things only: Do not make them too sturdy and do not make the defense mechanisms a pain in the ass.

But on the other hand, you didn't want them to be easily found and destroyed by faeries, so you needed to set up traps that would go off if something approached or touched them. Too many traps, however, would exhaust the soldiers and could even lead to casualties, thus defeating the whole purpose.

For that reason, I had to keep an eye on Norgalle—such as where he placed the first set of supplies.

"Perfect," he said proudly, nodding to himself. He'd placed his chest down a dead-end tunnel. "I even impress myself sometimes. The brave soldiers who reach this crate will be handsomely rewarded."

"Wow!"

Teoritta expressed deep interest in the supply chest. It consisted of a box with an iron-reinforced exterior that was painted with white light-reflective paint, allowing it to stand out even in the darkness. He'd added ornaments made from light-storing glass that were just as flashy. I had to wonder if all that was necessary.

"Incredible! Norgalle, can I see it up close?"

"Please wait, Goddess. Approaching it without the right equipment is far too dangerous… Observe."

Norgalle rolled a rock toward the storage chest. Instantly, countless sharp spears shot up from the ground and pierced the intruder, while the chest's keyhole spewed out scorching blue flames.

"Hnnng?! What was that?" shrieked Teoritta, leaning away. My gut told me this wasn't going to end well.

"Woah there," I said. "Am I seeing things, or did fire just spew out of that chest?"

"You saw correctly. That's the part I am most proud of. Anyone who approaches without the proper caution will be skewered, then melted by flames so powerful they could liquify a rock. I call this execution device Zolinvolkov, which means 'the judge of fools.'"

"…And how do you disarm the traps?"

"I am glad you asked! It is extremely complicated. If you carefully test it by rolling over a stone, you will find that the ground triggers an attack in some locations but not others. However, that is merely a decoy. The moment someone touches the storage crate, the fool will be scorched by the flames of judgment! To avoid such a fate, you must first find this key, which will be hidden in a different location, where—"

"All right, that's enough. Time to take it apart. Tatsuya, hold on to Norgalle for me. I need to take the key away from him."

"Wh-what? Why?! How dare you!"

"What are you trying to do? Wipe out the entire Thirteenth Order?"

Norgalle was a prodigy when it came to tuning sacred seals, but at times like this, that became a problem. In the end, we had to disarm around 80 percent of the traps he'd made, leaving us with only the bare minimum.

As we ran around placing the supplies, the day quickly came to an end. Once we'd installed the two frontline bases, we broke for a meal.

Norgalle engraved a sacred seal into the ground and promptly constructed the cooking equipment.

"Here, my knight." Teoritta said proudly, a pot in her hand. "I have learned how to cook as well. Be grateful and enjoy."

It was a very simple meal. This was a war zone, and we penal heroes were at the very bottom of the pecking order. We couldn't expect much from our rations. Particularly when Dotta and Venetim were absent, we had to brace ourselves for some real slop. They usually managed to steal something a little better from the military.

Today we had leftover vegetable and meat scraps. We fried them in a pan, salted them, and added some light liquid seasoning we had on hand before wrapping it all in glutinous rice. This was paired with a tiny piece of cheese. Teoritta managed to cook the meal exactly how I taught her.

"This is nowhere near enough to fill our stomachs. How can they neglect the soldiers at the front lines like this?" King Norgalle seemed offended as he ate. "Our military provisions must be improved. This is a serious issue. Where is the minister of finance?"

"At the royal palace, I assume."

"This must be investigated! Is the budget being properly distributed? We cannot maintain morale on the front lines with rations like this."

"I agree. We'll start looking into it once the mission is over."

If you took every one of Norgalle's absurd fantasies seriously, there would be no end to it. The trick was bringing the conversation to an end quickly. You might even wind up believing him if you weren't careful.

Tatsuya was perfect during situations like this, quietly chewing his rice without reacting to the conversation.

"How is the mission, Xylo? Is everything going according to plan?" asked Teoritta cheerfully as she took a bite of the so-called meal she had cooked. How could she look so happy eating that crap underground like this? She was acting as if she were on vacation. "The source of the Demon Blight must be close, yes?"

"Yeah…most likely."

I visualized a map as I traced our route in my head. Not the avant-garde art piece Kivia had supplied us, but an actual map.

"We should reach the deepest layer by tomorrow at our current rate."

"Easy, right?" She snorted with pride. "My divine grace must have really helped… Don't you think? Surely the Holy Knights will all praise us when this is over, yes?"

"They might thank us a little if it goes well. They're the ones who are gonna kill the demon lord, though."

"About that, my knight…" Teoritta lowered her voice, her eyes burning. "How about we defeat the demon lord ourselves? Surely we could do it with my blessing and the skills of you and your allies!"

"Not only do I not want to do that, but it would be a violation of our orders."

"But…as a goddess, if I do not produce results and display my might—"

"No." I didn't want to make my situation any worse by violating another order. "If you wanted to fight the demon lord, you should have gone with her—with Kivia."

"Huh?"

"That's the main team. They're gonna be doing most of the fighting."

While Teoritta wouldn't be able to use her powers to their full extent without me, she still could have chosen to go with the others.

In fact, she would have been a valuable addition to the main force. Kivia had weighed the options and decided to respect the goddess's will. That had been the logical decision, especially with a priest on loan from the Temple present.

"So why'd you decide to stay with us?" I asked.

"…What do you mean?" She frowned, and the flames in her eyes grew stronger. "Am I not needed here?"

"I never said that."

That was when I realized that she wasn't angry—she was worried. Her voice was trembling slightly.

"I'm really thankful that you're here," I said.

"Right? Of course you are!" She promptly stood, not waiting for the rest of my explanation. "My knight Xylo, I have noticed you sometimes display arrogance toward me."

"Really?"

"Yes. You should depend on me and offer me words of gratitude and praise far more often." She pointed at me. "I will not be satisfied until you admit that I, Teoritta, am the greatest of all goddesses!"

I felt like I was being roundly criticized. Teoritta nodded, positive she was right.

"I am honoring you with my company to allow you that chance!"

"Wait. Hold up…"

I tried to come up with something to say.

It was not only difficult trying to explain but depressing. What should I tell her? I hesitated for a few moments to find the right words. Just then, Norgalle suddenly spoke up.

"Xylo!"

His tone was sharp and scolding, so I thought he was angry at my treatment of Teoritta.

But I was wrong. He raised the lantern in his hand—the engraved sacred seal let off a glowing red light.

"The main unit is contacting us," he said. "This is…not good."

"A distress signal?"

The sacred seal on the lantern had several functions, one of which allowed us to communicate with the main force. A red light signaled an emergency.

"Hurry. …—need backup…"

A crackling voice could be heard from the sacred seal, but there was too much noise to make out all the words. Metal clangs, roaring bolts of lightning. Were they in battle?

"Demon Blight…"

Norgalle, Teoritta, and I pressed our ears to the lantern.

"We're being attacked by..."

We could only hear Kivia's voice faintly in between the louder noises, but we had already heard enough to piss us off.

"...faerie-turned humans. ...possible survivors..."

Norgalle and I looked at each other and clicked our tongues. Our actions were almost simultaneous.

"I'm already so exhausted," I said.

"Ugggh. Guhhh," grunted Tatsuya. He seemed to be agreeing.

I'd thought things were going a little *too* smoothly. So of course something bad had to happen.

The Demon Blight would occasionally affect humans, too.

This was inevitable. Plants and animals alike were targets. Not even rocks or soil were exempt. Humans were no different. The only exceptions were those protected by a sacred seal.

Soldiers at the front lines like us were provided seals to stave off the transformation. Towns and villages had walls of protection similarly engraved with seals, and travelers tended to carry amulets of protection.

Humans who transformed into faeries changed far more drastically than any other living creature, and the more time passed, the more they lost their human features. The worst case I ever saw was a guy who looked like a slug with countless faces and organs growing out of his body. Some of my soldiers had vomited at the sight.

The faeries we encountered this time still retained a lot of their human features—too many, in fact.

That said, all of them had grown extremely tall, their skin was covered in a dazzlingly bright silver carapace, and ragged strips of clothing clung to them here and there.

There was a whole horde of them.

For the sake of convenience, these types of humanoid faeries consumed by contaminated minerals were given a special name to differentiate them—knockers. The scholars at the Temple's Academy had decided on it. For people fighting on the front lines like us, at least, it was important to distinguish them from humans.

I'd wager there were about a hundred of them here. Despite their appearance, knockers were surprisingly agile and used that to their advantage. That put the Holy Knights on the defensive, and they'd formed a line of shields and barricades on the ground.

"Xylo! Goddess Teoritta!" shouted Kivia as she thrust a spear into one of the human—*ahem*—humanoid creatures. The tip of the spear let out a powerful roar, shattering the carapace covering the knocker's body and sending it flying back. The spear must have featured a sacred seal with that effect.

"Looks like you're having a rough time," I said, stating the obvious.

I counted about twenty Holy Knights fighting a defensive battle. When dealing with this kind of faerie, one tactic was to split your unit into smaller groups and use a communication device, such as a sacred seal, to coordinate your attacks. Throwing a hundred or a thousand men at the enemy wasn't going to help in a tight, confined space. If anything, you risked losing your entire team to a cave-in or some other kind of accident.

"My knight." Teoritta was already grabbing my elbow. She looked like she might leap into the fight at any moment. "It is my duty as a goddess to save them!"

"You got it."

The sacred seal on the nape of my neck began to sting. The death of our supervisor, Kivia, would mean our deaths as well. But in order to save her...

"If you want us to help, then give us the orders, Captain Kivia. That's the rule."

"I know. Help us sandwich the enemy!"

My sarcastic tone earned a scowl from Kivia, but she promptly gave us directions. We jumped into action and joined the Holy Knights in a pincer attack.

"Very well. Go forth!" shouted Norgalle. He showed no intention to join, but he certainly sounded dignified. "Elite soldiers of my kingdom! Break our fellow humans free from this curse so that they may finally rest in peace!"

It felt really odd hearing him say the words *my kingdom*, but there was no point in letting it bother me.

Both Tatsuya and I entered combat at almost the same time. I leaped forward, carrying Teoritta in my arms, while Tatsuya charged across the ground, body tilted forward like a wild animal.

"Bwuuuh!"

He swung his ax with a strange battle cry, attacking the knockers from behind.

"Geeeryaaaa!"

The knockers' skin was made of some pretty tough mineral, but Tatsuya's power rendered it meaningless. His battle-ax was engraved with one of Norgalle's sacred seals—a seal of severance. As long as it functioned, his ax would be as sharp as a blade forged in the eastern islands.

Charging forward, Tatsuya took out one faerie after another as if he were smashing rotten trees. As for me, carrying Teoritta allowed me to move even faster. I effortlessly hopped into the air and flew over the knockers' heads.

"I need you to hold back, Teoritta. Just one sword'll be enough."

"Are you sure? I'd like to do more." She seemed dissatisfied, but she did as I asked.

She rubbed the air with her hand, generating a single sharp steel blade. I grabbed the hilt, then immediately threw it at the knockers.

This move may have looked careless, but I had a plan and a target. In a confined space like this, the power behind explosive attacks had to be limited, and I had the skill to do it.

Tatsuya was rounding up the knockers and pushing them into a corner so they had nowhere to run. The white flash of light from my sword was instantly followed by an explosion, taking out more than a dozen faeries at once. Although a few survived, they had lost most of their limbs, so Kivia and her men could handle them.

"Attack!"

The Holy Knights rushed forward as my feet returned to the ground. A group of Knights charging in formation like this was a force to be reckoned with. Even their armor, covered in sacred seals, was a weapon.

Equipment created with multiple sacred seals had come to be referred to as a seal compound. Various individual seals, such as those for offense, defense, and agile movement, were fused together and engraved into equipment.

Kivia's armor and spear in particular featured a compound geared toward close-quarter combat. She slammed knockers out of the way with her gauntlets as if they were nothing and spun her spear like it was a twig, easily shattering the faeries' tough skin.

A thunderous roar echoed each time the tip of her spear connected with an enemy. It was probably emitting some ballistic force.

Her equipment was most likely developed by the military, rather than sold as a commercial product. My best guess was that it was a surprise attack compound intended mainly for defense. It was the armor of a Holy Knight, meant to rush the enemy while protecting the goddess.

And so the battle was soon over.

Once every last foe had been taken care of, Kivia approached us with an imposing expression.

"...Thank you for coming to our aid. You arrived quickly."

"Yeah, I guess," I replied.

Fortunately, we'd been nearby. It seemed we'd saved them before they suffered any casualties. And yet her soldiers' eyes were cold and distant. They looked at us with obvious revulsion.

Makes sense, I thought. In their eyes, I was a criminal who had murdered a goddess for some unknown reason, and Norgalle was an infamous terrorist. They probably didn't know what to make of Tatsuya, but he must have looked pretty scary to them, fighting like a wild animal.

I figured Kivia was the same. Her face wasn't twisting in disgust like last time, but she was still suspicious of us. I could see it in her eyes. To her, we were no better than a bunch of unscrupulous mercenaries. We knew how to fight, but we couldn't be trusted. A band of criminals.

...I understand their dislike of us, but...

What was it about Teoritta that they didn't like?

The Holy Knights stared at her with a strange darkness I couldn't comprehend. Then again, there was a lot I didn't know about Teoritta as well.

Why were they carrying her in that coffin—that giant box? Why hadn't they woken her up? I tried to read their expressions for clues, but before I had the chance, Kivia interrupted.

"Xylo, I apologize for the inconvenience, but I would like to discuss the plan."

"Well, aren't you polite?" I replied sarcastically. "Why don't you just give us orders?"

"Because the situation is a bit more difficult now. Those faeries used to be human."

"Ah, right."

The same thing had been bothering me for a while, too.

Faeries that were once human grew more monstrous in appearance as time went by, and the enemies we'd just faced still looked very human. That meant they had turned recently. About five days ago, at most.

But this tunnel had been sealed off a month ago, and that could mean only one thing.

"You think there are still people trapped down here somewhere?" I asked.

"When those faeries attacked us, I thought that was very likely. And now we have evidence."

Kivia signaled behind her, toward a nook in the narrow passage. A figure in tattered clothing stood there, neither faerie nor Knight. It was an extremely emaciated man, and I could see he was shivering. Kivia nodded at me solemnly.

"It has become apparent that there are still a few dozen survivors—civilians who worked in the mines and didn't escape in time."

I couldn't believe it.

What was she saying? More than the subject matter, I couldn't get over how awkward it was to admit all that while the man was still here with us.

"Then we must save them," interjected King Norgalle in a grave tone.

Of course. His eyes were the epitome of seriousness—the stern gaze of a man who would not take no for an answer.

"My loyal subjects worked in this mine for the sake of our kingdom." He continued in his booming voice before the baffled captain. "Which means they must be saved at all costs!"

There's no way that's gonna happen, I thought.

I knew how the Holy Knights, Galtuile Fortress, and the Temple worked. They would never allow such a decision. They were serious about getting things done, no distractions. And I knew how they handled this sort of situation, too—they probably intended to slaughter the survivors.

"…Wait. I cannot allow that," replied Kivia, as expected. Her expression was grave, nauseatingly so. "Galtuile will not approve a rescue mission."

"Galtuile?" King Norgalle scoffed. "Preposterous. I, your king, am giving you a direct order."

The only people I knew of who spoke like that were Norgalle and the real king.

"Ignore those imbeciles," he continued. "The military should serve the government and respect my orders!"

No matter what he said, King Norgalle was the one who would be ignored in this situation.

"I have already contacted Galtuile," Kivia said with a soft sigh. "…They said that saving civilians is not our objective, and we are not to suffer casualties in service of such a mission. The survivors can wait until after we've dealt with the Demon Blight."

"Figured as much." I nodded. That was their usual answer. I didn't completely disagree, either. I liked how clear-cut things were when I was in the military.

"What do you think, Xylo Forbartz?"

"Me?"

I was a little surprised to be asked.

"Yes, you. I merely want your opinion. If we were to attempt a rescue mission…"

Kivia seemed concerned about the soldiers behind her. The other Knights had begun to look our way. That was when it hit me. Her expression was stiff. There was doubt in her eyes.

"…what do you estimate would be the extent of our casualties?"

She wasn't sure if she was making the right decision, so she'd asked me what I thought. It had to be serious for her to consult an outsider like me, instead of her staff officer or adjutant.

Could the captain—Kivia—be isolated even within her own unit?

I see. She must be in a pretty awkward position.

It was safe to assume that her unit was extremely new, since I'd never heard its number when I was in the Knights. That meant Kivia was freshly appointed as well. Plus, she was still young and must lack experience as a leader. She was probably still earning her soldiers' trust. Add in her recent failure at Couveunge Forest, and I could see why she might seek counsel from an outsider.

But this was a terrible move on her part. Simply asking me for my opinion had her soldiers staring daggers at her.

So this tells me...

I felt an overwhelming sense of gloom.

...Kivia wants to save as many survivors as possible, but her soldiers don't want to go along with something so risky... I'm inclined to side with them, to be honest.

The Holy Knights consisted of hereditary nobles and specially promoted commoners.

They didn't want to lose their status, especially not if it was hard-won. And that's exactly what would happen if they disobeyed direct military orders. Their reaction came as no surprise.

There's definitely something wrong with Kivia.

That was my conclusion.

"Xylo Forbartz, state your opinion," she ordered, leaving me with no choice but to comply.

"Be prepared to suffer a ton of losses if you decide to rescue the survivors," I told her honestly. There was nothing else I could do. "You would have to retreat while defending the miners, surrounded by faeries. And in a narrow passageway like this..."

Imagining the situation for only a few seconds made clear how awful it would be.

"I can't predict the extent of your losses. It'd depend on the Demon Blight."

"I see." Kivia frowned. "But Holy Knights fight for the people. We—"

"Captain Kivia, my apologies. May I speak?"

A reproachful voice came from behind her. It was one of the men who'd looked displeased this whole time. He wasn't a soldier, though. He wore a simple white robe—a single piece of cloth with a hole for the head only. An iron pendant in the shape of the Great Sacred Seal hung around his neck, proof he worked for the Temple. He must be the priest on loan to Kivia's unit.

Among the Holy Knights, such priests acted as both advisers and engineers for tuning sacred seals.

"I do not wish to be rude," he continued, "but there is no need to ask this man his opinion. I believe we should continue the current mission as planned."

His gaze seemed to plead, *Stop making me state the obvious.*

This priest was still young and definitely didn't want to die here, so I completely understood why he wasn't interested in listening to a penal hero and risking his life for some ridiculous plan.

"Galtuile has given orders to place scorched terrain seals and use them to close off the tunnel, correct?" he continued.

"Yes." Kivia nodded. "I'm aware."

I recognized their strategy. It was commonly used against faeries of this type.

The only goal was to kill the demon lord. Essentially, they would set a few scorched terrain seals at designated spots and detonate them in unison, destroying the demon lord's entire structure. This was a surefire way to eradicate an outbreak of Demon Blight along with its attendant faeries.

The issue was...

"That would mean abandoning my people!" shouted King Norgalle. Like most members of my unit, he was stubborn and full of spirit. "I shall say it once again. You must change course and rescue the civilians! It is your king's order! Ignoring me is an act of t-t-treason!"

"...How terrible." The priest looked at Norgalle and placed a hand on his head. "I cannot bear to see him like this... Norgalle Senridge... To think that the last disciple of Sage Hordeaux and an esteemed genius of the Academy would end up like this..."

He spoke as if he knew Norgalle.

Come to think of it, research concerning the tuning of sacred seals was mainly conducted at the Temple's Academy. Tuning techniques could only be studied in the military or at the Temple. Did that mean King Norgalle was originally from the Temple?

I couldn't help wondering how he wound up here. But my curiosity was only mild. Right now, I had to find a way to calm him down, which I knew was impossible. Could anyone talk King Norgalle into backing down? Maybe if Venetim were here.

After thinking it over, I came to a single conclusion.

"This is unacceptable!" shouted Norgalle, red in the face. "Y-you… you traitors! You fiends are plotting to overthrow the government! I swear I shall have you all executed! This is unforgivable!"

"Relax, Your Majesty."

"Silence, Xylo. Or do you plan on betraying me as well?! Because if you do, I know just what I'll do—!"

"I know of something I'd like to do, too… Kivia, allow me to put forward a proposal to the Holy Knights."

I was well aware what I was about to say was stupid.

And yet, I was saying it anyway. I had no idea why, and no good reason.

Whatever ideals I once had were lost the moment I was found guilty of killing the goddess and removed from the Holy Knights. When I was a Knight, I thought that if I fought, I could protect someone. I believed that through killing the demon lords, I could help create a future where we didn't have to live in fear.

But the moment I learned of *their* existence, I realized how absurd all that was. *Them*—the people who set me up to kill a goddess while I was fighting a war for the survival of mankind. I was determined to pay them back for what they did to me, but any pretty notions about why I fought were long gone. There was something wrong with me back then, when I risked my life for some nameless, faceless strangers.

And yet…

For a while now, I'd felt a gaze I couldn't ignore.

It didn't come from the Holy Knights. This gaze belonged to a goddess.

Teoritta had been watching me without a word. She looked afraid— or perhaps expectant. *I wish she would stop*, I thought. Was she staying silent because she knew it would be more effective on me?

I doubted it. Teoritta must have been genuinely afraid.

Well, I guess that makes sense, too.

I knew how goddesses worked. On the one hand, they lived to be praised by humans. But on the other, they were just as afraid to be rejected and criticized. It was a deep-rooted fear, especially when that criticism came from their chosen knight. Rejection from the one they'd chosen would be soul-crushing.

That was why Teoritta couldn't say a word. She could sense that no one here besides Norgalle would agree with her.

Oh yeah, that idiot.

Norgalle was still kicking up a fuss. And what he was saying was right. If this really were his kingdom, then I would probably agree with him. He'd be a popular ruler, that much I knew.

But if he kept yelling like this, he was going to die. The sacred seal on his neck wouldn't put up with him talking back to the Holy Knights— especially if he disobeyed orders.

Why am I always surrounded by numbskulls?

I felt my blood boil. Why was I always like this? Why did I always cave and ruin everything?

Teoritta and Norgalle were idiots for risking their lives like this. Did they really want to die that badly? Couldn't they keep their damn mouths shut?!

Before I knew what I was doing, I had pushed King Norgalle out of the way and was standing before Kivia.

"This is my proposal: ...Let *us* save the surviving workers."

I'd gone and said it. To tell the truth, I didn't give a crap about any of them. I wasn't a good person like the goddess or Norgalle. I was just annoyed.

"The penal unit alone will take care of the survivors. We already finished setting up camp for you at the deepest layer of the dungeon. You don't need us for anything else, right? So you guys can stick to your original mission."

King Norgalle nodded with satisfaction, and the flames in Teoritta's eyes burned. I was beginning to feel a little *too* warm under her gaze.

"This is our decision and has nothing to do with you, so feel free to bury us alive if we don't make it in time. That sound fair?"

Kivia's frown deepened, but the priest smiled wryly, as if to say,

Knock yourselves out. That made sense. I'd laugh at someone, too, if they said what I just said. In fact, I'd be thinking *Have fun dying!*

"Even if we fail, only us heroes will die."

"…Xylo! My knight!"

Teoritta grabbed my arm. Actually, it was more like she latched on to my arm and was now dangling off it. She weighed about as much as a small dog.

"That's my knight," she continued. "Your bravery is commendable. My judgment was true, after all."

She looked ready to jump for joy. In fact, she was already bobbing up and down.

"You will allow it, yes? Kivia! Priest! You are to praise us for our honorable deed should our rescue prove successful!"

"Obviously, I'll be leaving the goddess with you," I said to Kivia.

"What?!" Teoritta's jaw dropped in shock.

This was the obvious decision. There was no way they would allow me to take the goddess on such a foolish endeavor, especially when it'd probably end with us buried alive.

I lifted my arm with Teoritta attached and held it out toward Kivia. The goddess weighed so little.

"Stop right there, my knight! You tricked me! Mmph…! This is unforgivable!"

She thrashed about, but what could I do? I hadn't tricked her, either.

"I want you to welcome us back with open arms once we succeed."

Kivia silently turned her back, and the priest followed suit, smiling wryly and shaking his head. That was their answer. And just like that, I had dug my own grave once again—this time even deeper.

The miners' hideout was nearly at its limit.

Deep in the mine, at the end of the tunnel and down the tracks, was a shack-like "fortress."

Digging equipment had been laid out to create a kind of defensive barrier, along with large mine carts originally meant to transport workers. The carts were each as big as a small hut, and they were lined up side by side to block the enemy from getting in.

But this wall was already in shambles. It was obvious that if a large faerie attacked, it would fall. The sacred seals holding back the Demon Blight were dim, barely any luminescence left in them. Seals ran out of power quickly without access to the sunlight that fueled them.

That was why the survivors were now under attack.

Norgalle, Tatsuya, and I managed to arrive right as plump centipede boggarts were running amok and on the verge of tearing down the wall. As their fangs bore holes into the mine carts, I suddenly heard a scream.

"Attack!" ordered King Norgalle. "Go forth and save my people!"

What he was saying sounded ridiculous, but it wasn't wrong. So Tatsuya and I followed his orders. What else could we do?

The battle ended in a flash.

"Bfffah!" cried Tatsuya as he lunged forward.

He split a boggart's head wide-open before swinging his ax again and slicing another's body in half. Then he jumped and pulverized the jaw of yet another.

The area fell silent in under thirty seconds.

That probably made it sound like Tatsuya was the only one who did anything, and, well, that was true. But I had another job to do, and I was the only one who could do it.

Once I'd secured the miners, I explained to them that the others with me, who looked like they'd turn into faeries any moment now, were actually allies and here to save them.

There were twenty-four survivors, but they were extremely exhausted. Fortunately, none of them were too weak to walk. I was afraid to ask what had happened to those who were. Did they already die? Or were they disposed of?

"...I never expected to get help," admitted an elderly man who seemed to be in charge. Perhaps he'd been the overseer. He looked like he was still caught in a dream—or a nightmare.

"Are you with the Holy Knights?" he asked.

"In a way," I said. "They gave me the orders to come get you."

I didn't tell them the truth. If they found out we were penal heroes, they'd probably sink right back into despair.

"I need everyone to gear up before we head out."

In my head, I went over what we needed to do next.

To escape, we had to give the noncombatants a means to protect themselves. It would be impossible to protect this many people if all they were doing was holding us back.

I looked over the resources in the area. Some men were already carrying shovels, and there were enough pickaxes and sticks to go around. That should be enough. Even a rock would have worked. Any one of these things could be transformed into a weapon for protection, and we had the technology to do it.

"King Norgalle here is a specialist in tuning sacred seals, so he can help get you all equipped. I want every one of you holding a weapon."

"King...Norgalle...?"

"That's what they call him," I said.

The workers looked confused, but there was no time for explanations.

"Fear not, my loyal followers!"

King Norgalle's voice did sound a bit like a leader's... Sort of. If you didn't pay too much attention to him.

"Once we escape, you will all be rewarded for your hard work. Now grab a weapon and follow my elite warriors!"

What a grand speech. Even though I knew it was pointless—no, precisely because I knew it was pointless, I patted Tatsuya on the shoulder, and he looked at me with his vacant eyes. He was simply reacting to outside stimulation.

I had no idea what had happened to him, but I'd heard he was a human from another world summoned by a goddess.

Some said he got on the goddess's bad side. Others that he was the most talented person in his world at killing. And still others that he specialized in beating and killing women as a hobby, and that was both the reason he was summoned and the reason for his downfall and sentencing. Those were the rumors, at least.

The truth didn't matter anymore.

Tatsuya had neither an ego nor the ability to think for himself. He was merely a hero. He would never feel despair, even during the bleakest of times. He didn't have that function. He had to keep fighting, just like Norgalle and me.

"Tatsuya, you go on ahead and clear a path for us," ordered the king as he went about engraving simple seals into a pickax.

He'd created a basic protection seal and a seal able to wreak a modest level of destruction—enough to destroy a boulder or two. But Norgalle's skills made them even more powerful and long-lasting.

This should be sufficient to inspire confidence in the miners when facing a faerie, even if it wasn't up to the job of actually fighting them.

"Watch each other's back!" Norgalle shouted. "No man left behind! And, Xylo, you—"

"I know," I said, nodding as I counted my remaining knives. Given the situation, it would be best if I stood at the very back—what you'd call a rear guard. Tatsuya wasn't fit for the role, and there was no way I could leave a task like that in Norgalle's hands. I knew the extent of the king's combat skills. He was a rather large man, and that was it.

"I'll take the rear. If anyone wants out, let me know right away." I

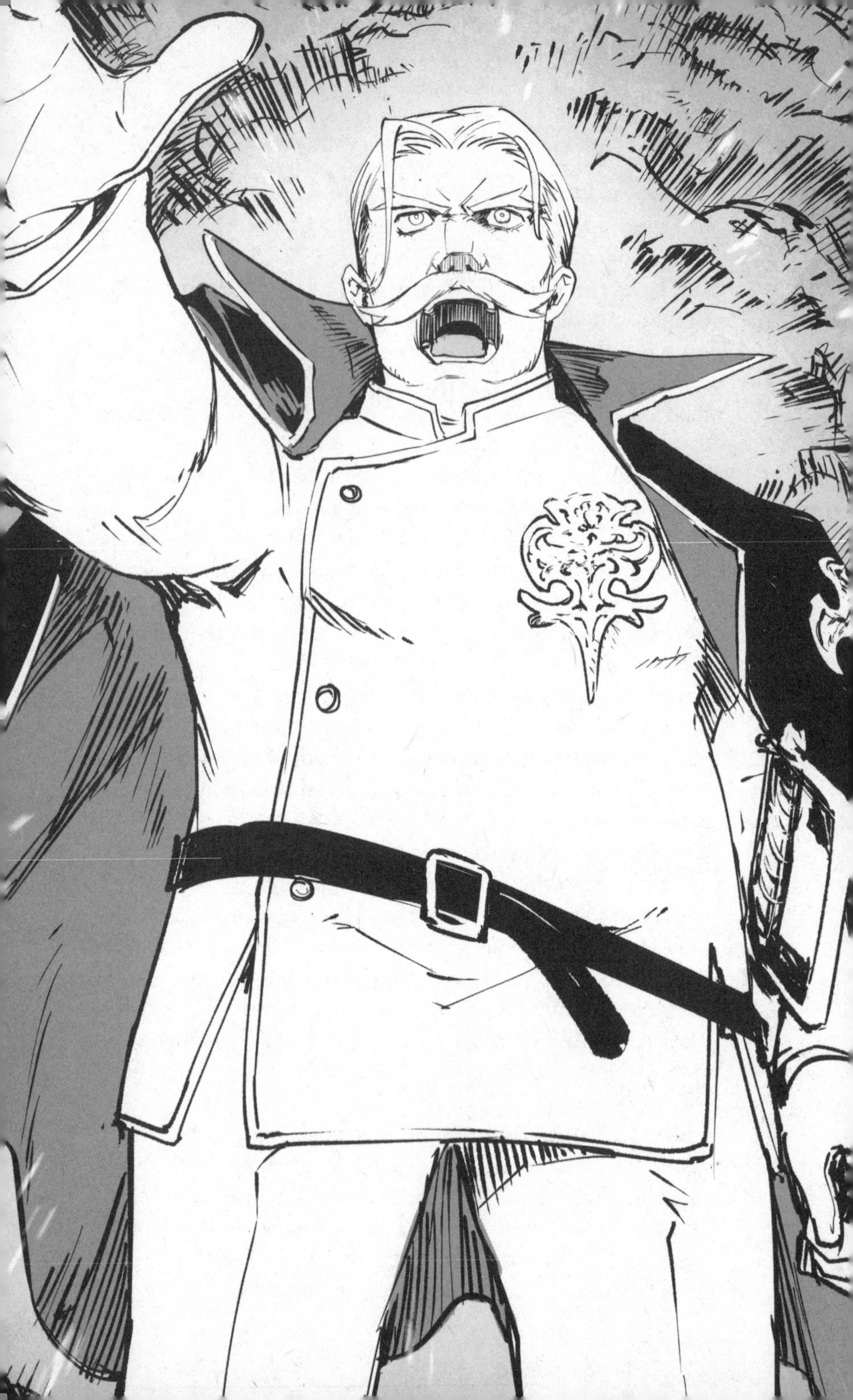

looked over the workers, making a point of joking around. "I'll be sure to put you out of your misery before things take a turn for the worse." The workers looked even more miserable now.

"Xylo, I believe in you," King Norgalle assured me as he engraved another seal onto a flimsy stick. "Once we make it home safely, I will promote you to commander in chief—the greatest of honors."

"Thank you, Your Majesty."

How else was I supposed to reply? But there would be no glory or honor in this battle.

Even if the mission went well, we'd only have saved twenty-four haggard men. And the chance of things going wrong was much higher. We weren't going to kill the demon lord, either, since that wasn't our assignment, and the Holy Knights were probably going to blow up this entire tunnel along with it.

All our mission had was risk: the risk it would all be a huge pain in the ass, and the risk it'd go south and we'd all suffer.

Now this is starting to feel like punishment.

I laughed at myself and pulled out a single knife. Norgalle hadn't finished tuning the sacred seals, but we couldn't afford to wait any longer.

"We should probably start moving, Your Majesty."

I could feel the vibrations in the earth around us.

Something was coming, and that "something" was almost certainly a faerie. I was proven right almost instantly as the mud wall behind me cracked open, revealing the jaw of a vicious centipede boggart. One of the miners shrieked and fell backward.

"Get up! Now!" I shouted.

I threw my knife, piercing the creature's head and using Zatte Finde to blow it clean off. I was already down one knife.

"Next person who falls gets left behind." My declaration echoed down the narrow tunnel. "You need to be able to protect yourself. That's what King Norgalle was telling you."

All at once, the miners let out battle cries, perhaps trying to drown out their own fear. Their shouts combined with Tatsuya's growl, producing a hellish din as he dashed ahead.

I could sense boggarts approaching us from all directions. It was time to show off my moves. I was going to get us out of here with ease and brag to everyone about it later. I looked over at King Norgalle.

"You'll be the first to die, Xylo."

What words of encouragement from my king.

"I will follow," he continued. "And Tatsuya will be last. But our lives are meaningless compared to those of my loyal followers!"

What a king. I could barely communicate with him, but I kind of liked the guy.

The miners we'd come to rescue were left behind for one reason: The order to retreat had come too late.

The Allied Administration Division had an order of priority when evacuating civilians. The first to be evacuated were children, the sick, women, and the elderly. After that were the engineers responsible for tuning sacred seals, merchants who possessed useful equipment, and military personnel. Working people like miners were put off until the very end.

This had likely been decided after much back and forth between the Temple and the military. The Temple would have insisted the weak be saved first, according to their teachings, while the military would have emphasized practical benefit.

Conflict between the Temple and the military had been a major issue ever since the establishment of the Federated Kingdom. It wasn't a problem of which was right or wrong. The domains they controlled were simply far too different.

But when nobles began investing in one or the other, things got out of hand. The chancellor had called for reform and begun taking action to fix the situation, but upon his sudden death five years ago, chaos broke out once again.

"There were...fifty of us originally," said the miner in charge. He was running—tottering, really—on unsteady legs.

The fifty of them had gradually started to go mad.

"...One man started saying he could hear voices at night, until one day...he disappeared while we were all asleep... When he finally came back, he had transformed into a monster."

Voices?

I focused on this detail. It could be a clue revealing the nature of the Demon Blight affecting the mine. Some instances of the Blight could interfere with the human mind.

In this case—

"Xylo! The next wave is coming!" King Norgalle shouted. The miners' screams drowned him out.

As they fled in a long line, an eerie noise came from the mud wall to their side... It was the sound of centipede boggarts moving underground, and it looked like I was the only one who could do anything about it. Tatsuya was busy crushing the boggarts blocking our escape route, and King Norgalle had neither the ability to fight nor the experience to command.

"Ready your shovels for battle."

I gave orders to the miners, doing my best to put on a relaxed, authoritative front.

About five people in the middle of the line had decent shovels on them. They were lighter than the pickaxes, and there was iron at the tips of their blades. They could do a good amount of damage.

"Once it shows its head, hit it. Here it comes. Take a half step back... A little farther. Perfect. Now, go!"

I barked out the final *go*, pumping them up.

The miners' shovels slammed against the boggart, right into its face. The sacred seals seemed to be functioning as intended, creating a fissure in its hard jaw.

It was the boggart that was screaming now. It tried to pull its head back into the hole, but I wasn't going to allow that. I immediately threw a knife into its head, keeping my seal's explosive power to a minimum. It was enough. Its head exploded, bodily fluids gushing into the air.

That put an end to the enemy's attack.

"Perfect," I shouted. "Catch your breath and patch up the injured! You can have some water but only a sip."

I picked up my knife from what was left of the boggart's head. The iron blade was so hot I could have bent it with one finger. This was a drawback of Zatte Finde. The item used as a catalyst for the explosion could easily be scrapped as a result of the blast. When I was a Holy

Knight, I used to receive special knives designed for this purpose with my supplies. Now, I had to use whatever was available.

"Is this the correct path, Xylo?" asked King Norgalle in a whisper. He sounded displeased. "This isn't the way we came."

"We're taking the quickest route out of here. Tatsuya wouldn't go the wrong way. He doesn't make mistakes like that."

Our destination had already been decided, and I had already given that information to Tatsuya.

We were purposely taking a different route than the Holy Knights would be using to withdraw. This was not the path we'd dug a shortcut into and where we'd placed the frontline bases. The Holy Knights were going to set up scorched terrain seals in the deepest parts of the tunnel, and the demon lord would surely notice them moving and preparing their seals.

As a result, it would likely focus its attacks on them. The plan had been to let the Knights attract most of the enemies, and it had ended up working. The faeries came in droves, but there weren't too many of them for us to handle.

But we still had to hurry, and we were nearing our limits. The miners were fatigued, and the boggarts seemed set on finishing us off. We were slowly encountering more and more of them. I figured it was only a matter of time before they swarmed us.

But if we could make it through that, we would be home free.

"I need you to listen up while you rest," I told the miners. They were panting with exhaustion. "We're going to form a line here and temporarily take out our pursuers. I need anyone who can still fight to raise their hand… All right, I want you three to go with Tatsuya. The others will form a detachment… Tatsuya, follow the plan."

I saw Tatsuya's head flop in a nod and shifted my gaze back to the others.

"Sorry, guys. This will be the last time you have to fight. Can you do it?"

Nobody wanted to die. As the miners exchanged glances, I could see they were still clinging to hope… Wait. Hope?

"If you all say we can do it, then we can do it," replied the overseer.

"You people…aren't with the Holy Knights, right? I've heard about you before. The sacred seals…on the backs of your necks…"

"Oh, you know what this is?" Lying wouldn't help now. "Sounds like we're famous. I guess I'm not surprised. I bet you heard we were a group of the nastiest villains around, huh?"

"That may be so, but you still came back to save us." The overseer smirked a little at my joke. Just seeing he was confident enough to smile was a relief. "So whatever happens to us, I figure at least our deaths won't be as bad as they could have been."

"Don't talk like that. I'm not gonna let you die." I waved my hand dismissively.

"Exactly," Norgalle added with a grave nod. "I need you all to live and continue contributing to society."

I couldn't say it pleased me that we were on the same page for once, but what could you do? There was no time to complain. Our next guests were nearly here.

I could hear them digging not only from ahead of us but from above and below as well.

"Tatsuya, take those three and go!" I shouted. "Use the path on your right!"

I gave the ground a rough kick.

Sounds like we've got even more of 'em this time.

I could tell by the echoes. I used to have something even better at locating enemies with sound—a probe seal called Loradd. This sacred seal had already been suppressed, preventing me from using it, but I remembered the feel of it. The things you learn when your life is on the line really stick with you, and even now I could manage a rough estimate.

"They're here."

The dirt crumbled around us as enemies emerged from both walls, the ground, and the ceiling. We were completely surrounded with nowhere to run. Just as I'd expected.

Let's do this.

Most of the boggarts that appeared went after me. It was a full-fledged attack. It looked like they were starting to figure out who was the biggest threat.

They were a little clever, but that was it.

"Fall back fifteen steps! Don't panic. I'll take care of the ones behind us."

This was important—we had to avoid being surrounded, so we needed to take care of the enemies behind us and regroup. But falling back while maintaining order was no easy task—a fact I knew all too well. Even the smallest bit of confusion could lead to a panicked retreat. The best way to prevent that was to install a good rear guard.

And the only person here who could fill that role was me.

"Take this!" I shouted, throwing a knife at the enemies behind us with just enough power to open up a path. The vicious explosion lit up the tunnel for a moment as the miners swung their pickaxes and shovels, running like madmen. I stood alone at the end of our line with my weapon at the ready. It was only a stick, but Norgalle had engraved a simplified sacred seal on it, and I'd attached a knife to the tip, creating a makeshift spear.

"Don't get cocky."

I took a step back as the boggarts continued to charge and closely watched their movements. I thrust my spear, piercing one of the creatures in the head, then took another step back to dodge the next one. Then another step back. One faerie's fangs brushed against my calf as another tried to coil around me until I kicked it away. I was running out of breath. I could pull off only one or two more strikes at this rate.

But that was all I needed. Everything was going to be okay.

"Attack! It's time to fight back!"

"Charge, my elite warriors!"

"Haaaaaah!"

The instant I gave the signal and Norgalle issued his pompous order, the miners charged forward with a powerful battle cry. The overseer had clearly been serious earlier. After falling back those fifteen steps, the miners were able to avoid being surrounded and had enough space to launch a counterattack.

They swung their shovels and pickaxes in unison, pulverizing the boggarts' heads. Shouts mixed with the sounds of metal clanging. But as the boggarts started to put up resistance, the inexperienced miners found themselves in a head-to-head battle, putting them at a disadvantage. There was too much of a gap in their abilities.

But the strategy was still a success. We had spoiled the enemy's surprise attack and bought enough time.

"Guuuhhhhhhh!"

A roar echoed from the depths of the tunnel.

Tatsuya and the other three miners were charging toward the boggarts from behind. We had merely pretended to retreat and lured them into our trap. Meanwhile, our other unit had gone around to ambush them. While it was an old trick common throughout history, it was still very effective.

The boggarts were confused. A few even began to fight one another until Tatsuya swiftly leaped forward, swinging his ax and turning their heads into dust.

"Aaauuuuuuh!"

His drawn-out war cry echoed through the tunnel. This was the critical moment. Sink or swim. I unsheathed one of the knives I'd been saving.

"See."

I raised it into the air...

"You."

...imbuing it with the power of my sacred seal...

"In hell!"

...and threw it.

The boggarts recoiling from the detachment's attacks were engulfed in the flames of the explosion and reduced to ash.

How many more?

This was where my strategy ended. From here on, it was going to be a brawl. I rushed straight into battle, pounding the ground with my feet and leaping into the air. After barely managing to dodge the faeries' attacks, I brought down my knife. Then I fought, killing one enemy after another, as if to prove to them that I was their biggest threat.

Not yet. I need every last one of them focused on me.

Tatsuya and I proceeded to kick up a rain of blood like we were in competition. He howled, and I followed suit.

"Over here!" I shouted. "You're boring me to death!"

This way, we were taking the monsters' focus off the miners. I moved in a frenzy, to the point that I thought my heart was going to explode. I needed the enemy to look only at us.

But we didn't make it in time. It happened in the blink of an eye.

A few boggarts slipped through our attacks. They opened their jaws, exposing their sharp fangs and bizarre organs. The miners' efforts alone couldn't completely stop them, and a single man who missed his timing was bitten. The boggart's jaw latched on to his leg, and he screamed, causing every other boggart to rush in his direction. This was bad.

Dammit.

I forced myself to turn around.

I knew it was a stupid decision, even for me. I now had my back to the enemy, ready to be stabbed from behind, when steel swords suddenly emerged from their heads.

At first, I thought these were a new type of boggart that I had never seen before.

But I was wrong, of course. The swords fell from a void, piercing the faeries' bodies. They shrieked in agony, and their fluids shot into the air. I strained my eyes, trying to figure out what was going on, and saw sparks in the darkness. Beyond Tatsuya, at the end of the tunnel, I could see glowing eyes of flame.

"I apologize for keeping you waiting," announced Teoritta, her voice high with excitement.

Her cheeks were flushed, and she was panting slightly. Not even her pride as a goddess could hide her fatigue—proof of how fast she must have rushed to get here. Or maybe she'd had to escape the Knights and had a difficult time of it.

"The goddess of swords, Teoritta, is here. All of you, feel free to praise me to your heart's content! My knight Xylo, you may now squeal with joy, for I have arrived."

What a ridiculous statement... She really knew just what to say.

There were both pros and cons to Teoritta's arrival.

One pro was that we weren't working against the clock anymore. The Holy Knights could no longer detonate the scorched terrain seals without burying the goddess alive, too.

Another pro was that we now had a large supply of high-quality iron swords.

"I shall engrave my sacred seals! Pierce the ground with swords and construct a fence!" King Norgalle was acting like a military engineer for a change. "Allow me to thank you for gracing us with your presence, Goddess!"

"You can count on me, Norgalle." Teoritta flashed a bold, brilliant smile. It bothered me a little how these two seemed to be on the same wavelength. "With me and my knight together, there's no way we can lose."

As long as we had Teoritta's swords, we could engrave them with protective seals and construct an iron fence.

Right now, we needed to improvise a defensive position for ourselves. More faeries would be coming, and we needed to block them and kick up a ruckus. That would allow us to meet back up with the Holy Knights, who would probably be looking for us.

Now, on to the cons of Teoritta's arrival—basically everything else.

"What are you doing?" I didn't bother to hide my irritation. "Teoritta, what happened to the Holy Knights? Why are you here?"

"I am a goddess, Xylo," she stated proudly. "I ran away. Do you honestly think a few humans could stop me?"

"Teoritta..."

"Now shower me with praise." She stuck out her head as glittering sparks illuminated her smooth golden hair. "...You were in a pinch, and I saved you, didn't I? Did I make it here in time? Was I useful?"

"You're getting no praise from me." I pushed her head away.

That must have made it clear I was mad. She looked like she was going to cry.

"Wh-why are you angry, my knight? Was I too late? But..." She bit her lip, determined to protest. "...It is your fault for leaving me like that! I will not allow you to treat me that way! What you did was an act of betrayal, and if you ever do it again—"

"I've said it before and I'll say it again. I'm not expecting you to make yourself useful."

I needed to be clear with her. I stood right in front of her and glared. Flames flickered in her eyes—no, those weren't flames; they were tears.

She was crying. *Dammit.* Now it looked like I was bullying her.

"You don't need to do me favors. I don't want you to serve me."

"...Then what?" Teoritta attempted a glare of her own. "What do you want from me?"

"Stop trying to die. You don't have to help anyone or 'be useful.' Just shut up and live. Don't stupidly throw your life away for someone else!"

"Yes, I understand." I'd thought I was giving her a stern talking-to, but Teoritta just nodded, looking very pleased with herself. "It is precisely because you are this sort of person that you are worth risking my life for. I was not wrong when I chose you."

"That's not what I meant at all. I'm trying to tell you to stop that. Don't ignore me."

"I am a goddess." She didn't need to tell me that. Her tears were already dry. "I was born to serve mankind. I am not embarrassed, nor do I pity myself. Everyone accepts me for what I am, so why don't you?"

"Because I hate goddesses. I knew one once. She said she was fine with dying if it meant saving someone, too. Whenever I see someone like that, it fills me with rage."

I was out of excuses, and now I was lashing out. And yet Teoritta nodded as if she understood.

"Was she the goddess you served before me?"

"Yeah, the one I killed."

"And it was what she desired, yes?"

She was right.

I was surprised by how sure she sounded, despite having no knowledge of the situation.

"I understand how she felt."

"Oh, you do? Don't make me laugh. Doesn't make a lick of sense to me, throwing your life away for someone else like that."

Even I realized what I was saying didn't hold water.

I was the very one who'd accepted the goddess's way of thinking and killed her, and I knew Teoritta could sense that.

"But I *do* understand. I am a goddess, too, after all. And now I know that you claim to hate goddesses because you are worried for me."

"Then...you also know how much that crap pisses me off, right?"

"Yes. But it does not matter how you feel about me," Teoritta said with a smile. Her expression was both confident and somehow defiant. "I want to be praised by everyone. I want applause and admiration. Maybe that is how goddesses were designed to be. Either way, I want to live believing that I am great. So I am sorry, Xylo, but there is no way you can stop me from doing what I desire, even as my knight."

"I see."

I must have had the stupidest look on my face.

Feeling sorry for Teoritta, thinking her existence was twisted—all these thoughts I harbored were the "objective" drivel of an outsider looking in. None of that mattered to Teoritta, because this was who *she* wanted to be.

"All right."

I still didn't like how goddesses functioned.

But I had to acknowledge one thing, at least—Teoritta really was something. She was trying to live by her own rules, no matter how much it might hurt her.

I placed my palm on her head.

"I have a ton of things I want to say. But for now, I need a hand from a powerful goddess. Things are gonna get ugly from here on out. It's gonna be hell. You up for it?"

"Mmm. Heh-heh, I wouldn't have it any other way." She moved her head around under my hand, forcing me to pat her. "Now, be mindful and act worthy of being my knight! That barbaric personality of yours needs some work."

"You can kiss my ass," I said with a laugh. But just then—

"Xylo!"

—King Norgalle stood up, a sword in his hand.

"Get into position!" he called out. "Something's here! Do not let it get even a single step closer!"

"That doesn't sound very realistic," I shot back.

This man acted as if it was only natural that he would give the orders and that his "retainers" would handle the rest, even if it cost them their lives. What a carefree guy.

I lightly kicked the ground.

From the echo, I could tell there were a lot more enemies than before.

"Th-they're here!" shouted a miner.

But something had changed since last time: We now had a fence with protective seals carved into it. Even if faeries came from underground, they still couldn't break through that fence, unless they wanted the holy light to fry their bodies to a crisp.

"Shall we begin?" Teoritta proudly puffed out her chest and lifted her head. As she rubbed at the air, yet more swords emerged, piercing the ground. "Is this enough, my knight?"

"Yeah."

I decided to stop complaining and lecturing her. After all, a simple human like myself couldn't possibly stop a goddess.

Plus, I was her knight.

"Xylo, if my self-sacrificing devotion bothers you"—*Self-sacrificing.* Those were the words she used—"then all you need to do is protect me. Work hard to prevent what upsets you from ever happening."

"I guess you're right."

Now she was starting to make me laugh.

A self-proclaimed king and a goddess—I was surrounded by the most arrogant people, and I had no say in the matter. I pulled one of the swords Teoritta had summoned out of the ground and swiftly threw it.

There was a flash of light, followed by an explosion. I was able to increase the power of the blast a bit more, since the target was far away. It took out a whole group of boggarts in a single blow. Their hard shells turned to dust, becoming one with the dirt around them. After I threw two more swords, the enemies started to hesitate.

Things always work out. I can do this.

My Bellecour Thunderstroke Seal Compound was perfect for defensive battles like this. I could keep going forever. I could crush any enemy that came our way. The miners were fighting bravely, and Tatsuya was as effective as ever. Even King Norgalle's encouraging shouts almost seemed like they meant something. The wall of swords kept the boggarts back.

"Vwaaah…!"

Tatsuya roared by my side as I threw another sword.

"Aaawoooooo!"

What incredible momentum. He flew forward, swinging his ax as if the word *tired* wasn't even in his dictionary. He cut down the enemy to his side, then charged forward the next moment and swung his fist down into another boggart's head. He kept doing this over and over again. What were his fists even made of? He was somehow able to break through their shells and smash their heads in with his bare hands.

For a moment, I felt as if our eyes met, and I smiled.

We were both warmed up and ready to go, so I briefly glanced back at Teoritta.

"Teoritta, if this is really what you want"—I reached out and plucked a new sword from the ground—"then you need to follow your knight's orders. First, I decide where you risk your life. And…"

I threw it. There was no way I'd miss. Another blast followed.

"…I decide where you die, too."

"Very well." There was no concern in her voice. "That is no problem at all, my knight. That is what I was born to do."

Blind trust.

It was too much, and yet it was what I needed right now. I needed the burden and responsibility to motivate me.

"Excellent! Then let us do this, men! Charge!"

We now had the advantage, and King Norgalle had let it go to his head. I really wished he hadn't said that.

"Advance forward toward the exit!" he continued.

"Wait, Your Majesty." I stopped him in a panic.

It was true the boggarts had thinned, and it looked like we could rush through toward the exit, but…

"We have the advantage because we're fighting defensively. We need to keep—…"

I started to make my case, then stopped. It suddenly dawned on me that King Norgalle might have made the right call.

What's that sound?

A faint but unpleasant din had caught my attention.

At first, I thought it was just the reverberation from Zatte Finde's explosions. But it was sharper and more piercing—like the scraping of metal—and it was rapidly growing louder, to the point that my eardrums were starting to hurt.

It almost sounded like a scream. Or maybe a voice…but whose voice?

No. Something's wrong. Don't listen to it!

I knew this type of attack.

I caught myself unconsciously trying to confirm what it was but covered my ears and stopped myself. With a swift survey of my surroundings, I saw that the miners could hear the "sound" as well. They had to be in pain. The whole lot of them had fallen to the ground.

King Norgalle was curled up on the dirt as well, his face twisting in agony. He'd dropped his lantern, and its sacred seal was flickering. Only Tatsuya remained normal as he mechanically continued to crush the boggarts.

The next threat was closing in on us.

"…Teoritta!"

I looked back at her, still covering my ears.

She softly gripped my hand, alleviating my pain somewhat. The sound began to fade. She was using the protective and healing powers all goddesses possessed.

"It appears it has come to us."

She was forcing a confident smile, perhaps trying to give me courage. She was so strong. Unfortunately, it wasn't very effective, since the rest of her face was as white as a sheet.

"The source of the Demon Blight is here."

Something was slithering deep in the darkness. I could see countless tentacles—or perhaps they were the vines of a tree.

The creature gave a high-pitched shriek. At last, I knew what the voices from a moment ago were saying. Their words were conveyed to me not by sound but by feeling.

I found you.

That was what it said.

I found you, it screamed over and over.

Something in the darkness had found Teoritta.

The sound was grating, even with Teoritta's protection—a testament to this demon lord's skill at manipulating the mind.

It felt like something was screaming at the back of my head. Like it was in pain—like it was crying. It was like the feeling of loneliness, and it was stabbing me right in the middle of my brain. It—

No.

Don't think about it.

I purposely shut out the voice. I had no other choice. I had encountered a demon lord with a similar attack once before—one that contaminated the human mind.

The overseer had said that there used to be fifty miners until they started disappearing into the night one by one, claiming they heard a voice calling them. That was what this voice did to people.

"Don't move!" I shouted to those around me. The miners were either writhing on the ground in agony or trying to stand up and fight through the pain. I grabbed one of those trying to stand.

"Don't move. Stay down."

"W-wait…" He was moving his hands, pleading with me. "Don't you hear that voice coming from over there? It's trying to tell me something!"

He stared into the darkness, anxiously scratching at his head, so I grabbed him and held him down.

"It's just your imagination. Ignore it."

"I can hear it, but it doesn't make any sense. Wh-what is it trying to tell me?!"

"If you go over there, you're going to die. That much makes sense, right?"

Tentacles were extending out from the darkness.

They looked like vines. In fact, they *were* vines. This demon lord must have originally been a plant. But it was like no plant I had ever seen before, and it was massive. Was this really the source of the Demon Blight? Its vines were as thick as logs. One hit would do terrible things to the human body.

Tatsuya leaped around with extraordinary speed, severing each squirming tentacle-vine that met his ax.

"B-but something... Something..." It was as if the panicking miner couldn't even see the scene unfolding in front of him. "It's saying something! But I—I can't... I... Ah! Ahhh! Ahhhhhh!"

He began violently scratching at his ears until they bled. Then he tried to push me out of his way and take off, leaving me with no choice.

I punched him back down onto the ground.

We can't stay on the defensive.

No sense pretending.

Almost everyone was on the ground covering their ears, and the ones who could move were trying to stagger their way toward the demon lord, forcing me to knock them back down.

Those mentally strong enough to fight through the pain would hear a voice—the voice of the demon lord—calling them.

The jarring screeches weren't its actual attack. Its true weapon was its voice. It was preventing anyone from moving, and it would likely kill and eat anyone who managed to approach it.

It was only because of Teoritta that I was managing to overcome its effects.

There was a certain bond between a goddess and their chosen knight, and the power that protected Teoritta's mind was just barely keeping me from losing my own. The rest was thanks to the fence of swords and Norgalle's sacred seals. Tatsuya wasn't having any problems, either, but he was a special case.

Regardless, at this rate everyone was going to die. And like hell I was gonna let that happen.

"Change of plans! It's time to strike back! Your Majesty!"

I pulled a sword out of the ground and kicked the crap out of Norgalle while I was at it. He groaned, but his eyes were still rolled back in his head.

"Wake up! It's time to get to work!"

I picked up his lantern and thrust it up to his head. It should have had a powerful protective seal carved into it, but it wasn't doing the trick. Norgalle groaned softly and grabbed the lantern, but he was still in no shape to move.

"M-my throne... My throne...," he mumbled. "I won't let you steal it...from me...you thieves...! You shall pay with your lives, you cursed usurpers!"

Great. His imagination was running even wilder than usual. He wasn't going to be any help like this.

Maybe I could shatter his eardrums?

If that could keep him from hearing the sound and free him from its influence, it might have been worth trying. But you use more than just your ears to hear, and we were up against a demon lord—who knew what kind of unfair, illogical abilities it possessed. Besides, there was no time to test such hypotheses.

"Dammit! Teoritta!"

"I am here." Teoritta grabbed my arm as sparks shot from her fingertips. "State your wish, my knight, and I shall grant it."

"We need to snipe the enemy from here and back up Tatsuya."

The ominous sound would probably only get worse if we left the fenced area. But would I be completely incapacitated? I couldn't check, either, since there was no coming back once I stepped out.

"Tatsuya can handle this. I need more swords."

"That's what I like to hear, my knight. You can count on me."

Teoritta summoned more sharp, glittering swords. These ones had slender blades suited to throwing.

Been a while since I've fought a long-range battle like this.

I used to have even better seals, like Carjisa, which had greater range and power, or Yak Leed, which could penetrate even a castle wall.

Guess I can't waste my time crying over spilled milk.

I tightened my grip on the sword in my right hand and held it over my head. I could see Tatsuya leaping into the darkness, further proof the grating sound wasn't affecting him. He was a human-shaped weapon focused solely on attacking the demon lord.

This must be why they used heroes to fight the Blight.

"Tatsuya!" I shouted, launching my sword. "Keep pushing forward! Kill the demon lord!"

My blade missed the squirming tentacles, but it pierced the nearby mud wall. The bursting light of Zatte Finde scorched the darkness, ripping the nearby tentacles apart and sending sap flying into the air like blood. The demon lord's screeching grew louder, and I staggered, but Teoritta caught me before I fell.

Her eyes sparkled, as if to say, *Aren't you glad I came?* But I didn't have time for a comeback. I had to throw another sword, and another, and another. I had to back up Tatsuya.

Just like I thought. I can't leave this fence.

I wanted to do more to help, but I knew Tatsuya could manage.

I threw another sword, and another, and another.

While my aim wasn't precise, I made up for it in numbers, blowing off numerous tentacles in rapid succession. I was quite literally carving a path for Tatsuya to strike, and I wasn't going to let any boggarts get in his way, either.

Light and explosions trailed one another down the dark tunnel. Tatsuya's shadow leaped along with him in stark relief. His eerily long arms and legs painted the wall like some sort of dancing monster.

"Guh."

He reached his target in almost no time, grunting with his mouth half-open.

"Gah!"

The frenzied swing of his ax tore through the creature's tentacles until it reached the root—what appeared to be the bulb of the plant.

That was when I realized my mistake.

Seriously?

Tatsuya buried his ax in the bulb, splitting it with ease. It exploded, but the tentacles didn't stop moving. Because that wasn't the demon lord's heart.

Was it a lure?

But that would mean...

"Bfff... Gah!"

A muffled voice grunted behind me. It was the overseer being slammed against the wall. More tentacles and a bulb even bigger than the one Tatsuya had destroyed were peeking out from the ground below.

It broke through our fence! We're out of time...!

More than a few of the swords making up our fence were bent and broken, and the light of their sacred seals had faded. They were out of energy, and once its luminescence was gone, a sacred seal was useless. Even the king's extraordinary work was no exception. We must have used up every last bit of natural light stored in the steel.

I unsheathed a knife and turned around to see a bulging eye emerge from the massive bulb as it tore through the dirt.

There it is.

This was the heart—the demon lord's true form. Its tentacles reached out and grabbed another miner before it swung him around. The moment his body hit the ground, I could tell his neck was broken.

Dammit.

I tried to aim for the eye, but there were too many vines. The bastard was reinforcing its defenses. The only one who could get through something like this was Tatsuya.

"Xylo, watch out!" shouted Teoritta as she latched on to my arm.

Wriggling tentacles were heading our way. I swung my sword, tearing through the vines and exploding them.

I sure am popular today. Can't catch a break.

The area protected by the sacred seals was already on the verge of collapsing.

We needed more hands. Tatsuya was battling the tentacles at the other end of the passageway, and over here we had only the unconscious miners, the goddess, King Norgalle, and me.

"Aaaaaahhhh!" Even Norgalle was slamming his head against the ground and screaming. "It is all mine! It all belongs to me! I will protect my nation! Over my dead body, you cursed usurpers!"

Norgalle was useless to us right now. His mental state was only getting worse, and communication would be futile.

Things were falling apart like a chain reaction.

"There she is!"

I heard a sharp voice, followed by countless footsteps—it was Kivia and her Knights following our path.

"There's Goddess Teoritta," she said. "We'll ask questions later. For now, we're here to help, Xylo!"

"Don't! Stay back, you idiot!" I yelled.

Kivia was so earnest, but right now that wasn't what I needed. I couldn't let her step into the range of the demon lord's voice. But was there anything I could do to stop her?

We're all gonna die.

The likelihood was only increasing. Teoritta gripped my arm tighter.

"Xylo." She was fired up, and sparks were flying off her. "You can rely on me. It is time. You need my help, do you not?"

She was going to summon more swords—maybe a whole bunch of them. Would she be able to slice off all its tentacles and pierce its eye-heart?

Was it possible? Did we even have any other options? Teoritta's hair was sparking ceaselessly. I could tell she was reaching her limit. I had to make a decision, but I hesitated.

That was when Norgalle shouted:

"Cursed usurpers!"

King Norgalle was also at his limit, mentally. He raised his lantern, shining by the power of its sacred seal, and twisted the lid slightly open. I could see flickering blue flames spilling out of the crack. This must be another of those dangerous-sounding contraptions he'd tried to explain when we were setting up the supply chests—the trap that spewed fire. The instant it saw the fire, the demon lord's eye opened wide. It twitched and started backing up.

That was when it hit me.

Fire!

This was a demon lord that had formed from a plant, so it was very likely weak to fire. We didn't need to hit it with some powerful attack; we only had to burn it.

"Your Majesty! Pass me the lanter—!"

But before I could finish my sentence, the demon lord's vines slithered across the ground and grabbed Norgalle's leg with fang-like thorns. I couldn't reach him in time.

Snap!

Before he could finish twisting the lid, the vine ripped his right leg clean off. He screamed and dropped the lantern. I dove to catch it.

The demon lord twisted its body, trying to get as far back from the lantern as it could. It was fast. Would I make it in time? It didn't matter. I had to do it or die trying. I sprinted as quickly as I could, slipping under a thorny vine as it wriggled before me.

I won't let you escape. An arm or two is nothing—

Midway through my thought, a rumble passed through the ground below me.

It sounded like something was being carved away and broken into pieces.

That was when I noticed a vine being pulled up from the ground. The parts of the demon lord were apparently connected like sweet potato roots, and as a result, it couldn't retreat any farther. Its scream echoed in the back of my head as it thrashed about, trying to sever its own vine.

I swiftly glanced behind me and caught sight of the cause.

"Grrr!"

It was Tatsuya. Unbelievable. Just how strong was this guy? He had grabbed one of the tentacles and was dragging it back as if it was nothing. His shoulder muscles swelled and rippled. He wasn't going to let the demon lord get away, no matter what.

"Gwoooaaaaaah!"

Another one of his nonsense screams. Actually, I was starting to feel like they weren't so meaningless after all. It was just a feeling, but it seemed like he was telling me to hurry up and kill the demon lord.

I was more than happy to oblige. I fixed my sights on its vines as they whipped around in agony.

"Teoritta!"

"I am here."

Our conversation was brief, but that was all a goddess and their knight needed to communicate.

"Put an end to this, my knight."

Teoritta spoke, and a sword emerged from the void. This time its blade was curved like a nata hatchet. I instantly grabbed it and swung, slicing the vine as it flew toward me. The next one was coming, but there was nothing it could do to me now.

I'd already picked up Norgalle's lantern.

"See you in hell."

The instant I removed the lantern's lid, pale blue flames shot out and mercilessly scorched the demon lord. The roaring inferno illuminated the darkness for around ten seconds as the enemy's ear-piercing screeches slowly faded. That was more than enough time to reduce the demon lord to ash.

Everyone fell silent. Kivia and the Knights stood in mute amazement, unable to process what had happened. Norgalle, meanwhile, had bigger issues to worry about. Tatsuya was the only exception.

"Gah... Hfff."

He let out a grunt like a yawn as he dropped to his knees. It seemed even he was exhausted.

I swept my eyes over the extinguished lantern, the scorched demon lord, and the walls and ground nearby. Small rocks were glowing red and melting.

Only Norgalle was dumb enough to make a trap for a supply chest this dangerous.

Nothing worth mentioning happened after that—well, except finding out that the king's torn-off leg was shredded so badly by the thorns that it was beyond salvaging. That was funny. He was sent away for repairs immediately due to massive blood loss.

But honestly, it was hard not to feel depressed when I thought about what would happen next.

Teoritta and the rest of us had violated the rules, and there would be no excuses.

The concept of vacations did not exist for penal heroes.

After all, we were meant to be bound and locked up in a cell.

But we were sometimes put on standby in between punishments or in the lead-up to being handed an even heavier sentence.

Although we were still prohibited from leaving our designated areas, we could get a little rest—or something like it. We could drink tea in the cafeteria or use the training facilities. Tatsuya, for example, was almost always out catching rays.

I, however, didn't feel like going out. That was because Mureed Fortress, where we were stationed, was way too crowded.

What a pain.

On days like this, nothing beat reading a book.

Although we were penal heroes, as part of the military, we could easily get our hands on books for entertainment. And so I decided to lie down on the floor and lose myself in the pages.

Today was the day of the Great Exchange. Held once every ten days, the Great Exchange was essentially a small market where you could buy things from visiting merchants dispatched from the Verkle Development Corporation, instead of the permanent fortress shops usually available. It was held in the courtyard, and you could buy anything from daily supplies to nonessential luxury items. The most popular products were alcohol, cigarettes, mail delivery services, and sweets.

Soldiers would purchase these goods using a pseudocurrency known simply as military notes, issued by Galtuile for use in place of actual money. This currency could then be taken by the recipients to a designated government building in any city and exchanged for real money.

Tons of soldiers gathered at the Great Exchange. Naturally, members of the Thirteenth Order would be among them—yet another reason I wanted to avoid the whole thing.

Besides, I had a job. I had to watch over King Norgalle. After losing his right leg, he'd come back from repairs along with Dotta and seemed to be having trouble with everyday tasks.

"Commander in Chief! Commander in Chief Xylo! Where are you?!" hollered King Norgalle, awkwardly slamming against the floor of the corridor as he walked. "The merchants are here, and I want a drink! Red wine! On the double!"

Ever since he'd returned from repairs, his delusions were even more severe, and he was now calling me "commander in chief" and Tatsuya "general." He seemed to have lost quite a few of his memories and could hardly recall anything that happened in the tunnels. He had also decided we heroes were his royal guards. To make matters worse, his right leg hadn't regenerated successfully, so he was now sporting a wooden prosthetic. The Temple was currently in the process of selecting a corpse from which to harvest a replacement limb. It was only taking so long because the guy was so damn massive.

"Commander in Chief Xylo! There you are!"

King Norgalle threw open the door to my allocated room. His entire body was still wrapped in bandages, and I briefly wondered if they were needed just to hold him together.

"The merchants are here. Go fetch me my wine."

"Got any money, Your Majesty?" I reluctantly sat up and crossed my legs. "You know our kingdom's treasury is empty, right? Can't even afford booze."

"What? Is poverty really that bad? Where is the minister of finance?! What is he doing?!"

Technically, it was King Norgalle's fault, since his military notes would disappear as quickly as they came. He always wasted them on alcohol and luxury foods. But of course he didn't remember that, not with *his* memory.

"If you want wine that badly, you're gonna have to take out a loan."
I provided him with a compromise. "I don't have time to help, though,
since I've gotta run my eyes over this important literature. Get Venetim
or someone to help you out."

"The chancellor is currently busy keeping an eye on Dotta."

"Oh."

That's right.

Dotta was back, and today was the Great Exchange. That meant
someone had to monitor him. Wrapping him up in chains wasn't
enough—he needed someone constantly keeping an eye on him. Venetim was the commander, if only in name, so the task naturally fell to
him. It wasn't like Tatsuya could do it.

"Looks like Tsav's your best bet, then." I suggested our other recently
returned team member. He'd been on a separate mission until now. "You
can borrow money from him."

"Tsav is completely unreliable. He spends his money like water, and
he is a terrible gambler. I highly doubt he has any funds left."

"Nah, I heard he was finally barred from the gambling house here.
He shouldn't have anywhere to spend other than the market. If you go
now, you should be able to catch him before it's all gone."

"I suppose I have no choice," said the king, nodding gravely and
turning on his heel. My problem was now Tsav's problem.

Tsav was our sniper.

He was an amazing shot, but he'd been sentenced to the penal hero
unit, so you could easily guess what kind of guy he was—a former assassin and a real piece of shit.

He'd been sent to the western battlefront alone, but I had no idea
how well he'd done. He'd probably fulfilled his mission, at least, seeing as
he came back with all his limbs intact. I guess he must have hit his target.

Whatever the case, I'd finally scored some peace and quiet.

I lay back down. *Time to read a book and relax until the Great
Exchange is over,* I thought.

But I was a fool. It was precisely at times like this that people would
come bother you one after another.

"My knight!" Teoritta flew into my room, her steps light and airy.
"There you are, Xylo. I was looking all over for you."

"What do you want?"

"Will you not attend the Great Exchange? I assumed you would be out shopping."

"I don't want to see any Holy Knights."

If all they did was scowl at me, I wouldn't care, but I didn't want anyone picking a fight. I wasn't in the mood for sarcasm or criticism, either.

I wish they'd just gimme a break.

I didn't trust my temper in a situation like that.

"Then get up and play with me."

Teoritta gazed arrogantly down at my face, casting a shadow over where I lay on the floor.

"What about you, Teoritta? Aren't you going?"

"...I am a goddess! I have no interest in such things."

Yeah, she's definitely lying, I thought. But I couldn't blame her.

It was true that goddesses weren't free to use the Great Exchange. People expected them to maintain an air of authority, and they'd need permission from a Holy Knight or a priest, on top of being supervised.

I assumed Kivia and the priest loaned to her unit were a little busy at the moment. They still had to decide how to deal with me and Teoritta going forward.

"If you are free, then allow me to bestow upon you the honor of entertaining me... You must be brimming with joy, yes?"

There was a small box in her hand. It seemed to contain a game-board and pieces.

Such games varied by region but were generally called zigg. Gameplay consisted of moving marked pieces on a board to try to take over your opponent's territory. The rules were simple, so anyone from kids to adults could play. It was a good time killer. Quite a few soldiers enjoyed it, and some even used it to gamble.

I was somewhat fond of the game myself, and when I saw Teoritta with nothing to do while we were on standby, I'd taught her how to play. That was three days ago, and ever since then, she had been bringing the board to my room whenever she had time on her hands. *What have I done?* I thought. But it was too late.

"I have been practicing. You shall not win so easily this time."

"We just played last night."

"That was before Venetim taught me a very useful strategy earlier today. Heh-heh. It is an ancient technique called hidden spear, used often in the royal palace of Meto, and…"

I figured Venetim was lying to her, but I decided to keep my mouth shut. And besides, "ancient technique" was just a nice way to say "out-of-date."

As Teoritta hurriedly began setting up the board, I put out a hand to stop her.

"I'm busy right now. I'm reading."

"What? …A book? You can do that later," she said. She seemed interested in what I was reading, however, and tried to sneak a peek. "I never expected you to be a fan of books. What are you reading? Is it interesting?"

"Poems. A poetry anthology."

"A poetry anthology…! Xylo, you? …Reading poems?"

Teoritta was taken aback, her eyes wide. She seemed genuinely caught off guard. Was it really that surprising?

"What kind of poems? I must know. I shall allow you to read them to me."

"No."

"Hmph!" My blunt reply earned a pout from the goddess. "Very well, then. I can read them myself… Surely you will allow me to read by your side! …Right?"

"Uh, I don't think these would be very interesting to a goddess."

I closed the book. It was an anthology from the old days entitled *Dragon-Drunk*.

"These are the poems of Altoyard Comette. He was a raging alcoholic, and after being fired from his duties at the palace, he holed up alone in the mountains. In his later years, he became delusional and started wanting to become a dragon. Night after night, he would practice flying, until he eventually fell off a cliff and died."

"Uh-huh… What an eccentric individual he must have been."

"Almost every poet back then was like that."

And those were the kinds of poems I enjoyed. I might've tried to become a poet myself if I hadn't joined the military. It seemed like a comfortable, easygoing way to live.

"Anyway, we can play some zigg if you're really that bored."

I wouldn't be able to relax with someone reading over my shoulder, so I gave in and sat across the gameboard from Teoritta. My original aim was simply to kill time until the Great Exchange was over anyway.

"Really?!" Her lips were curling into a beaming smile when all of a sudden—

"...Xylo Forbartz."

—Yet another visitor appeared at my door.

It was a tall woman with long black hair who I had never seen before. I wondered for a split second who it could be, then realized my mistake. I didn't recognize her in her military uniform because she was usually wearing a full suit of armor. Her hair, too, was now tied back in a braid, further confusing me.

It was Kivia, and she'd come alone.

That meant she probably wasn't here to arrest me... But then why?

"There you are. I thought you'd be at the Great Exchange... I wasn't expecting Goddess Teoritta to be with you, either."

"What an honor, having the one and only captain of the Thirteenth Order come all the way here to see me." I couldn't keep the sarcasm from my voice. "Did you already decide what to do with us? Or are you here to give us our latest orders?"

"...Both. But I came in person for a different reason." Kivia knitted her brow. She probably wasn't a fan of my tone. "Follow me, Xylo."

"Where to? The underground torture chamber?"

"No," she replied seriously. It was like she didn't know I was joking. What she said next, however, caught me by surprise.

"I...would like to speak with you. That is all. Anywhere is fine." Then she fixed me with a sharp glare, as if she was challenging me to a duel. At least that was how I interpreted it. "So? Will you speak with me or not? I need an answer now."

The hell? I thought. It wasn't like I had the right to refuse.

"Sure, I'll talk. But could I pick the place?"

"Tell me where. I will try to be as accommodating as possible."

"The Great Exchange in the courtyard. I want to do some shopping, and I want to take Teoritta with me as well."

"What?!"

"Mmph…"

Kivia was at a loss for words. Meanwhile, Teoritta sprang to attention, raising her head. The flames in her eyes brimmed with hope as she looked back and forth between Kivia and me.

"Xylo, Kivia, I would love to talk. Shall we head out immediately? I think we should go now!"

After about ten seconds of silence, Kivia agreed. "…Fine. I can meet your demands… To the courtyard!" she declared.

It was as if she was ordering us to march into battle.

Heroes lived—or rather, were imprisoned in a place called Mureed Fortress.

It was originally built to block passage to the royal capital from the northern territory. Protected by a river on one side and cliffs on the other, it was a natural place for a fortress. For this reason, it was also referred to as the Nest, and no matter what else you said about it, the view was incredible. Nothing beat the sight of the Kad Tai River from the steeple at dusk.

This river was the fortress's lifeline. It was how we got supplies from the port city of Ioff, and it was an important preemptive line of defense against the Demon Blight coming down from the north. The expansion of the Demon Blight and the accelerating loss of territory in recent years had only increased its importance.

And that was precisely why the greedy Verkle Development Corporation had to get in on it. They were sending crowds of merchants to the Great Exchange with plenty of goods aimed at maintaining soldier morale.

Now all I need is a woman, Dotta and Tsav would say, but even if such a shop existed, there was no way they would let penal heroes use it. The most you could do with the few military notes we had was gamble or buy some booze.

"Xylo, look at that!"

Teoritta was skipping among the merchant stalls. They were

decorated with brightly colored signs, flags, and strips of cloth, lending the bland courtyard a festive look. It was certainly working for Teoritta, judging by her utter excitement.

"Is that food? Or is it some kind of decoration?"

Teoritta was pointing at a crimson piece of sculpted sugar candy. It looked to be in the shape of a strawberry, and when the sun hit it just right, it could easily be mistaken for a piece of jewelry.

"It's candy," I said. "You've never seen candy like that before?"

"Candy like that did not exist when I was created. It looks almost like a gem, doesn't it?"

She gazed intently at the candy, her eyes filled with curiosity. *Interesting.* They say that goddesses like her were created long ago—at least three hundred years in the past. The Temple claimed they were the last children of a race of gods who lived a thousand years in the past, but that was, without a doubt, a lie. I felt sure goddesses were man-made.

Otherwise, why would they be so ready to sacrifice themselves for the sake of humanity? It was all too convenient. I didn't know what happened after they were created, but somehow the technology used to make them was either lost or concealed. Maybe it happened in a large-scale attack by a demon lord or in a war between different groups of humans.

I wasn't too familiar with that era of history, and I hadn't been interested in learning more. Until now, that is.

"What about *that*, Xylo? It smells wonderful. That long, stringy food…"

"Those are noodles. Cuisine from the West. They cut wheat into thin strips, then fry them in butter and some kind of paste."

"Oh wow! Then…uh, what's that?! There are tons of people lined up over there. Do you see it? The sign with the bear! It appears to be very popular, whatever it is."

"That's…"

The line was made up of mostly female soldiers. This led me to believe the stall was selling some kind of sweet, but there were so many people that I couldn't see what it was. The sign outside the stall featured a mascot animal that did indeed look like a bear.

"I've never seen a sign like that before. No clue what it could be."

"You don't know?" said a voice. "That's Miwoolies Creams."

To my surprise, the voice was Kivia's.

"They sell frozen desserts," she continued. "The shop is really famous in the First Capital. They freeze whipped cream, then drizzle honey and sprinkle nuts on it. It's simply delectable. That cute bear is their mascot, and they're currently inviting suggestions to name it."

"Incredible! The development of civilization is such a wonderful thing!" Teoritta's eyes were sparkling. "Doesn't it look delicious, Xylo?! I think so. You've never had it before?"

"This is the first I'm even hearing about it. Is the place new? I wasn't expecting you to be so well informed, Kivia."

"...Is it so surprising?" She sounded a little offended. "Yes, I eat frozen desserts from time to time. Is that a problem?"

"No, I never said it was."

"You better be ready for a fight if you're criticizing me for eating sweets! What? Is it a problem that I like cold desserts and that I own goods with that bear embroidered on them? Are you saying there's something wrong with me submitting names for the contest?!"

"I didn't say any of that!"

It seemed like my comment had dredged up some trauma for Kivia. She must have been teased in the past. It *was* surprising that she'd submitted a name for the mascot. She just didn't seem the type to—

"Ahem. What are you daydreaming about?"

"Are you gonna police my thoughts now...?"

I decided not to say another word about it. I didn't want to accidentally offend her again. You never knew what was going to trigger someone like her.

I shifted my gaze toward Teoritta for help, but she was staring hard at the stall with a serious expression. No wonder she was so quiet.

"Xylo." Teoritta's small hand wrapped around my arm. Her gaze never left the frozen dessert stall. "Are you not curious how it tastes?"

This was a bizarre way of telling me that she wanted to try some, but it was very in character for a goddess—or for Teoritta, at least. Due to some misplaced pride or shame, she wanted to make it sound like I was the one interested, not her.

"I guess I could go for one. How about you?"

"Of course! I could never refuse an offering from my knight."

"Then pick out two flavors you like... Wait." As I got out some military notes to hand her, I looked back at Kivia. "Make that three. Right, Kivia?"

"I... I'm fine," she replied. "I'm trying to save. I have a long-term budget planned out." I'd been joking, of course. But once again, after what looked like a brief, agonizing internal struggle, she responded with total seriousness.

I gave up and passed Teoritta the notes. Knowing her, I figured she'd want to do the shopping herself.

"Teoritta, do you think you could use these and grab two frozen desserts?"

"Of course! Ah, what would you do without me? I will be right back!"

She dashed off with a spring in her step, her golden hair fluttering in the wind, and lined up in front of the stall with the others. Everyone's eyes were drawn to the goddess, but she paid them no mind, as if it were only natural for them to stare.

"...Xylo, there is something I need to tell you," Kivia said, staring at Teoritta's back from afar. It sounded like she was finally going to get to the point. "My opinion of you all has changed somewhat. You're not simply a pack of villains. You're... How to put this—?"

"We're also stupid pieces of shit, right? Yeah, I know."

"That isn't true. At least, not in your case," she replied with a straight face. This woman really didn't understand the concept of joking.

"I still haven't forgotten how you saved my men back at Couveunge Forest, nor have I forgotten what you did for us at the Zewan Gan mines. You saved the miners we were going to abandon."

"We ended up losing more than we saved, though."

"But you still did it, and I believe you deserve respect for that. The wounded soldiers who managed to retreat back at Couveunge Forest were very grateful, you know."

"I'm glad." I smiled slightly. This felt like the first good news I'd gotten in a while. "They made it out alive, huh? I guess it wasn't all for nothing, then. Was that all you wanted to talk about?"

Kivia didn't reply. She glared sharply at me as though I'd offended her. *What did I say this time?*

"What's with the look?" I asked.

"Don't be ridiculous. I'm not looking at you," said Kivia. She frowned and cleared her throat. "I was simply surprised to see you smile, since you always seem so angry."

"The world can be an aggravating place."

"...If you could only fix that attitude of yours, then—... No. Forget it. At any rate, I simply wanted to commend you on your skills. You continue producing great results... Perhaps Goddess Teoritta, too"— there was a hint of pain in her voice when she said Teoritta's name— "was saved by forging a pact with you."

"What's that supposed to mean?"

"...Goddess Teoritta was discovered by a group of adventurers in some ruins to the north."

I knew about adventurers.

They were basically professional grave robbers operating in groups who claimed what they were doing was work. *Adventurer* used to be synonymous with *thief,* but people's view of them had gradually changed as the war progressed. Now it was hard not to support them, since they were willing to brave dangerous locations to find ancient artifacts.

Sometimes they even found something incredible like a goddess.

"We, the Thirteenth Order, were given the task of excavating those ruins, but there were administrative and operational issues due to friction between the military and the Temple."

"Sounds rough. Not my problem, though." I laughed through my nose, and Kivia shot me an irritated stare.

"What are you talking about? Of course it's your problem. Have you forgotten you were the one who killed Goddess Senerva?"

"...What are you trying to say?"

"Because of that, the military started wondering... If a goddess could be killed, then could more be created?"

What a terrible idea. That was how I felt, at least, and it looked like Kivia agreed.

"The military requested to analyze Goddess Teoritta's body. The Temple, however, is opposed."

Analyze her body?

I figured—no, I was almost certain, since the military was involved, that would mean dissecting her in order to unlock the secret of how goddesses were made. They'd work carefully so as not to kill her, but that meant she'd be alive during the dissection.

Sounds just like the monsters back at Galtuile.

It was aggravating how well I knew them. They were so maddeningly practical.

"The military's opinion was winning out, but the situation is gradually changing now that you've proven the goddess's value. You've already defeated two demon lords in a very short period of time."

"...And what were they thinking up until now?" I couldn't help asking. I was starting to get irritated, and I couldn't stop myself from pressing her. "We had to prove she was valuable? So they thought Teoritta was useless before? Why was *she* chosen to be dissected? She was just discovered the other day! They couldn't possibly know what she could do—"

"We knew she could summon swords because of writings in the ruins where she was discovered." Kivia seemed to be trying her best to remain calm. "She is noticeably inferior when compared to the other twelve goddesses. There is even a more powerful goddess with the same abilities."

I understood what she was trying to say.

That was how the military thought. Even the Temple was likely to agree. Visions of the future, lightning and storms, warriors from other worlds, war machines—compared to that, Teoritta's swords were far too limited.

"Scumbags."

It dawned on me as I said this that the real scumbags were us heroes. Though as far as I was concerned, the military and the Temple had no right to say so.

It was then that I finally realized why Kivia and the Thirteenth Order had been acting so strangely. At last, I knew the reason behind their suicidal behavior back at Couveunge Forest. It must have been their way of atoning for what they were doing. Or maybe they were just filled with despair.

The Thirteenth Order's task had been to deliver the goddess, whom they were supposed to protect, to be dissected. That was also why they hadn't awoken her. As soldiers, they couldn't disobey orders, but they must have thought they could win over the Temple or the northern nobles if they sacrificed themselves to defend that territory.

But the scumbags back at Galtuile—

"What does it matter if she's not useful?" I said, looking at Teoritta. She had just bought two frozen desserts and was rushing back toward us, smiling proudly. "Who do they think they are? Dammit. What else do I need to do to prove to those Galtuile Fortress lowlifes that she's worth more in one piece?"

There was no point in getting mad at Kivia. I knew that, but I couldn't stop myself.

"Okay, tell me about our next mission," I said. "If we succeed again, they won't need to dissect Teoritta, right? What do you want me to do?"

"Defend," spat Kivia. Maybe she was angry, too. "You heroes are to defend this fortress to the death. Alone."

The room was small and dark, not much different from a cell.

...What a gloomy place.

That was the first thought that came to Venetim Leopool's mind.

Aren't they going to make me stand before that hammy "veil of truth" for my trial?

He'd intended to talk his way out of this mess before the jury and the confessor.

I'll tell the biggest lie there ever was—something for the history books.

That was what he'd planned anyway. But it seemed that wasn't in the cards anymore.

There were only two people in the room with him now.

Sitting across from him at a desk was a young man with an overly cheerful smile, and standing behind him was a woman in a simple white robe—common garb for priests—with her arms crossed. She was staring at him with sleepy, emotionless eyes.

Something isn't right.

It was no surprise Venetim felt that way. After all, this was nothing like the trials he had heard about. There were no jurors, and he didn't even have to swear to tell the truth.

This feels more like an interrogation than a trial. Is there still some information they want to get out of me?

He'd already told them everything—lies, truth, lies he'd convinced even himself were true.

"You have my apologies, Venetim Leopool," said the young man, placing his elbows on the crude desk and lacing his fingers together as if he was about to pray. His voice sounded somehow insincere. "I really wish we could have spoken somewhere nicer, but it is what it is. I've always wanted to meet you. I have a lot of respect for you."

"O-oh... You do, huh?" Venetim replied, nodding vaguely. There wasn't anything else he *could* do.

He wasn't the kind of person who could carefully select his words before he spoke. When people heard he was a con man, they tended to get the wrong impression. Venetim wasn't a levelheaded thinker or a witty wordsmith. He didn't have those talents. Even when he was deceiving people, he simply said whatever came to mind.

This time was no different.

"What exactly do you mean, 'you have a lot of respect for me'?" He had some serious doubts about that. "Do you plan on making a living by swindling people, too? Because if you do, you shouldn't be looking up to people like me. After all, I got caught."

"Yes, you are right about that," said the man, laughing low in his throat. His expression was cheerful, but there was something eerie about his laugh. It was almost like the hissing of a snake.

"I suppose I went a little too far this time," said Venetim. "I guess trying to sell the royal castle to a circus was a bit—"

"Actually, that has almost nothing to do with this. It was pretty funny, though."

The man waved his hand, and the woman dressed like a priest silently started moving. She lined up stacks of paper on the desk, one after the other. They were all records of Venetim's crimes.

"The nature of your crimes is unprecedented. I'm honestly surprised someone could be so reckless." The man laughed again, snakelike, as he ran his eyes across the papers. "First, you made an agreement to sell land to a circus wishing to perform in the royal capital. To that end, you counterfeited an entire palace relocation plan... It's impressive, to say the least."

Venetim could still remember it as if it had occurred only the day before. The scam had gotten out of hand before he knew what was happening.

Originally, he'd only planned to set up the land sale, collect the advance payment, and pull his usual disappearing act. However, the more he talked, the more complicated things became. Before long, they were discussing palace relocation plans, demolition work, and potential buyers for the leftover stone and iron. He had to start lying to all kinds of tradesmen just to keep up the act.

I felt like I was walking a tightrope. Things were so busy...

He'd issued quotes, raised seed money, and prepared a letter of attorney from the chancellor's representative as things snowballed beyond anything he'd imagined. By the time the circus troupe finally arrived, there were carpenters, construction-related vendors, and even protestors all jumbled together. They had created quite the scene.

Venetim was too afraid to witness the chaos he had created, so he stayed away and tried to bide his time until it was safe to leave the capital. But he was easily captured before he could make it out.

"You've done a lot more than just that. Investment fraud, counterfeiting antiques, lottery fraud, financing violations... You have over a hundred lawsuits filed against you by the Verkle Development Corporation alone."

"I'm sorry... I truly regret my actions."

"Don't be. It doesn't matter anymore. What I want to know is why. What's your motive?"

To Venetim, "it doesn't matter anymore" sounded extremely ominous.

"...I hate seeing people disappointed. I've hated it ever since I was a child." This was a story he'd told countless times, but the details always changed. When he really thought about it, all these stories seemed true, and at the same time, they all felt like lies. "I would make up whatever lie I could on the spot to avoid disappointing people. And I tried to make the lies consistent."

"That must have taken a great deal of effort. Keeping everything consistent with this circus plan must have been awfully difficult. But you managed it."

"Well..." Venetim gave only a vague answer. He couldn't think of anything else to do. He was far more interested in who this man was and if he was going to be put on trial.

"Um. Will I get the death penalty, then?" he asked.

"Hmm? Oh. No, unfortunately not." The man leaned forward. "You aren't actually being tried for fraud."

"...I'm not? Then—"

"This was what got you into trouble."

Another sheaf of papers was tossed onto the table. This one Venetim recognized. It was a newspaper. *The Livio Chronicle*. Not the most prestigious of publications. In fact, it was at the bottom of the barrel even among third-rate newspapers. It regularly published dubious scoops on the occult, conspiracies, scandals, and self-produced gossip about the Demon Blight.

Venetim had been working for them as a journalist for the past year, since he was very good at coming up with fake stories.

"Uh..." Venetim tilted his head in confusion. "Why are you showing me this?"

"This is an article you wrote—'The Demon Lords' Secret Invasion.' Spies under the influence of the Demon Blight are already among us and pretending to be human. And the Temple, Galtuile, and even the royal family have already been compromised. I think that about sums it up."

Venetim recalled writing the article. The paper was out of ideas for scandals between knights and goddesses, and they couldn't come up with any more dirt on the royal family, so they'd asked him to write something that would scare people. And that's just what he'd done.

I guess I deserve the look he's giving me...

Perhaps there was some truth to Venetim's stories about hating to see people disappointed.

"And you included names, too! High Priest Marlen Kivia, General Delph, and even Governor-General Simurid. Impressive. That's quite the imagination you've got... To be straight with you, fraud, scandals, conspiracy theories—I don't care about those. But this..." He laughed, rattling his throat. "We can't have the truth getting out."

"Huh?"

"Especially from someone like you, who's so good at making people believe their lies. You've done enough to convince us, after all."

Venetim felt this was all very unfair.

"Wait. I never—"

He tried to get up, but he couldn't. The woman in priest garb was suddenly standing right next to him, tightly gripping his shoulders. Immense pain shot through his body, and Venetim wailed.

"You were going to ruin all our hard work... And so I have a gift for you. It's a special restraint that will ensure you can never talk about any of this again."

The man snapped his fingers theatrically.

That was when Venetim noticed the sadistic glint in the man's merry smile. It was the expression of someone who enjoyed seeing the fear in his victim's eyes.

"Unfortunately, you'll be suffering a fate far worse than death."

The grin on his face widened. He clearly didn't think any of this was "unfortunate."

"Venetim Leopool, you are being sentenced to serve as a hero."

"Defend this fortress to the death."

That was what the messenger told us—a man from Galtuile who had an impressive beard.

Honestly, I didn't like the look of the guy from the moment I saw him. I didn't trust well-dressed, dignified men. Maybe I was cursed so that I couldn't, even if I wanted to.

"The Demon Blight is approaching, and the penal hero unit is to defend this fortress to the death, alone."

Venetim and I were standing side by side like idiots, listening to this man bluntly order us to die.

"Xylo, relax…," whispered Venetim. "I implore you to remain calm… Please don't punch me in the face or beat me to death, okay?"

"What kind of person do you think I am?" I said.

Did I really look like someone who would suddenly get violent for no reason?

Maybe I did. I'd killed a goddess, and that sure counted as meaningless violence. Maybe he thought I was the type of guy who let his moods dictate his actions.

"…Ahem. I apologize, good messenger," said Venetim. "I understand you wish for us to protect the fortress at all costs, but…"

Venetim cleared his throat and continued like he was on the verge of death. At the very least, he sounded like he had a hole or two in his stomach and was bleeding out.

"What exactly is our objective?"

"Your mission is to remain here. That is all," replied the messenger solemnly. "Keep fighting until the very last man and then fight some more."

"Ah, you wish for us to hold the enemy off and draw the battle out, hmm? How long should we keep them busy?" Venetim was persistent and friendly, too. He was even smiling... He was probably just afraid to face reality.

"Until you're dead," stated the messenger. "The Thirteenth and Ninth Orders will be conserving their strength at the rear. They will execute a special attack the moment every one of you is dead and the fortress falls."

Well, that's a very mean-spirited plan, I thought. But if the sacred seal hanging from the man's neck was real, then there was no doubt he was a legitimate messenger from Galtuile.

"And...what kind of special attack are we talking about, if I may ask?"

The messenger nodded gravely back at Venetim. "Poison. The Ninth Order's goddess will perform her miracle."

I had heard rumors about this.

The Ninth Order's goddess was able to summon any kind of poison from the tips of her fingers, but it was apparently very difficult for her to cover a range broad enough to take out a demon lord. That was why they needed to set up a trap. *So they're planning on doing that here? At this fortress?* They would probably combine it with a bomb featuring a sacred seal. Calling it a special attack was a bit overdramatic—they'd simply be detonating the bombs.

"This fortress shall become the grave of Demon Blight Number Fifteen, Iblis, and you heroes are being granted the honor of becoming the foundation."

Neither Venetim nor I said a word. Our jaws were already too busy dropping.

The plan this time was to lure the demon lord and its associated faeries to this fortress, contaminate the place with poison, and go down with the enemy.

So we're basically just buying time with our deaths? That's ridiculous.

"This plan is unbelievably inefficient." The words were out of my mouth before I even realized it. "You're going to use this whole fortress just to trap and kill a single demon lord? If you use a poison strong enough to do that, the fortress will become uninhabitable."

"Demon Blight Number Fifteen, Iblis, is extremely powerful." The messenger was clearly disgusted with my argument.

Venetim anxiously elbowed me in the side. This was his fault, however, for bringing me along just because he didn't understand military affairs.

"During the previous battle, it survived an attack from the Ninth Order," the messenger continued. "Are you aware of its astonishing regenerative abilities?"

I knew, but only through rumor.

Iblis's existence was confirmed early on during the war against the Demon Blight. It roamed slowly across the land, consuming or destroying everything in its path, and was famous for its ability to survive any attack. The Knights had tried to wipe it out in the past but were never able to finish it off.

Iblis had especially long dormant periods, so the matter had been shelved for some time afterward. It only moved around a few times each year in remote areas, keeping damage to a minimum and making it a low priority.

But for some reason, it was suddenly heading straight toward this fortress, as if it had a clear purpose in mind.

"Last time, we sniped at the Demon Blight from afar while the goddess's miracle hit it with a lethal dose of poison."

The sniper in this case was probably Tsav from our unit. He had been lent to the Ninth Order and helped out with their activities. It seemed he *had* done what was asked of him.

"The mission was a success, but that didn't matter in the end. Although Iblis temporarily entered a state of suspended animation, it came back to life before its death could be confirmed."

I was starting to understand where he was going with this, and I had a feeling the conclusion was going to piss me off.

"The result of that mission and a vision from the third goddess, Seedia, led Galtuile to amend their strategy. They concluded that the only way to defeat Iblis was to use a substantial amount of poison to *kill it continuously*. The goddess will be using a special poison…similar to a living creature."

I knew it.

"There is no other possible way to kill it," he concluded.

"Are you out of your mind?" I said. "What's gonna happen to us when—?"

"P-please wait, good messenger." Venetim cut me off. "If we manage to lure the enemy into position as promised, wouldn't it be all right if we evacuated the area?"

"I cannot allow that," he insisted.

"Why? It shouldn't be a problem as long as we complete our mission."

"I cannot allow it. This is what Galtuile has decided. If even a single penal hero leaves Mureed Fortress, the sacred seals on your necks will automatically activate, killing every last one of you."

Are they out of their minds? I thought once again.

What was the point of that? There was something odd about all this. Why were they so dead set on all of us dying? It seemed completely pointless. Would our survival somehow inconvenience them?

Perhaps this was *their* doing. The people who set me up.

They must have really hated me—hated all of us. It was like they were doing everything they could to kill us. Part of me understood how they felt, but like hell was I playing along. What could I do, though? I didn't have the time to die here.

That's right—Teoritta.

She was in danger of being dissected alive unless we could prove her value. Taking down the demon lord along with the fortress wouldn't be enough. The Ninth Order's goddess and her poison would probably get all the credit anyway.

Or was that what they were after? Did they come up with this plan to make Teoritta seem less useful?

"Very well. We will carry out our mission as planned," replied Venetim casually while I was thinking.

Is he for real? I thought, unconsciously glancing at his face. He was smiling as he talked, really buttering the guy up.

"However, I would like to request a few changes to improve the plan," he continued. "First, that rule about everyone dying if a single person leaves the fortress. That could be a little problematic."

The messenger knitted his brow, but Venetim didn't give him the chance to reply. Venetim's biggest advantage as a con man was how loud he could be. He was able to project his voice in such a way that it drowned out everyone else.

"As you know, we are a group of criminals—sick individuals with various personality disorders. It's quite easy to imagine at least one of us folding under the pressure and deciding to take the easy way out by leaving the fortress early on. If that happens, we won't be able to lure the enemy here."

He's got a point, I thought.

If their publicly stated aim wasn't killing all of us, but defeating the demon lord, then this was a fact they couldn't ignore.

"You're free to appoint a supervisor, but one of us could still escape. That's why I think the whole group should only be put to death if everyone tries to leave the fortress."

It was impressive how Venetim could pull arguments like this out of his ass. He spoke so quickly, I didn't even have time to consider if what he was saying made sense.

"In addition, there is the issue of Goddess Teoritta. She has forged a pact with Xylo here and will likely insist on remaining in the fortress no matter what anyone says."

"…I will do my utmost to convince her," replied the messenger.

"She won't listen to you. Our goddess's mighty compassion is far too powerful for her to leave us behind."

Although his phrasing sounded a little off, Venetim maintained an absolutely straight face as he formed the Great Sacred Seal with his hands. He traced a circle in the air, then ran his finger straight down the middle as if he were cutting it in half. Forming this seal—the first sacred seal—was a common sign of worship at the Temple.

"Our continuous success as of late is all thanks to the protection of the great goddess Teoritta, and I would like to request permission for her to stay with us."

"I am in no position to grant that permission."

"Then who is?"

"The goddess falls under the Thirteenth Order's command, and—"

"Xylo, get in touch with Captain Kivia. I will handle things here." Venetim patted me on the shoulder and whispered, "I think I can get us the okay to let Teoritta withdraw once we complete our mission. What else do you need?"

"More soldiers," I replied. "We don't have enough people. There's no way we can do this alone."

I wasn't expecting much from him when I said it, but he easily agreed to give it a shot.

"All right. What else?" he asked.

"Weapons and food."

"All right. What else?"

"A pardon."

"All right. What else?"

He's just randomly nodding in agreement with whatever I say. He looked incredibly serious, too. I snorted.

"I'm kidding about the pardon...but I do want cavalry and artillery. What about Jayce and Rhyno? Do you think you could get them?"

"They still haven't returned from the western front, so I highly doubt they'll make it back in time."

Jayce was our unit's cavalryman and Rhyno our artilleryman. They had been sent together to the western front to fight. Jayce was especially valuable, since he was a dragon knight. His personality was less than ideal, but you could really count on his dragon partner. If he were here, we could afford to take a few more risks. But no use thinking about the impossible.

"All right, just leave it to me." Venetim proudly bumped a fist against his chest. "I'll take care of things. All you need to do is believe in me."

"Those words mean almost nothing coming from you. Do you really think you can do it?"

"How should I say this? No one would ever believe me, but..."

He suddenly lowered his voice even more.

"...I know a secret. A really big secret. I was one step away from saving the world once, and this is nothing compared to that."

"Yeah, I bet."

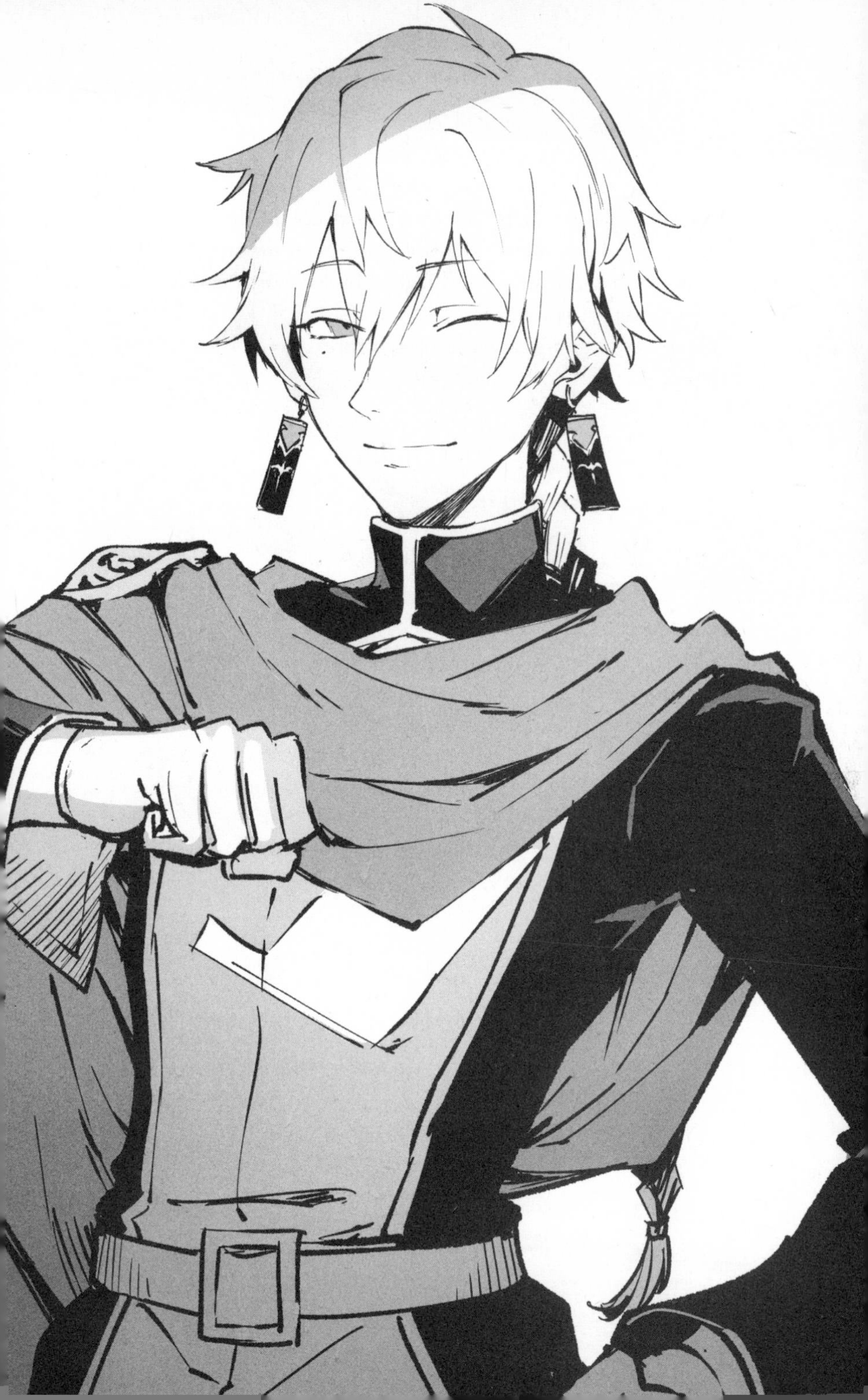

I knew he would, of course.

Indeed, Venetim went on to successfully negotiate all of my demands, save the pardon. And Kivia informed me later that he was ordered to grab the goddess and leave Mureed Fortress the second it became necessary to evacuate.

This guy was going to get himself stabbed in the back on the battlefield one day. No doubt about it.

"Come on, you know me. I'm basically a nice guy, right?"

I could hear Tsav's voice from behind me. He'd been talking constantly for a while now, like he'd stop breathing if he wasn't flapping his lips. I was at my wit's end.

"I'm too nice, in fact. It really gets me down. I always felt like something wasn't right, ever since I started training. It's a real problem. I mean, I'm a superelite killer, raised from childhood by an order of assassins."

It was a terrible day to have ears. I tried to walk a little faster, but Tsav didn't seem to catch on that I meant for him to shut up.

"The more I looked into my targets and who they were, the more I was like, 'Man, I can't kill this guy. He has a wife and kids and a sick grandpa, to boot!' It was times like that when my pure nature would come out."

Dotta, who was walking ahead of us, looked back at me, fed up. His eyes were saying *Maybe we should have left this guy back at the fortress.*

We'd heard Tsav tell this story a few dozen times, and I would have already knocked him out cold if he wasn't such a good sniper. Luckily for him, his skills were supernatural.

"That's why I've never killed my target. My success rate is zero percent! ...But the order would be mad if I went home without proof I'd done my job, you know? ...So I'd find some random person, turn them into mincemeat, and bring that back instead. Then I'd have my target secretly run away. I'm such a good guy, right?"

Tsav was an assassin who couldn't kill his targets.

And yet you can kill some innocent bystander? This question had occurred to me before, but it truly seemed not to bother him. I'd asked him once, and he'd replied, "Well, of course..."

The guy was a real piece of work, to be sure.

Tsav probably didn't differentiate between humans and livestock like cows or pigs. If he grew attached to someone, he couldn't kill them. But if it was someone he didn't know anything about, there was nothing stopping him. He was the kind of person you'd never want to get involved with, but unfortunately, that was a luxury I couldn't afford. It was times like this when I remembered I was a criminal and this was my punishment.

"But get this! The order of assassins kicked me out of the group! Just what kind of scumbags—?!"

"Tsav."

That was when I finally looked back at him. We had reached our destination, and he was annoying me, so I figured it was about time he shut up.

"Shut up."

"Ah! Sorry, bro."

He scratched his straw-colored hair and offered me a slight smile, revealing a few missing teeth. He was a cheerful guy but kind of a goofball, and he kept calling me "bro" for some reason. Tsav was just that kind of guy.

"Was I talking too much again?"

"Xylo, I think it's about time we gag him." Dotta frowned and pointed at Tsav. "He never shuts up. I had to share a room with him before, and it was awful. He talked *all* night! He didn't even sleep!"

"I can stay awake for three days straight," said Tsav. "I underwent training for that."

"See?! It's literal torture!" Dotta said, stricken. With Dotta and Tsav together, the noise level was as high as it could get, but I didn't have any other choice. Our mission was to scout the area outside the fortress, and I couldn't do that with Norgalle, the one-legged king. Venetim was out of the question as well. He had absolutely no stamina. And Tatsuya was useless during missions like this.

That was how I ended up with these two.

"Dotta," said Tsav. "We should be friends and get to know each other better. We're on the same team."

"I'd love to, if you promise to be a little quieter from now on."

"I'm not really a fan of silence. You see, my training under the order was basically like torture. My past is super sad. Back then, they'd throw me in a dungeon underground—"

"Hey." I had to interrupt. "I already told you to shut up once, didn't I? Don't make me repeat myself."

"Look what you did," said Dotta. "You made Xylo mad…"

"Oh gosh! I'm sorry, bro! Dotta, you too! Hurry up and apologize!"

"Why do I have to apologize?"

Tsav swiftly lowered his head into a bow. And yet they continued to argue. All I could do was sigh. Messing with these two was a waste of time.

I crouched down a little, straining my eyes at the scenery before us.

We had been walking for about half a day after leaving Mureed Fortress, and although it was cloudy out, I could see Couveunge Forest and the Zewan Gan mines. Slightly to the west were the mountains of Rettar Mayen. Blackish smoke currently hovered near their base.

It technically wasn't smoke, of course, but countless faeries gathering together. When they moved in droves like that, they flung black dirt into the air like smoke. Now they formed a great army, tearing into the ground with their steps and knocking over the trees in their path like a mudslide.

Their movement appeared sluggish, but that only made me feel more keenly the promise of destruction they brought. They cut into the foot of the mountains, turning the area into a valley. They flattened nearby settlements, buildings and all.

Demon Blight Number Fifteen, Iblis, had to be somewhere in the center of this throng.

"They're getting close."

While I was crouching, observing the enemy, I suddenly heard a voice from above. It was Kivia. Dotta needed someone to keep an eye on him and make sure he didn't run off, so she had ended up coming along.

"They're going to reach the fortress faster than I thought."

As she traced the map in her hands with a finger, I stood up and joined her. Judging by its route, the Demon Blight seemed to be heading straight for Mureed Fortress. Almost as if it was chasing something.

"At this rate, it should be here in about three or four days," I said.

"…Y-yeah." Kivia blinked a few times and cleared her throat. "I'd say that sounds about right when you consider Iblis's speed."

"It's coming straight here as if something or someone is guiding it. It's fishy, especially when you consider how it's behaved up until now."

"Yes, I agree. I wouldn't be surprised if Galtuile knows something. Perhaps there's a Demon Blight that can function as a commander guiding it."

"Great. Just what we need. By the way…"

Each time I spoke, Kivia would lean away from me. She was practically falling over, her eyes staring in the opposite direction.

"Why are you moving away from me?"

"I—I… Your face is way too close. Stand back a little."

But before I could reply, Dotta shrieked.

"Eek!"

He pointed toward the forest. "I just saw something! I think it was a faerie."

"Ohhh, yep. That's what it looks like, all right."

Tsav, standing by Dotta's side, was leaning forward and gazing in the direction Dotta had indicated. These two had crazy good eyesight. I guess they were just built different or something. It was hard to believe they were human.

"It looks kind of like a dog to me," said Tsav. "What do you see, Dotta?"

"Same here. Looks like a cir sith."

Cir sith was the name people used for all small doglike faeries. While they weren't exceptional fighters, they were very perceptive and agile. Therefore, they would usually go ahead and scout an area before the demon lord arrived. Their senses seemed to be linked up to the demon lord's somehow.

"A cir sith?" asked Kivia. "How many are we talking about? Are you sure they're there?"

The captain strained her eyes as well, but I didn't think she'd see anything. I couldn't, either. If I still had my old sacred seal meant for scouting and capturing enemies, then maybe. But I didn't have the abnormal natural eyesight of Dotta or Tsav.

And if they said they could see something, then I had no doubt it was there. You couldn't trust them as far as you could throw them, but they didn't lie for no reason like Venetim.

"Well, it looks like we've got some killing to do," I said. Things would get messy if the faeries spotted us and came flooding in. "Tsav, can you hit it from here?"

"I don't know... I think I can do it, but I'm not gonna make any promises. So don't kill me if I miss, okay?"

"What kind of person do you think I am?"

"I think...you're a great guy. Really."

His answer was a little less than convincing, but he proceeded to unsheathe the long staff strapped to his back. It was a type of lightning staff with a sacred seal engraved into it, but its range and power were in another league compared to Dotta's. Its product name was Daisy, and it had been developed by the Verkle Development Corporation as a sniper weapon. But King Norgalle had tuned this one to such an extent that all of its sacred seals were unrecognizable.

"Can I shoot it already? If I keep looking at it like this, I'll stop wanting to kill it. You know what they say: That Tsav's a really empathetic guy. Nicest assassin there ever was."

"Just shoot it already," I said. "Or can you not shoot unless you're running your mouth?"

"All right, here goes nothing."

It was almost instantaneous. A bolt of lightning soared from the staff toward the forest far in the distance, threading through the trees in a flash. *Pop.* There was a dry, deflated sound.

"Got it," he said before glancing at Dotta out of the corner of his eye. "I hit it dead-on, huh. How'd I do?"

"…It went straight through its head… Wow. You make it look easy."

Dotta sighed in relief, spyglass in hand. He was a very simple person.

Tsav might have made it look easy, but he'd just hit something around 1,200 standard rattes away.

The Federated Kingdom had adopted rattes as the unit of measurement for distance, and one standard ratte was equivalent to one step forward for an adult of average height. The skill you would need to shoot a target through the head from 1,200 steps away while avoiding obstacles was beyond human understanding.

"Looks like there are more, though," Tsav said to Dotta, keeping his lightning staff in position. "Dotta, how many do you see?"

"Oh, you're right! I see them—four more! And they've spotted us…!" Dotta began shaking Tsav's shoulders in a panic. "They're coming this way, Tsav! Hurry! Do that thing again!"

"Don't rush me. I can't fire multiple shots in succession with this thing… It's made specifically for distance and power. But don't worry. I'll take care of them before they get here."

Dotta and Tsav were a pain in the ass when you paired them together like this, but they got the job done. Dotta would do whatever he could to save himself, and Tsav was probably the best lightning staff wielder I'd ever seen. It was actually pretty aggravating how useful they were.

In other words, everything was going to be all right with them on the job. So while chatterbox Tsav's attention was on his sniping, I decided to use the time to talk to Kivia.

"I'm gonna go set some traps His Majesty gave me once we're finished scouting. I want to take out as many of the faeries as we can before they reach the fortress." I peered into the distance at Iblis. Its faerie forces would only increase as it approached. "I know it's probably pointless with numbers like that…but it's better than doing nothing. Anyway, I hate to bother you, but I need your help."

"It's fine," Kivia replied. "That's my job. However…"

"What?"

"I find myself more confused about you by the day." Kivia was looking at me like she was having a hard time accepting what she was seeing. "You are still trying to fulfill your role even under the circumstances.

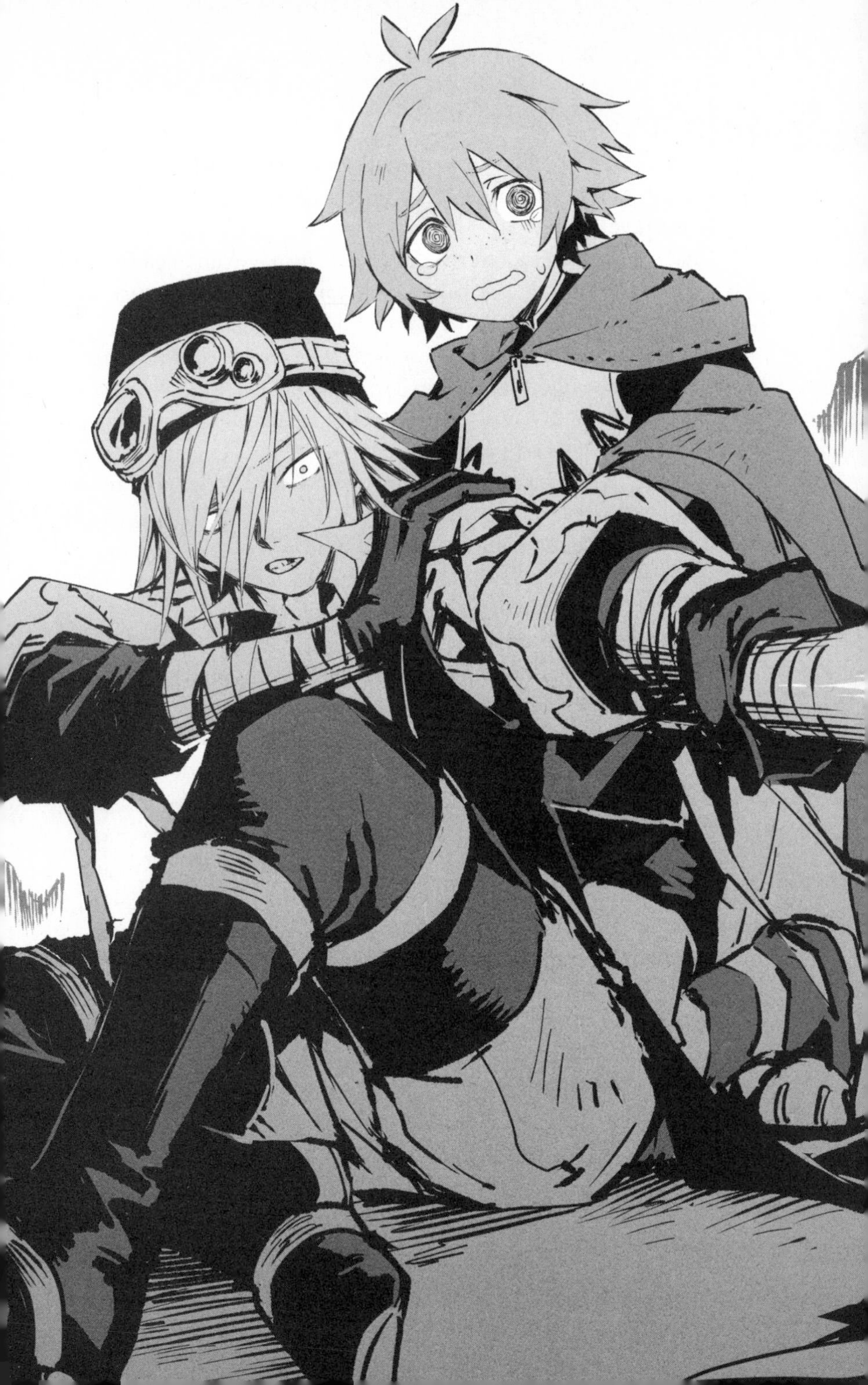

You haven't given up. And your attitude toward Goddess Teoritta...
You're nothing like the goddess killer I heard about."

"What'd you hear?"

"That you were an upstart who acted hastily in pursuit of glory and
that you put your unit at risk before eventually going mad and taking
the goddess's life. But I can't imagine you doing such a thing."

"You never know." I smiled bitterly. But a certain word in Kivia's
explanation had caught me off guard: *upstart*. That was something
hereditary nobles said. Kivia... Was that the name of some prominent
family I had simply never heard about?

"Hey, Kivia. Which noble family are you from? I don't mean to be
rude, but I've never heard the name."

"That's because I'm not from a noble family."

"Don't give me that. Do you really think Galtuile would let just
anyone become a captain of the Holy Knights?"

"My uncle's a high priest."

A high priest, huh? Now it all made sense. That was pretty much the
highest rank within the Temple. A few dozen people held it, and they
alone were privy to exclusive sacred council meetings. So Kivia wasn't
born into a family of nobles, but a family of priests. No wonder I'd never
heard of her. Her attitude toward Teoritta finally made sense, too.

What had happened in her life that led her to join the military?
And not as a military priest, either, but as a captain in the Holy Knights.

"That's why...I was wary of you at first. I was worried you might
harm Goddess Teoritta, but it appears my concern was unnecessary."

"I see. So does that mean you can stop watching me like a hawk?"

"Watching you?"

"I've noticed you staring at me this whole time. I haven't been able
to relax since we left the fortress."

"...I've been doing no such thing. Perhaps your ego is deluding you,
because nothing like that ever happened. Ridiculous. You're so self-
centered. You should reflect on that."

"You think?"

Kivia rattled off her words without pausing to breathe. I felt she
was being a little unfair, and I wanted to object. What did I need to

reflect on, exactly? But before I could form my thoughts, Tsav had finished the job.

"Bam. I did it, bro! Pretty incredible, right? I landed every shot!"

The tip of his lightning staff was still red-hot. Despite activating a sacred seal and accurately sniping from such a distance, however, Tsav didn't seem exhausted in the least.

"That was all of them…right?"

Dotta was still glancing around anxiously. If he didn't see anything, then I sure as hell wouldn't. At any rate, it seemed safe to assume the threat was gone for now.

"All right, we go on horseback from here," I said.

Kivia was still staring daggers at me, but we had a job to do, and I needed to focus my attention on that.

"Let's finish laying these traps and head back," I continued. "Kivia, you know how to ride a horse, right? Follow me. Dotta, Tsav—you two wait here. Don't you dare even think about running away."

"You got it!" said Tsav. "I'll make sure to keep an eye on Dotta."

"I couldn't run away even if I wanted to," Dotta added. "The area's crawling with enemy scouts now… Without you here, Xylo, I'll be too scared to even move."

"Good. Kivia, let's go. I need your help. I won't be able to set up these traps by myself, and—"

"W-wait." Kivia looked confused. "I know how to ride a horse, but where are the horses? We weren't supplied with horses for this mission."

"*Someone* acquired them and stashed them over here."

I looked at Dotta, who immediately averted his gaze awkwardly. Kivia breathed a heavy sigh.

In the end, fifty Holy Knights remained at Mureed Fortress.

All fifty were from the Thirteenth Order. They had stayed behind at Kivia's request, and every one of them was trustworthy—at least according to her. I didn't know how true that was, but they could at least help with odd jobs. We had a lot to do in very little time. Plus, you could never do too much when it came to inspections and maintenance of the fortress's equipment.

Meanwhile, the Ninth Order seemed to have zero interest in helping out. When we returned from scouting, we happened to run into their goddess and captain leaving the fortress.

"Excuse us."

Hord Clivios, the captain, nodded to Kivia on his way out.

I was familiar with his family name. The Clivioses were nobles with a vast stretch of land in the south, and their wine was delicious. Dotta and Tsav would grovel and beg with tears in their eyes for a single glass.

"You're quite the eccentric, Captain Kivia," he said, as if truly baffled by her. There was probably a hint of disgust in there as well. "I find your desire to watch the penal heroes die in poor taste, though. But, well, if that is what you wish, then I will pray for your safety."

The captain of the Ninth Order seemed to think we were nothing more than gamecocks, and us fighting was merely a show for his enjoyment. At the very least, he didn't acknowledge us as part of the military's forces.

I felt basically the same whenever I looked at Dotta or Tsav. Including them in the military seemed to be causing more problems than it was solving.

"...I will pray for your safety, Kivia."

The goddess of the Ninth Order bowed as well. She was a woman with flowing black hair and eyes of fire, but she was nothing like Senerva or Teoritta. She had a very gloomy, cheerless personality.

"Stand back, Pelmerry. That's the goddess killer."

The captain of the Ninth Order slipped in between the goddess and me.

I understood where he was coming from. He thought I was some sort of hardened criminal who could kill goddesses. And I could. I had.

"Our work here is done, so we're leaving," he said. "Stay close to me. Got it?"

"Yes, Hord. I will not leave your side. Did I successfully fulfill my role?"

"You were perfect. Absolutely perfect."

"Perfect? Then...will you not say, 'That's my Pelmerry. Good job'?"

"Of course. That's my Pelmerry. Good job."

He rubbed the goddess's head, and their exchange continued like this until they had left the fortress along with seventy-four large casks filled with poison.

The plan was like this: Lure Iblis to Mureed Fortress, then simultaneously detonate all the casks. The poison should stop the demon lord in its tracks and continue to kill it, neutralizing it.

And the best part? We penal heroes were the ones who had to do it. *Hilarious.*

"Sounds like we're in for a rough time," said Tsav, as if the whole thing had nothing to do with him. We were walking side by side. "I'm guessing we're all gonna die. This sucks. I'm getting pissed off just thinking about it. Want to kill one of the Holy Knights?"

"Why would we kill a Holy Knight?"

"To feel better. I see you kicking rocks when you're stressed, bro. It's the same thing."

"Rocks and humans aren't the same."

"Hey! That's discrimination! You should be more open-minded."

I had to remain calm, no matter how annoying he got.

"You know, humans are just another part of nature," he continued. "Humans and rocks are practically siblings, so I don't think you should treat one group like they're special."

I couldn't listen to his drivel any longer. Humans and rocks were not equal. Humans were special. Humans were different from rocks and plants—even livestock. Why? Because I was human. Of course, an idiot like Tsav wouldn't be able to understand that. Plus, he seemed to have forgotten that the sacred seals on our necks would activate and kill us if we ever harmed someone without specific orders to do so.

"Xylo!"

By the time we reached the now evacuated control room, Venetim had already made himself at home. Teoritta came rushing over like she was a little dog and we were her family just returned home.

"Oh. Hey, Goddess." Tsav waved and put on a goofy smile. "It looks like you were a really good girl while we were gone. How were things here? You didn't eat too many snacks, right?"

"Hmph! I'm not in the mood for your endless prattle, Tsav! I'm angry. Xylo, you sneaked out and left me behind. How far did you scout?!"

She'd barely met him, and yet Teoritta seemed to have already figured out how annoying Tsav was. She ran over and grabbed my elbow.

"How could a knight leave his goddess behind for two whole days? That is unacceptable. Do not let it happen again! Listen, you—"

"Goddess Teoritta." Kivia peered into Teoritta's eyes. The goddess was still hanging from my arm. "Please have mercy. We were simply fulfilling our duty to ensure your victory. Although I understand they are sinners, please grant the penal heroes permission to rest... Xylo, why don't you drink some water? You need to take a break. You've been working nonstop."

"Mmph." Teoritta furrowed her brow and began looking back and forth between Kivia and me. "Xylo... It seems you managed to have a lot of fun scouting with Kivia."

"There's no such thing as 'having fun scouting,'" I shot back.

"Precisely," added Kivia. "Goddess Teoritta, we only did what was necessary. We weren't there to have fun. We only rode so far away in order to set traps. It was all for the mission."

"Uh-huh." Teoritta looked at Kivia like she wasn't convinced, probably because the captain was saying everything in a single breath the same way Venetim did. "Is that so?"

"Yes, Goddess Teoritta. Here, I brought you back some fruit I picked in the forest. They're very sweet."

"You picked fruit. In a forest. Together. Interesting. That sounds like a lot of fun."

"No! I was merely fulfilling my duty by—"

"Xylo! My knight."

Teoritta tightened her grip on my arm, hanging off it as if she was dangling from a branch. I could tell from this contact alone that she was under a great deal of emotional strain. Small sparks were beginning to fly off her.

"I saw the Ninth Order," she said.

"Okay."

"Not okay! I saw it happen seven times in a single day! Are you listening? Seven times. I saw their goddess get her head rubbed seven times!"

Teoritta began shaking my arm. *I really wish she hadn't seen those two*, I thought. Now she was going to demand to be spoiled.

"I…am not asking for that many…but at least half should be possible, yes?"

"All right. You did a good job waiting for us these past two days."

What else could I have done in this situation? I rubbed Teoritta's head as I shifted my gaze to Venetim, who was sitting at the commander's desk.

"How are things going?" I asked him.

"A lot better than I thought they would."

He was leaning back in the chair listlessly, as if he were dead tired, but I knew it was an act. The con man was excellent at faking gestures and mannerisms.

"We have Knights from the Thirteenth Order on our side now," he continued. "But what really surprised me was all the miners from Zewan

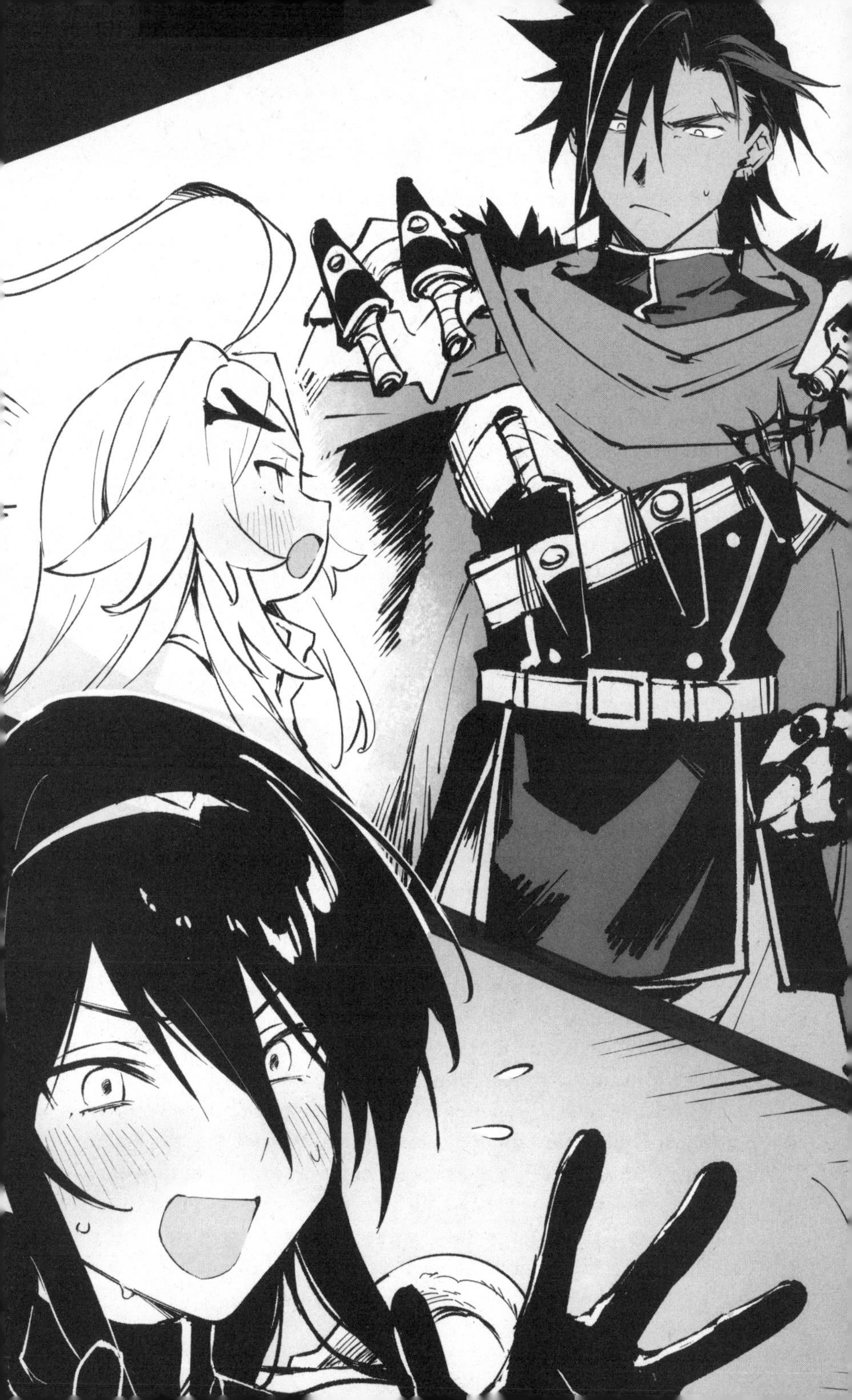

Gan who came to our aid along with their friends. A hundred of them in total."

A little earlier, the miners from Zewan Gan had shown up, along with their acquaintances and people from their union, giving us a total of a hundred more men. They said they wanted to help the penal heroes with their work. They were currently underground helping King Norgalle in his workshop.

What is with these people?

There had to be something wrong with them. They seemed to think we were some sort of honorable band of knights who saved their lives. I told them I was no such thing and they should get lost, but they wouldn't listen. All I could hope for now was that Dotta wouldn't cause too much trouble. He was outside the fortress on another mission at the moment, but I was already worried about when he got back.

"Man, I'm getting lonely," said Tsav. "I wish there were more people here. Even an extra hundred miners feels like nothing. We're gonna lose for sure. I know it."

"What are you talking about? How could you lose with me here?" Tsav's thoughtless comment had annoyed Teoritta, of course. "You may rest assured that I will be watching over you and granting you my blessing. I will lead you all to victory, no matter what!"

"Hmm... Well, you sure have grit, Goddess. Hey, bro. Are all goddesses like this? Is the world gonna be okay?"

"I think Teoritta's a special case," I said. "And no, this world isn't gonna be okay."

"H-how rude! Even you, my knight?! You should be defending my honor!"

Teoritta's fists rained down on my back as Tsav continued. "So... Venetim, what should we do now? Should we start running away?"

"Running away?" Venetim looked a little panicked as he briefly glanced at Kivia. "We will do no such thing! Tsav, whatever happened to fighting for justice? We must stop Demon Lord Iblis and become a shield to protect our people and our territory!"

"Oh! Is that how it's gonna be?" Tsav laughed dryly, then turned back to look at me. "I don't think I can do it... This guy's too funny.

Funny people are my weakness. I don't think I can shoot him even if he runs away. Can you do it for me, bro?"

"Who cares?" I said. "It's not like he's any use to us in battle. If he wants to run, let him."

"Excuse me?" Venetim said, frowning.

"Yeah, good point." Tsav nodded without hesitation.

"Venetim, you won't mind if I come up with our strategy, right?" I asked.

"I will defer to you, Xylo," he said, nodding gravely. This was all a bluff—he didn't know the first thing about strategy. "No matter what happens, we must defeat Iblis. That is our duty! For the future of the kingdom! For humanity's tomorrow!"

Kivia's eyes narrowed in exasperation, growing colder the more Venetim spoke. It seemed she was starting to pick up on the fact that he was all talk. He had yet to present a single plan of action addressing any military issues.

"...So what would you like for us to do, Xylo?" he asked.

"I want you and the king to stay put. All you need to do is relay the orders I give you. The king will continue doing what he's good at."

I visualized a map of the fortress and its surrounding area.

"I need Tatsuya to seal off the underground passage. Have him take around twenty Holy Knights. That should be enough. Tsav, I want you on top of the castle walls. Shoot anything that approaches."

"You got it! Looks like it's time for me to shine." Tsav gripped his lightning staff as if he was enjoying himself. "By the way, what happened to Dotta? I thought he'd be teamed up with me."

"He's busy with another task... Ahem. We'll have the miners and Holy Knights hold off the enemy at the front gate for half a day if possible. I don't think it'll be a problem with the king's traps and weapons."

"Very well. I will have it done," agreed Venetim like he was a real commander. *"I will have it done,"* my ass. "What about you, Xylo?"

"I'll handle the demon lord." I looked back at Kivia and Teoritta. "I'm gonna kill Iblis before it even reaches the fortress. That's the only way everyone will make it out of this alive."

A loud voice could be heard from the courtyard. It belonged to King Norgalle.

"You are my best and bravest! The warriors, the soldiers—the champions of my kingdom!" he shouted with unnecessary force. He walked with a cane, dragging his fake leg behind him and offering words of encouragement to the clearly bewildered soldiers.

The miners, however, knew what was up. They exchanged glances, whispering to one another and nodding eagerly in response to what King Norgalle was saying. I could hardly believe my eyes.

"We must protect our land and our people!" he continued. "The future of mankind rests on your shoulders!"

The miners roared wild battle cries as King Norgalle clenched his fist and raised it into the air.

"Go forth! I shall bless this battle! We here today—yes, all of you— are true warriors!"

◆

Things got even busier after that. We were lacking in almost every area, but our biggest problem was manpower. We had miners and Knights at the front gate and underground, but that was the extent of it.

Mureed Fortress had a back gate as well, and we needed people for its defense and for tasks other than combat—delivering supplies, relaying messages, maintaining and fixing equipment, and collecting the wounded. You could never have too many people in the rear.

But we weren't military—not officially—and we were all expected to die here. We were criminals with no rights, so there was no way we could get any more people. Not through legitimate methods anyway.

That meant we had no choice but to use more unscrupulous means to get what we needed.

I tried a few different things. First, I rounded up some prisoners from a nearby jail—around thirty of them. Obviously, this wasn't normally allowed, but Milnid Jail was quick to agree to bribery. They handed over the prisoners for us to use however we pleased, under the pretext of placing them under the Thirteenth Order's surveillance.

They were all criminals on death row—bandits who had profited from the chaos of war. They openly stole, killed, raped, and engaged in human trafficking, and their whole group had been imprisoned as a result. They'd been sentenced to death but had sacred seals engraved on their bodies and were put to work due to a labor shortage.

They were thus of higher social rank than us heroes, and they made sure we knew it. It was obvious the moment I met them in the courtyard: They were not pleased to be receiving orders from us. Just bringing them here was an unforgivable offense. They looked extremely unhappy.

"C'mon. You gotta be kidding," one of them said, glaring at me. He seemed to be the bandits' boss.

"Yeah, we may've done some bad things," he said. "I mean, we weren't put on death row for being nice guys. Even butchered the soldiers who came to arrest us." He looked at me threateningly. "But we ain't gonna take orders from some filthy heroes. We're criminals, but you're even lower than that. Damn goddess killer! Why do we gotta—?"

"Whoa! Not so fast." There was a crackling noise. Something went flying, then landed on the ground with a wet, heavy sound. "Please stop talking. You're gonna piss off my bro here…"

Tsav was holding his staff at the ready. The man who'd been threatening me—no, the man next to him was missing his right shoulder and everything below it. His right side had been turned into a pile of meat scattered across the ground. A second later, screams broke out.

"I don't want my bro getting angry because then he's gonna take it out on me. So do you think you could do something about the attitude?"

"…Wh-what?" The boss was at a loss for words as he looked to his side, his mouth agape. His face was red, covered in splattered blood.

"Why him? Why not me?"

"Huh? Oh, uh… Because you're bigger and louder." Tsav looked like he needed a few seconds to think of a reason, but his face lit up almost instantly with a cheerful, goofy smile. "I figured you'd work harder, since you're so aggressive and you have so much energy… Right, bro?"

"…All right," I said. "That was partially my fault for not explaining things to you beforehand. And it seemed pretty effective, so there's that. But…" I mercilessly kicked Tsav in the shin. "Do *not* do that again."

"Ouch! ...Oh, right! The arm wasn't enough, huh? I should've just killed the guy. That's what you're saying, right?"

"Wrong. We need all the help we can get, and here you are blowing people's arms off. Take the guy to the infirmary and use a sacred seal to stop the bleeding."

I gave Tsav a stern warning and left the courtyard.

To be honest, we'd been given carte blanche to do as we pleased with these criminals. We could treat them as harshly as we wanted. They were already on death row, after all. We could even directly harm them, and it wouldn't be an issue. And if they managed to survive the mission, we could waive their death penalties.

We told them all of this. What it really meant, however, was that the powers that be were absolutely sure we would all die when the poison was unleashed on the fortress.

At any rate, it seemed best to let Tsav take command of them. The sacred seals on their necks would prevent them from getting too violent.

I decided to head to the control room next.

The fortress was essentially empty now, but it was especially quiet on the uppermost level. Seated in the commander's chair was Norgalle, with Venetim standing behind him.

"I arranged for some prisoners to help, Xylo. Have you met them yet?" asked Venetim. He was the one who had bribed the jail.

"Good work," answered King Norgalle on my behalf with a solemn nod. "While they may be criminals, the nation is in danger. If you can control them, use them."

"...What is His Majesty doing here?" I asked. "He should be back in his workshop tuning sacred seals."

"I tried to stop him, but he won't listen," answered Venetim.

I can believe that, I thought. Not even Venetim could change the man's mind once he'd made it up. I doubted anyone could stop him.

"We still lack soldiers." King Norgalle groaned, his expression grave. "What happened to my plan to increase the military? Chancellor Venetim! I need answers now!"

"Uh... I believe we should discuss it with Xylo first, Your Majesty," he replied, holding up some sort of cylinder. It was a letter sealed with a familiar family crest: an elk leaping among waves.

"Xylo, this letter is addressed to you."

"No."

"...Oh, but, well... This noble has singled you out and offered to lend you some soldiers. The letter's from a Frenci Mastibolt. Personally, I think...we should accept her offer, but..."

His speech was beginning to falter because of the glare I was shooting him. I must've looked royally pissed off.

"We can't ask her for help," I said with a firm shake of my head.

But Venetim didn't seem like he was going to back down just yet. "Ahem. Did I mention how many soldiers she is offering? Up to two thousand..."

"Forget about it. And burn that letter."

"Why? Xylo, what is your relationship to this lady and the Mastibolts? That's the night-gaunt family of the south, right? Why would—?"

"We were engaged a long time ago."

In response to my tone, Venetim finally stopped pressing me.

"Plus," I continued, "they wouldn't make it here in time even if we asked. Got it? This conversation is over."

"I agree with the chancellor," King Norgalle cut in. "There are likely some farmers among such a large group of soldiers, and it is about time we start preparing for the winter."

I decided to set aside King Norgalle's words for now. He had a point, but I needed to end this conversation about soldiers and get him back to his workshop as quickly as possible.

"So you cannot secure Jayce or Rhyno?" asked the king.

"I sent a carrier pigeon just in case," said Venetim. "And it wasn't free, just so you know."

"Bring me the best in the nation. That is your job, Chancellor."

"...Jayce is extremely busy, and, well...he said he doesn't want to overwork the young lady. He even threatened to kill me... Rhyno, on the other hand, completely ignored my message."

"Yeah, sounds like them," I said.

"What? Rhyno! That insolent fool! Tell him I want him here this instant!" the king demanded.

I had no idea what Rhyno was thinking. He was, in a way, even harder to read than Tatsuya. Out of all of us penal heroes, he was the most— How should I put it? As Tsav would say, he was "bad news."

I couldn't deny that he was different from the rest of us heroes. He had applied of his own volition—a volunteer hero.

"What about mercenaries? Did you contact any?" the king continued.

"I did," said Venetim, "but none of them will work without a hefty reward."

"Then open the treasury! And if that isn't enough, go tax the nobles and the Temple."

"What do you want to do, Xylo?"

"Dotta's working on getting us some money," I said.

"Hurry," demanded Norgalle. "Circulate some reliable currency and increase its value. That's the only way we're going to get rid of the bad money running rampant in this nation."

"I really hope Dotta makes it back in time…," I said, glancing out the window of the control room.

The sun was already setting, and I could clearly see the sea of faeries slowly approaching, their backs to a crimson sky. The miners were currently at the front gate, digging holes and installing logs engraved with sacred seals as a kind of simple anti-cavalry barricade.

"It's about time they moved to safety," I murmured.

The miners' lives were much more valuable than those of us heroes or the criminals on death row. I planned on keeping them near the front gate, but I didn't want them to participate directly in the battle until they absolutely had to. They weren't soldiers. They should focus on providing backup for the Holy Knights. Honestly, I didn't want them fighting at all. In a way, they were being deceived by Norgalle.

But I understood their motive. They were doing this to survive.

The men who worked in the mines of Zewan Gan had likely come from local settlements. If they lost Mureed Fortress, they would have to abandon their homes and evacuate. In that case, they wouldn't be guaranteed a minimum standard of living. They might not even be able to find work where they ended up.

That was why I was so suspicious of the military's motives. Contaminating the fortress with poison to stop Iblis meant forcing all those living nearby to give up their livelihoods.

"What are the guys back at Galtuile thinking?" I said. "This plan's gonna ruin lives. Mankind will be wiped out at this rate."

"…Perhaps there are those who wish for just that," Venetim whispered eerily from beside me. "Are you a fan of conspiracy theories, Xylo?"

"Hell no." I sighed in exasperation. I knew Venetim used to write weird articles for some paper, and to put it bluntly, he was absolutely useless as a source of information.

"Demon lord worshippers? Coexisters? It's all nonsense," I said.

Both of these groups supposedly worshipped demon lords and believed we could coexist with them. Nobody supported such things openly, of course. But there were always rumors of secret societies and the like.

"What are you trying to say?" I continued. "That there are idiots like that high up in the military?"

"…Quite a scary thought, isn't it? There's no way something like that could be possible, though…" Venetim's lips curled into an even more unsettling smirk. "But imagine if such forces were hard at work to ensure humanity's loss. Wouldn't that explain these chaotic, incomprehensible orders?"

I didn't answer him. It was true the current situation was hard to explain otherwise.

Suppose there *were* some wicked people among the military's top brass. If that was true, then the unfair nature and fuzzy details of our orders in Couveunge Forest and the Zewan Gan Tunnels would make sense. The people who set me up were surely pulling the strings. *Those dirty bastards.* I didn't know anything about demon lord worshippers or coexisters or if such groups even existed, but I knew *they* were real.

For now, though, I needed to focus on what was happening right in front of me.

"Call for Teoritta."

The time for preparations was over.

I felt gloom seep into my heart. In the end, we hadn't secured much help. We were slightly better off than we had been, but we were still essentially fending for ourselves.

Maybe that was fitting for a unit of penal heroes.

"Teoritta and I will go after the demon lord," I said. "Open the rear gate when the time comes."

"Please don't run away, Xylo," said Venetim.

"Can't make any promises."

I was lying.

Truth be told, I probably could have lived a half-decent life—if I could have only run away.

There was one particularly effective strategy for protecting a fortress from the Demon Blight.

That was to build a moat and raise the drawbridge, making it difficult to physically approach. This would leave the demon lord's army at a loss for how to continue. They would have no choice but to rely on amphibian faeries, such as fuathan or kelpies, or flying faeries, like oberons. If that wasn't an option, the demon lord itself could use some kind of special attack, or the horde could ignore the moat, surround the fortress, and try to trap everyone inside.

Iblis, our current foe, had an army of around ten thousand. The Ninth Order had taken out a great deal of them, but we were still vastly outnumbered. Plus, the demon lord at the center was estimated to be the equivalent of a little more than thirty thousand faeries on its own. Normally, a single fortress like this wouldn't stand a chance.

However, the horde didn't have many faeries that could travel through water, and it quickly became evident they had almost none that could fly, either. This was a common trait among outbreaks of Demon Blight which started in dry locations or in tundra.

That should have made our defensive strategy simple: Draw water from the Kad Tai River into the moat, then raise the drawbridge and hold out until reinforcements arrived. If possible, I'd prefer to receive help from the relatively open-minded Sixth Order.

But that plan was dead in the water from the get-go.

There were two reasons. First, we couldn't expect any reinforcements. Second, the whole plan was to neutralize Iblis with poison after luring it into the fortress. That meant we had to let the enemy inside. We'd filled the moat with water, but we couldn't do anything else. We weren't allowed to seal off the front or rear gates. We had to fight the Demon Blight head-on with the drawbridge still down.

From atop a hill under an overly bright moon, Teoritta and I watched as the throng of faeries approached. The moon was a dull green that night, as if to signal the arrival of even drier, colder weather.

The demon lord's army slithered under its light.

The first in line was a herd of horses tarnished by the Demon Blight—coiste bodhars. They had great mobility and were capable of breaking through barriers. Their hooves could even shatter iron shields, and their mouths were typically filled with fangs. These coiste bodhars were now getting ready to break through the front gate.

"Ready your weapons!"

King Norgalle's fierce shout echoed directly in my ears thanks to the sacred seal on my neck. It was like a communication device for our penal hero unit that you couldn't turn off, no matter how much you wanted to.

"Aim, but hold your fire," he continued.

I could see around fifty miners on top of the walls of the front gate, seal-engraved lightning staffs in their hands.

"Has Venetim lost his damn mind?" I muttered despite myself.

There was a man up with the miners commanding them—a large man with a mustache and a cane to help drag his wooden leg. It was King Norgalle himself.

"Guess he wasn't able to keep the king off the battlefield."

I still couldn't decide if that was for better or worse, but the high morale among the miners was obvious. They were nervous but more than willing to defend the front gate.

"Not yet. Keep luring them in."

And Norgalle's orders were spot-on. The coiste bodhars were approaching the drawbridge. Seeing the terrifying beasts they had become made it hard to believe the creatures used to be herbivores. And yet the miners didn't randomly start firing in a panic. They were doing an excellent job following instructions.

"All right."

Norgalle's timing was good. The enemies were at exactly the right distance.

"Fire!"

They unleashed bursts of lightning with their staffs.

The attack was powerful, despite the miners' lack of fighting experience. Norgalle himself had tuned the seals, after all. That man could take someone else's seal and change every detail with ease, increasing its power exponentially.

Lightning soared through the air, shooting down a few coiste bodhars. Around 70 percent of the shots missed, but even then, they did a good job. The goal was to destabilize and slow them down.

"Fences up!" It wasn't King Norgalle who gave this order but Kivia. Her voice was tense, and it carried. *"Activate the sacred seals!"*

The Holy Knights standing by in front of the gate began to move, and fences made out of pointed logs were raised, blocking the coiste bodhars' path. Whatever collided with these seal-engraved logs or tried to pass by them would be shocked with a powerful jolt of lightning.

This, of course, was yet another one of Norgalle's traps.

His ability to tune sacred seals on his own was extraordinary, but it seemed his true talent lay in leading others. Norgalle could make blueprints anyone could understand, even for something as complicated as engraving sacred seals. He could take any bum off the street and make them into a master craftsman in the blink of an eye. If a group of people gathered under him and followed his orders without fault, they would operate like a giant, well-organized factory.

The miners were flawless. They were following his orders to a T.

"Perfect! Good work, men!" shouted Norgalle.

It sounded like even the king was satisfied with how things were turning out. He'd also tinkered with some of the fortress's equipment to link together several weapons engraved with seals. Once activated, they could kill dozens, hundreds, or if we were really lucky, thousands of enemies.

That was more or less what we had prepared to defend Mureed Fortress: We would slow the enemy down with Norgalle's sacred seals.

I was the one who had come up with this method of defense. I felt that, with only around two hundred people, we had to rely on the power of the seal-engraved war machines if we wanted the fortress to hold out for any time at all. And Norgalle's anti-cavalry barricades were doing just that, keeping even the large faeries back. I could see the charred remains of the coiste bodhars it had stopped.

The fact that the sacred seals engraved in the logs could be activated over and over without a second of delay was once again down to Norgalle's incredible talents. By using the limited seal-engraved weapons in tandem, he had managed to increase our attack power dramatically, and the effect on the enemy went beyond physical damage.

I could see the boggarts and barghests hesitating after witnessing the power of the sacred seals. Even these faeries, which would charge to their death if the demon lord ordered it, seemed unwilling to commit suicide by pointlessly running into our traps.

That meant the demon lord wasn't giving effective directions.

"It's not over yet! Prepare to fire!" Norgalle's voice resonated brightly. *"Wonderful shots, men! Your bravery has struck fear into the enemy's heart!"*

"Is the king gonna be okay?" asked Tsav. He sounded a little troubled. Tsav was handling the rear gate with the thirty criminals under his command. They were on top of the fortress walls with their lightning staffs ready to snipe. *"Don't you think he's standing a little too close to the gate? Please keep a close eye on him, Venetim."*

Despite his endless chatter, Tsav was continuously sniping the enemies trying to go around the fortress and enter through the rear. His accuracy was unparalleled. He would strike each circumnavigating coiste bodhar and fuath swimming across the moat in either the head or the heart, like he had no intention of trying for anything less. The prisoners took shots under his guidance, too, which at least served as deterrents.

I hated to admit it, but Tsav actually had what it took to command as well. He'd managed to make those unruly prisoners listen to his orders in only one day. Their attacks were more or less synchronized, too. And surprisingly, they rarely took pointless shots at enemies out of range.

"*Hey, I tried to stop him. I really did,*" complained Venetim, sounding like he was holding back tears. *Here come the excuses,* I thought. "*But the king wouldn't listen to a word I said.*"

"*Enough, Chancellor! I am the king! By standing with my men at the front lines, I will spur them to action!*" exclaimed Norgalle.

The fact that what he was saying was true was what made it so scary. The morale among the miners protecting the front gate was at an all-time high.

"*Well, it sounds like you did a bad job, Venetim,*" said Tsav. "*He's not budging. I mean, if you can't smooth-talk someone into doing what you want, what good are you?*"

"*Excuse me...? Tsav, that was very rude,*" Venetim shot back.

"*I'm just saying it makes me wonder.*"

Tsav kept sniping, even as he ran his mouth. I was genuinely impressed by his ability to focus on shooting, all the while continuing to give orders to his men.

His skills were downright abnormal.

Each shot took out one—no, two enemies and sometimes even three. He'd shoot clean through the legs of large faeries, knocking them over and causing them to crush the smaller ones to death. Froglike faeries were shot midjump, before they could even dive into the moat. And he pulled it off effortlessly, chattering away all the while.

"*To be honest, the king is far more valuable than us. If something happens to him, this fortress is history... What do you think, bro?*"

"I came up with a little plan so that doesn't happen."

"*Oh, nice! What's the plan?*"

"*Now!*" shouted Kivia, as if in answer to Tsav. Her piercing voice rang out, and the Holy Knights immediately reacted in a very knightly fashion.

Basically, they got on their horses and took off. Their armor was covered in sacred seal compounds, lending them increased defense as they sowed chaos among the demon lord's army. Every swing of a spear was followed by flashes of light and fire.

I had no complaints about Kivia's leadership. Her knights rode deep into the Demon Blight, surrounding themselves with enemies—but it was a feint. They quickly pulled back or broke through. They continued like that, gradually luring the enemy out before turning around and striking back.

Kivia's team consisted of only around twenty knights, but their armor was special. It could emit flames that illuminated the darkness and prevented counterattacks. The demon lord's army was soon thrown into disarray, preventing them from getting any closer to the fortress.

"...Kivia has honestly impressed me," said Teoritta from her place by my side. There was a note of discontent in her voice.

"It'd be great if they could take out the entire army for us," I said, half joking. It was said that a single knight fully-equipped with these defensive seal compounds could do roughly the same work as thirty normal soldiers in close combat. At times, that number might be even higher.

"Kivia's leadership is like having an extra thousand soldiers on our side," I continued. "If this battle ends without me having to move a muscle, you'll hear no complaints from me."

"...Xylo!" Teoritta slid in front of me and glared daggers into my eyes. "Have you no backbone?! I have granted you my blessing, and I shall not allow you to spew such cowardice!"

She poked me in the chest with a finger so hard it kind of hurt.

"If you lose to Kivia, your reputation will suffer!"

"To hell with my reputation."

I cracked a wry smile. The battle was going far more smoothly than I'd imagined.

The miners were boldly firing bolts of lightning under Norgalle's passionate guidance, and the anti-cavalry barricades were holding the enemies back. Furthermore, Tsav's precise shooting was keeping the rear gate protected, ensuring the faeries would have to suffer high casualties if they wanted to break through our defenses. It didn't seem like it would be hard to keep them busy until the demon lord itself showed up—

The moment I thought this, our luck ran out.

"*Huh? What's that?*" Tsav murmured curiously. I caught sight of a squad of a few hundred enemies rushing through the center of the demon lord's army. They were on horseback. Humanoid figures were straddling coiste bodhars with saddles, stirrups, and bows in hand, and nocked on those bows were fire arrows.

"*...Are those people?*" Venetim said, clearly surprised.

He was right. There were humans riding those coiste bodhars. Not faeries—actual human beings. That much was obvious even from my vantage point.

But...

I had never heard of anything like this before. Humans, untransformed by the Demon Blight, fighting in the demon lord's army.

What are they doing?

They released their burning arrows, piercing the seal-engraved fences and setting them aflame. Our defensive barriers were being reduced to ash.

The battle had only just started, and we were already about to lose our outer shell of protection.

"The hell is going on?"

I couldn't contain the irritation in my voice.

Humans were using weapons and working together with the Demon Blight.

This was extremely unusual. Humans transformed into faeries were one thing, but this was something else entirely. This meant there were forces in society aligning themselves with the enemy.

Though it was extremely rare, I knew there were a few creatures associated with the Demon Blight that understood our language and possessed a similar mentality. Therefore, it was certainly possible for such creatures to strike a deal with humans for their mutual benefit. Of course, if you asked me, only crazy people would try something like that. But it could theoretically happen. Or maybe the Demon Blight was messing with their heads?

I really hoped it was the latter, but I hadn't heard anything about Iblis having powers like that.

"Xylo," Teoritta said. Her face was pale. She clearly considered this a serious issue, and I knew why. "We have a big problem. I cannot attack humans. My mechanisms do not allow it."

"I know. I'll figure something out." I tried to reassure her, but I knew this was a big problem. "...Kivia! Can you hear me? What's going on out there? Who are they? The Ninth Order didn't say anything about this."

I had to call out to her a few times before she finally replied. Communicating via sacred seal was far less reliable if you were talking to someone other than another penal hero. I'd heard it had something to do with the wavelength used.

"...*I don't know what's going on, either,*" she replied.

Just what I wanted to hear.

Kivia and her men were moving away from the front gate as quickly as possible. A dozen or so knights who had been waiting in ambush joined them in pushing back the incoming faeries.

"*However, I'm sure they're some noble's private army. That much is obvious from their riding and horseback archery skills.*"

What's more, there were two hundred of them.

They were wearing only light armor, but they were still fully equipped and sported helmets, making it impossible to see their faces. And to top it all off, they were riding coiste bodhars and shooting fire arrows. It wasn't long before King Norgalle's anti-cavalry barricades were in flames. The scene was nightmarish.

"What the hell is some noble's private army doing teaming up with a demon lord?"

"...*I don't know,*" Kivia replied.

"So nobody knows anything! Got it! That means I can attack them, right? I'm gonna catch one and make them talk."

"*I suppose that's one option. But it appears we're too late. They're withdrawing! We won't be able to catch up with them now.*"

"Dammit."

The group of enemy cavalry immediately pulled back after lighting the fence on fire, and Kivia and her knights were too heavily armored to catch up with them. It was now clear that attacking the fortress from the front gate was not their role. They appeared to be heading toward an underground passage, the gate of which I'd purposely left open. They were probably planning to use it to sneak into the fortress.

A stroke of luck at last.

This was the best outcome we could have hoped for, since it meant we didn't have to fight the humans anymore.

"*Xylo, we're in trouble!*" said Venetim. "*They've infiltrated the underground passage!*"

"I can see that. They seem pretty familiar with the fortress."

"Yes, and that's the problem! What are we going to do if they find me?!"

"You're so obsessed with self-preservation… But, well, you don't need to worry about that."

"Yeah, Venetim," Tsav chimed in. *"Did you even listen to the plan? Tatsuya will protect you. He'll slaughter them all."*

"Precisely," said King Norgalle. *"And in addition to General Tatsuya's defenses, you have my explosive sacred seals as well. Your position is impregnable."*

Venetim didn't say another word. As always, he was completely unfit to command.

At any rate, the underground passage was safe. Those defending it should be able to hold out even if the enemy brought faeries with them. And if things looked like they were going south, we could blow it up and seal it off. But first we needed to lure them in.

The enemy's behavior made it clear that they didn't have much experience storming fortresses. They may very well be some noble's private army, but I doubted it was anyone allied with the military. Maybe they were connected with the Temple?

"So what's Team Aboveground supposed to do, exactly?" asked Tsav, sounding annoyed. *"I've got my hands full here and can't guard the front gate."*

He had a point. A horde of large faeries was rapidly approaching the front of the fortress.

These were what we referred to as kyracks. They were massive beasts shaped like bulls, covered in thick armor, and equipped with sharp horns. They acted like battering rams, so the last thing we wanted was to allow them to get close to the fortress. Unfortunately, lightning staffs had little effect on them.

"Venetim, you're the commander, right? How about some help?" Tsav said without a hint of worry in his voice. He continued to snipe each faerie that approached the rear gate one by one. *"Can we at least have the king get down from the wall? There are kyracks approaching. The front gate's not gonna make it."*

"Y-yes, you must come inside, Your Majesty!" urged Venetim.

"I will do no such thing!" King Norgalle shot back. *"Send reinforcements! This fortress, under my direct command, is the front line of national*

defense! We will lose not only our land but our spirits if they break through and I am forced to retreat!"

"*There aren't any reinforcements. And, uh…" You aren't even a king* was what Venetim almost said before swallowing back his words. It was a wise decision. All that would have done was anger His Majesty.

"*Prepare to fire!"* shouted Norgalle in a booming voice. "*Do not let those faeries come any closer!"*

Men started hustling around the fortress walls, accompanied by the unnatural sound of something scraping along the ground.

Mureed Fortress contained several seal-engraved cannons—known as runtels—that were produced by the Verkle Development Corporation. They were the newest model, which featured improvements stabilizing the cannonballs' average flight distance.

They were powerful, but with the number of people left, we could station only four facing the front gate.

"*Fire!"*

Norgalle himself had tuned the cannons, so both their power and blast radius were impressive. But that didn't mean much when the people firing were amateurs. In fact, they deserved praise simply for not blowing themselves up.

At any rate, while no one hit their targets, the cannons proved moderately effective. The sporadic shots caught a few kyracks in their blast, blowing them apart. The surviving faeries didn't make it out unscathed, either. For now, it seemed we'd made it—but that was merely the first wave. Unfortunately, the cannons were not able to fire in rapid succession, meaning a second wave would likely reach the front gate before the next round of shots was ready.

"*Blast it!"* shouted Norgalle. "*It appears our aim needs work, and our power is lacking! Where is my artilleryman Rhyno?! Chancellor Venetim, tell that fool to get over here this instant!"*

"*Have you not heard a word I've said, Your Majesty? He isn't here,"* said Venetim.

"*Then get me Jayce! Call for the air force! We shall take out the enemy where they stand!"*

"*He isn't here, either."*

"*Then…"*

I already knew what he would say next. I patted Teoritta on the shoulder. She looked back at me, and I winked. It was time.

"Commander in Chief Xylo! Kill the enemy general and make them withdraw their forces!"

"Guess I have to," I said.

This was quicker than I'd expected. Iblis was still crawling at the back of the horde, and I'd have preferred to wait until it reached the front line before launching my attack, with the men on the castle walls backing me up. But I didn't have a choice. The enemy was closing in, and I had to defeat the demon lord before its army broke into the fortress.

"Teoritta." I had to say it. "I didn't want you to have to fight yet."

"Personally, I was getting tired of waiting." There were already flames in her eyes as she stared ahead. "This is how a goddess and her knight's battles ought to be. We shall fight for humanity! For people far away whose faces we've never seen!"

She brushed back her glittering golden hair, causing small sparks. *There she goes*, I thought.

"Spoken like a true goddess," I said. "Maybe you should take the stage one day."

"I could say the same to you." Her eyes narrowed teasingly. "Think about what you are trying to do right now."

She pointed a finger toward the tip of my nose. "You are risking your life."

"Because I can. I'm immortal."

"That's a lie," she said immediately. "You would do this even if you weren't coming back, and yet you claim to be disgusted by a goddess's way of life."

"Can it with this stuff."

"I will not. It is obvious why you feel the way you do."

I decided to shut up and listen to her. I felt Teoritta deserved at least one chance to get back at me, since I had picked on her countless times in the past.

"You despise our nature simply because it reminds you of yourself."

"Tell me something I don't know, dammit."

Teoritta and I fought for very similar reasons. She was fighting because she wanted people to praise her, and I was fighting because I didn't want anyone looking down on me. I hated to admit it, but it was basically the same thing. We were risking our lives because we cared how others saw us.

I'm so pathetic. I was fighting because I cared what people thought of me... Just how badly did I want to show off? Did I want to become some sort of legendary savior? I still hadn't learned my lesson, even after what happened with Senerva.

No matter what, in the end, I couldn't escape from myself.

"Yeah." I nodded. "...You're a hundred percent right. You win."

"Of course I do." She huffed proudly, as if she couldn't be happier. "And that is why I chose you as my knight!"

This doesn't feel so bad.

I felt good, in fact. What I needed to do was clear: Win this battle and protect Mureed Fortress. That was how I was going to save Teoritta. I was going to show the guys back at Galtuile just how "useful" she could be. If that was what they needed, that was what I'd do.

Plus, we'd also be helping the Holy Knights and miners who ended up stuck here with us. And then—I guess we'd also be saving people whose faces we'd never seen and who might not even exist. Abandoning this fortress would mean forcing mankind to retreat. It would mean giving up on every settlement in the area. We could stop that from happening.

I lined up all the reasons in my head. With so many, I thought I might be able to fight with real valor for once.

I wanted to win a battle that had meaning. I wanted to save others so I could feel important. I wanted to believe that I wasn't a lost cause. Objectively speaking, my motives were unimpressive. But people could think whatever they wanted. This was my fight, not theirs.

"You are a hero, and I am a goddess. I must bless our fight... After all, this is our job, yes? We have no choice."

That was the first time I ever heard Teoritta joke around. She had a mischievous, childlike grin.

"Now you're getting it," I said. I lifted her up and kicked off the ground, soaring high into the air with Sakara at maximum output.

"That's the kind of spunk I want to see. I'm starting to feel like we're gonna crush this demon lord."

"Right?"

As Teoritta happily clung to me, I unsheathed a knife and threw it at a group of faeries gathering below us. Twisting my body, I threw two more, creating powerful flashes and loud explosions and disturbing the enemy's formation.

Our destination was Demon Lord Iblis.

I could see its massive body in the distance behind its army of ten thousand faeries. And I was going to kill every one of them to get to it.

The leader of the Thirteenth Order's infantry, Rajit Heathrow, saw a demon in the underground passage that day.

That demon was a penal hero known as Tatsuya.

Twenty infantrymen had been sent underground to seal off the passage under Rajit Heathrow's command. The moment they saw the intruders rushing in after them, they knew they were going to die—that this would be their gravesite. The sight of soldiers riding coiste bodhars filled them with astonishment and fear.

"Humans riding faeries?" muttered one man, his lightning staff at the ready. "Impossible."

Rajit felt the same way. He didn't want to believe his eyes.

Everyone was in shock. At this rate, they would all be trampled and crushed. They were outnumbered and too shaken to properly fight back. There was no way for them to win—under normal circumstances.

But that day, a man called Tatsuya was with them.

"Grrrhhh."

A growl echoed in his throat as Tatsuya leaped forward, his battle-ax raised. He moved so quickly that he was already on the enemy before the Holy Knights had even raised their weapons. They couldn't keep up with him—he was just too fast.

"Gwuuuuuuh!"

A strange battle cry rang out.

Tatsuya swung his long-handled battle-ax with one hand, crushing the first of the enemy's knights. He then grabbed another's spear with his left hand, dragging the man off his faerie and swinging the ax up into him, severing his spine and destroying his body. Tatsuya followed with another downstroke, finishing off the man's coiste bodhar as well.

After that, he started hopping around on all fours like some sort of insect.

"What is that thing?" moaned one of Rajit's men. They were all in shock. "Can a human even move like that?"

Rajit was having the same thoughts.

One moment, Tatsuya was leaping onto a wall and hanging there, and the next, his battle-ax was tearing into the enemy. Rajit had never seen a human being's shoulders move the way this man's did. At times, Tatsuya would even use the ceiling to kick off before slicing through a knight and his horse in one fell swoop. He deflected each of their spears, breaking them.

"Monster…!" shrieked one of the enemy cavalrymen. "Is he… Is he a faerie, too? He's too fast. Come together and defend!"

A few men were overcome with fear and made bad decisions. Cavalrymen did not specialize in defense, so gathering together only made it easier to mow them down. Tatsuya dodged the enemy's line of spears and lowered himself so he was almost crawling. Then he sprinted forward, swinging his ax upward and painting the ceiling with blood.

"…All of you, move to support!"

That was when Rajit Heathrow finally came back to his senses.

"Don't let them surround that penal hero! Fire your lightning staffs!"

By the time they started firing, the battle was thoroughly decided. Confined spaces like this were where Tatsuya shined most in battle. He kicked off walls, the ceiling, and anything else he landed on. His steel ax soared through the air like a bolt of lightning, cutting off the intruders.

Rajit and his soldiers didn't have to use their backup plan: blowing up the underground passage with sacred seals to render it unpassable. All they had to do was pick off the few enemies Tatsuya didn't finish and support him from behind. The battle eventually ended with the blood and meat of their enemies piled on the ground at their feet. A few soldiers threw up at the sight.

He was able to decimate an entire enemy unit without a moment's hesitation.

When every last enemy was dead, Tatsuya simply stood among the gruesome remains and gazed up at the ceiling, no longer moving. It was hard to believe he was human. A strange feeling twisted in Rajit's gut as he watched the hero stand in silence like a doll.

"Huuuuuuah."

What escaped Tatsuya's lungs sounded like a diver's first deep breath after returning from the depths of the ocean.

What is this guy?

Demon was the first word to pop into Rajit's head. There was no way this man was human.

◆

The moonlight grew dim.

Wind began to blow, pushing the clouds across the sky.

Teoritta and I weaved through these gusts as we soared through the air. We couldn't simply cut our way across the middle of the faerie horde. We had to fight as we went, making use of Sakara's limited aerial jumps wherever possible. This was what thunderstroke soldiers like me were best at.

Thunderstroke soldiers were a recent addition to the military. Their original purpose was to provide aerial fire support while leaping over the enemy's head using short-range jumps.

Their focus was on mobility. They were expected to supplement the abilities of dragon knights, who were extremely powerful but suffered from limited maneuverability. Thunderstroke soldiers were a decisive force meant to drive wedges into the faerie troops and attack demon lords head-on.

However, you needed a great deal of training in order to maneuver through the air with a flight seal and effectively attack at the same time. It wasn't something an average infantryman could easily get used to, and thus numbers were still limited. The concept itself was well-thought-out, however.

Such soldiers were quicker than cavalrymen and could move around the battlefield three-dimensionally, allowing them to target the source of a Demon Blight at the rear.

That was what Teoritta and I were trying right now. We had avoided the vast majority of the faeries, since fighting them would be a waste of time, and made our way directly to Demon Lord Iblis.

Still, almost every faerie that caught sight of us attacked on instinct. The area around Mureed Fortress consisted of nothing but flat plains and gentle hills with almost no cover. Thus, it didn't matter how hard you tried to remain hidden; there were some fights you simply couldn't avoid.

"They're here, Xylo," shouted Teoritta. She was currently latched on to my neck. "Large doglike monsters. And frogs!"

I could feel the wind brush against my ears as I looked straight down. There were a few barghests and fuathan, and they had seen us. In addition, another group from the horde was rapidly approaching. We had been killing every faerie that came near up until now, and it looked like they were finally sick of us.

Iblis, now close by, was staring at us as well. It looked like a giant black slug, but it felt smaller than I'd imagined—no bigger than an elephant. The red eyeballs covering its body were focused on Teoritta and me.

"Things are about to get serious," I said. "I hope you're ready."

"But of course." Teoritta stretched out her arm. "Go ahead, my knight."

Sparks flickered from the tips of her fingers.

I immediately grabbed a beautiful one-handed sword as it emerged from the void and threw it toward the ground, skewering a barghest and exploding it. But the instant I landed in the mess of blood and dirt it left behind, I was surrounded by fuathan.

Looks like I only have five knives left.

I unsheathed one and threw it in a single motion. There was a flash of light, followed by an explosion. I ran through the chaos, then leaped back into the air. The wind was howling. The roaring blast and radiant light seemed to have gotten the attention of a good number of faeries, and dozens were now rushing toward my next landing spot.

Teoritta watched everything, her burning eyes opened wide.

Goddesses were like having another pair of eyes for a knight. They kept watch on the knight's blind spots and could share their vision through a type of synesthesia. It was a method of processing information far quicker than having a conversation. This was nothing strange for a Holy Knight, but Teoritta still often put her thoughts into words. Maybe it was to relieve some of the tension—mine or hers, I didn't know. *I wish she wouldn't bother.*

"Bull monsters are coming this way, Xylo. And they're big."

"Those are kyracks."

These massive faeries could bring down even a castle wall with their shining lead-colored horns. They looked like small mountains moving under the moonlight.

"We're almost there." I looked ahead, and Iblis's red eyes were staring right back at me. "Hold on tight. Who knows what'll happen."

"I was never planning on letting go." Teoritta smiled as she summoned another sword. "You would be furious with me if I died, yes?"

Now you get it, I thought as I grabbed the new sword. The blade began to glow as I infused just the right amount of my sacred seal's power before launching it.

The explosion went off almost immediately, blowing off over half of the kyrack's head. It squealed and twisted its body, swinging its horns and stomping the ground. I had to land much farther away than I'd intended to avoid getting caught in its rampage. And that was a mistake.

Enemies closed in around me—no, wait. Something was coiling its way around my legs.

...It's a damn boggart.

The faerie's centipede-like head emerged from the dirt and tried to bite my leg. You couldn't see these things from the air, so this was a case of simple bad luck. They hid underground like mines.

I immediately activated Sakara and kicked the boggart before it could bite me. I felt its head crack under my kick, but that wasn't the end. More boggarts emerged from the soil—another, then another— and I had no choice but to deal with them. I began kicking them in between low-altitude jumps as I tried to make my escape. I didn't get far, though.

They'll surround me at this rate.

I could feel my legs burning from overusing the sacred seal. You were supposed to take a little time to cool off between jumps—around three deep breaths.

"Today must be my lucky day."

"Perhaps you have failed to praise and worship your goddess adequately?"

The worse the situation, the more I wanted to crack jokes, and Teoritta was quick to play along. Maybe it was because we shared a part of our consciousness.

"You're probably right. I'll have to do better next time."

I visualized what I had to do.

There were still tons of faeries to deal with, but Iblis was close. I'd have to take a gamble, and the odds weren't good. I needed to take out the faeries nearby, and to do that, I had to put some distance between us. But jumping again would leave me defenseless.

I had to find a way to keep the faeries from attacking me while I made my jump.

Will I even have enough strength left to deal with Iblis?

Doubt surfaced in my mind, but I immediately suppressed it.

A thunderstroke soldier was weakest on the ground. You were always wide-open the moment you made your next jump. I was essentially an isolated infantryman for the next thirty seconds or so, and I couldn't rely on Teoritta's powers. I had to save her strength for more important tasks.

Even if I run out of strength... Even if it's physically impossible, I'll figure out something.

I glared at the approaching faeries. Whatever I did, I had to deal with them first.

Pull yourself together. You decided to do this, right? So do it.

As soon as I thought this, I noticed a disturbance among the faeries. It was coming from the east, where the green moon shone in the sky. The faerie horde seemed to waver. Even a few of Iblis's eyes shifted toward the commotion.

...I don't believe it.

I'd caught sight of something dreadful under the green light of the moon. A fluttering flag with the crest of an elk leaping among waves. I knew that flag, and I didn't want to see it. It was the flag of a certain well-known family from the south: the Mastibolts—the family of the woman I was once engaged to.

"...Venetim." Even I could hear the rage in my voice. "Why are they here? You lied to me, didn't you?"

"*Well, let me ask you this, Xylo,*" said Venetim nervously. "*Why did you think I would tell you the truth? I knew you'd get mad at me.*"

Venetim's makeshift lies were the worst—the *worst*. The fact that they sometimes improved the situation only made them all the more aggravating. And speaking of aggravating...

"*Xylo! Help!*" came Dotta's piercing voice.

At the same time, clouds of dirt rose up behind the faerie horde to the north. Iblis's eyes were busy. The enemy's attention was more divided than ever.

"...Dotta, what did you do?"

"*I'm being chased by mercenaries! Help!*"

"Help with what? I told you to get some money together and hire some soldiers. What do you need help with?"

I'd told him to sneak into some noble's mansion, steal some valuables, and use them to hire mercenaries. Of course, I was well aware that Dotta was likely to run away, but I also knew he'd be no help back at the fortress. If anything, he'd probably just get in the way.

But now he was coming from the north with a group of mercenaries, heading straight for the enemy. Judging by the amount of dirt in the air, the group was predominantly cavalry.

"*Xylo, no. Listen to me. I had an epiphany. Why steal from some random noble to hire mercenaries when I could steal from the very mercenaries I was hiring? That would be much quicker, I thought—*"

"I've heard enough. You're rotting my brain as you speak."

I had already started running. Teoritta snickered under her breath despite the situation. I snorted a laugh, too.

The faeries were in a state of confusion, charging at me in a frenzy. I lightly kicked off the ground and threw a knife right in the middle of them, blowing them up.

The chaos lasted for about thirty more seconds.

The faeries weren't able to react in time to the reinforcements in the east or the band of angry mercenaries in the north. And yet they couldn't ignore them, either. Both were a far bigger threat than I was.

At last, the path to Demon Lord Iblis was wide-open.

Swords rained down on the earth.

As they fell, their blades glittered white under the green moon.

I ran, weaving my way between their sharp points. Meanwhile, the faeries struggled to defend themselves, their attention split between the two groups of reinforcements.

These attacks from outside had come suddenly, like a sucker punch to the face. And the cavalry at the rear had distracted Iblis itself, drawing the attention of a number of faeries as well. Their reactions were instinctual, animal. This demon lord's army was not very organized, and it appeared Iblis possessed little intelligence.

But then why?

There had to be someone else who gave the orders to attack this fortress. That was the only way to explain it. But now was not the time to worry about that.

It wasn't difficult to break through the faeries now that they were skewered with swords. I stepped on a fuath that lunged at me, smashing it into the ground and kicking off into the air. Just a little farther. Iblis was straight ahead. A large barghest darted into my path, and I threw a knife at it, blowing it into pieces. Then I jumped once more.

The demon lord was right in front of my eyes.

Damn, it's big.

I was wrong for ever thinking it was the size of an elephant.

Up close, I could tell just how huge it was. It was like a moving citadel. I'd be surprised if it could fit through Mureed Fortress's front gate. But I knew how to handle it. From this distance, I could reach it with Zatte Finde.

However, that also meant Iblis was close enough to strike back. The big slug's attacks were very simple. It used its weight to crush its opponents. The demon lord extended its soft, flexible body in an attempt to smash me. It was a simple charge—just a body slam—but it was effective.

"Teoritta!" I twisted around in midair. "Can you do it?"

"Of course." She nodded. She could sense what she needed to do. I felt her arms tighten around me. Sparks shot into the air, and a colossal, towerlike sword emerged from the void.

It fell onto Iblis's body, impaling it. The impact made a disgusting, wet sound as the creature let loose an otherworldly howl. Its charge slowed. The more it flailed about, the more the blade tore into its flesh.

I leaped, landed on the sword's hilt, and kicked off again, jumping into the air once more. Immediately, the sword rusted and collapsed into dust. Objects summoned by goddesses didn't last forever, though the length of time varied from object to object. This time, Teoritta had focused on size and strength and disregarded durability.

Swords like this were perfect for my style of combat, and it was clear that Teoritta was quickly learning how to fight by my side. This was yet another reason why Holy Knights and goddesses made powerful pairs.

"How was that, my knight?" She looked at me, her flaming eyes ready for a challenge. "My blessings are not to be underestimated. Wouldn't you agree?"

When I'd wished for Teoritta to summon that sword, I'd begun to remember.

Senerva, the goddess of fortresses. Her blessings had summoned structures from other worlds. We'd fought numerous battles together. I'd leap around the battlefield—literally—and she would summon large towers, just like this, for me to use as footholds. Together, we'd engage in aerial battles against the Demon Blight. It didn't hurt to remember anymore. And so I gave Teoritta my answer.

"Damn right. Now let's go win this thing."

"I expect nothing less. You have my blessings. Onward to victory."

I glanced back. Iblis was rushing at us, roaring as mysterious fluids spewed from its body. It was still moving, despite the fact that a giant sword had impaled it only moments ago. In fact, its wound was already closing up.

It was mindlessly charging straight for me. Its colossal body wriggled across the ground, leaving its army of faeries behind. Up close, it was like a mountain was coming to crush me, and while its movement appeared sluggish, it was so large that each stride it took was massive.

In effect, we'd already achieved our objective.

As my feet touched the ground, I turned to look up at Iblis. It gazed back down at me with its countless cloudy eyes. It was probably furious.

"I get it."

I threw a knife into the ground and nodded. Then I jumped back into the air, slowly enough so Iblis could catch up with me.

"I know how you feel. I hate battles like this."

Everything was chaotic, unclear, illogical. That was how all our fights as penal heroes went, and it was all because of *them*. Those assholes did this.

Iblis tried to crush me with its massive body and fell right into my trap.

The knife I'd skewered into the ground exploded, swallowing the area in blinding light and roaring sound. In the blink of an eye, it changed the very landscape. This was a trap I had set while out scouting earlier. With Kivia's help, I'd buried sacred seals tuned by King Norgalle throughout the area.

Weathering seals.

These seals essentially turned dry land into mud. Put simply, they created exaggerated pitfalls, making the ground unusable. It took time to restore the affected area, so they weren't used much on the battlefield. Destroying something was easy, but putting it back was hard. That was life.

But I wasn't going to let that bother me now.

I got the feeling Kivia wouldn't have helped if she knew what kind of sacred seals were inside the boxes. I'd turned the surrounding land into mud on a massive scale, and Iblis was right in the middle if it.

"Teoritta."

"I know."

Sparks flickered furiously off her golden hair as three swords emerged from the sky. They were colossal weapons with hooked tips, and the moment the demon lord saw them, it roared. But it was already too late. Iblis could writhe in agony and struggle to escape, but the mud kept it from getting anywhere.

"It ends…"

Teoritta held out a finger, and the swords rained down upon Iblis.

"…now."

The demon lord's body was impaled as the weight of the swords dragged it farther into the sinking abyss. This time, the swords had more than enough durability. The size and power were sufficient as well—there was no way Iblis could escape, no matter how much it struggled.

The gaping wounds in its body were tearing it apart. It began to heal itself, but the muddy swamp absorbing its body and the weight of the swords skewering it into the ground prevented it from doing much else. It struggled for purchase to move forward, finding none.

In the end, this was the way to deal with a demon lord whose only advantage was immortality: prevent it from moving. And to do that, why not simply make a big pitfall it couldn't crawl out of? It was painfully primitive, but this was all we'd needed to prepare.

Once our traps were set, we just had to get things moving: Deal with the horde of faeries, lure the demon lord to the right place, distract it, summon large quantities of swords, and—well, the list went on. But now that we had it in the muddy swamp and it couldn't move, we just needed to poison it. We didn't need to sacrifice the fortress.

"We did it." Teoritta looked up at me. She was breathing heavily, sweat dripping from her forehead. "…Right?"

She stuck out her head as if telling me to rub it. Maybe this was where we went wrong. Maybe it was too soon to claim victory.

Snap. An eerie noise could be heard coming from the hole.

Iblis was thrashing around in the mud. There was a laceration on its back. The soft flesh there tore open as wings emerged—no, those weren't wings.

Part of its body was separating.

Something resembling a small bat popped out and took off. That was when I finally realized the demon lord's true nature.

It transformed. It wasn't immortal, it simply adapted to change—though I suppose that effectively made it immortal. Was poison really going to stop it? Did this mean the third goddess's vision of the future had finally missed the mark?

I can't believe this little punk is gonna try to fly off.

Iblis had stripped itself of its large body, turned into a bat, and was flying away. And that wasn't all. It grew larger in the air as we watched, until eyes emerged all over its body and glared at us.

Here it comes, I thought.

"Dammit."

I unconsciously threw myself at Teoritta, pushing her away. That was when I realized our foe had claws as sharp as knives. Did I make it in time? I felt a sharp pain from the front of my shoulder through to my back. It didn't bother me too much, perhaps due to the adrenaline in my system. But there was a bigger problem.

"*...Bro? You still haven't finished up over there?*" Tsav's voice crackled, fading in and out. "*Things are getting serious back here. I'm doing everything I can, but...*"

I heard eerie cracking sounds and explosions in the background. Destruction. Norgalle's and Venetim's voices were mixed in as well.

"*Men, fall back! To the castle keep! The front gate won't hold any longer!*"

"*Huh? Your Majesty, please wait! Don't come here! K-keep holding the enemy off as long as you can!*"

"*Oh, is it already that bad?*" Tsav's voice again. "*Then I guess it'd be okay if I ran away, right?*"

"*Wait... Somebody...save me...!*" Now it was Dotta. "*The mercenaries are gonna kill me when they catch up!*"

What a bunch of morons. I almost wanted to laugh. The situation had really taken a turn for the worse. But this was my strategy, so I supposed it was my responsibility to fix it.

Iblis was circling in the air, probably evaluating our forces.

"Dammit." I sighed. "Teoritta, run for it. Get out of here. I'll try to buy you as much time as I can. It doesn't matter if a hero dies, but you're different."

"No, my knight." She shook her head. "You will not suffer defeat as long as I am by your side. I am a goddess, Xylo."

She was still watching the enemy, her eyes aflame. Iblis turned over in the air, still growing. Faeries were closing in on Teoritta from behind, and yet there was no despair on her face.

She's really something else.

It wasn't the most eloquent way of putting it, but it was how I felt. Teoritta still hadn't lost her will to fight. She was one hell of a goddess. Now she was pointing at the enemy, looking for all the world like a divine being descended from the heavens to guide the human race.

"We shall fight and win," she declared.

"You really are a great goddess."

"You are the same, my knight... You still remember the vow you made when you forged a pact with me, yes?" she asked with a hint of worry.

"I still remember," I said, grinning wryly. That was the truth, unfortunately—I remembered it well. I'd vowed to display my greatness as her knight.

"Just as I am a great goddess, you are a great knight. You must believe in yourself. We will not fall. We will not lose. We will not yield. We will win, no matter what. Don't you agree?"

"Yeah."

That was when I decided to let Teoritta guide me.

I'd made a vow, so I had no choice in the matter. I decided to have faith in myself—to believe again that I was a great knight, as I once had been. At the very least, I wasn't going to sit around and let that punk Iblis look down on me.

This was just my nature, it seemed, and not even dying was going to fix it.

The demon lord Iblis turned over in the air, flapping its wings soundlessly as its body expanded.

It looked like a mix between a bull and a wolf with colossal wings.

"We'll only have one more chance to attack, if that," I whispered to Teoritta.

It was the knight's role to make strategic decisions. If my goddess was still prepared to fight, then my job wasn't over.

Besides, giving up now meant dying, and that'd make me look totally incompetent. I'd be the target of all kinds of ridicule, and I was not going to have that. I didn't want to admit failure, especially not after acting like a real tough guy and leaving the fortress to go after the demon lord myself. I would die of embarrassment.

"The thing's still wary," I said. Its countless eyes were closely observing its surroundings as it glided through the air above us. "But it's gonna have to attack sometime. It can't wait for its army."

The surrounding area had turned into a quagmire, and the faeries would suffer too many casualties if they followed us here.

"It'll attack before that happens," I concluded.

This demon lord had low intelligence, but it could figure out that much. It was still smarter than your average wild beast.

"It'll probably swoop at us, giving us a split-second window to attack. If we fail, it might create an even more effective weapon."

The demon lord's claws, which had ripped into me a few moments ago, were only getting bigger. If its true nature was adapting to change, as I suspected, it must have sensed how effective they were against me. Its claws were now as long and sharp as swords.

"That's the situation. Still think we have a chance?" I asked.

"In that case…"

Teoritta lifted her head, her lips faintly trembling. I could see she was failing to hide her fear, but she put on a smile to show me the strength of her will. She was trying to give me the courage to fight. *The nerve.*

"…it will be a cinch. Who do you think I am?"

She was expecting a lot from me, and I couldn't let her down. I shot her back a wry grin.

"You're the goddess of swords, Teoritta," I said.

"Yes. I am the great goddess of swords, and you are my great knight," she declared, taking off her white mantle and throwing it to the ground. Her entire body was red with heat. I had never seen her hair spark so brilliantly. "I shall prepare you a special sword… This time it shall be truly amazing."

"One that can kill an immortal opponent? How?" I asked.

"…There is no 'how.' Nothing in existence can survive a strike from the Holy Sword."

"Another goddess foretold that nothing other than poison could kill it."

"Nothing of this world, perhaps." She had a point, but her smile was stiff. "Therefore, I will summon something from outside this world. There is nothing to fear, for it is merely a single creature."

She had said there was nothing to fear, but Teoritta was more afraid than anyone.

"I will grant you the space of one breath," she said. "That is your chance. I will not fail."

In other words, I better hit it in one swing. That meant it came down to technique—and that was all up to me.

"Is there anything else you need?" she asked.

"No."

All I needed was courage to conquer the fear. That was it.

But what I had probably wasn't courage, only unbearable anger. I'd lived my whole life tossed around by my own lack of patience. And so I answered simply.

"Leave it to me."

I was too embarrassed to tell the truth.

To be honest, I wasn't confident, and I wasn't a knight. I was a soldier. I'd learned swordsmanship as a Holy Knight, as was tradition. But I wasn't great at it—I was only average at best. Could I really make this swing?

I wanted more time to gather my focus—to get my breathing under control and prepare my attack. But there was no way my opponent would give me enough time.

Iblis flapped its wings forcefully. Its shadow was right on top of us. Against the backdrop of the green moon, the demon lord closed its wings, descending rapidly. Its massive, terrible claws glittered in the night. It moved quickly, but its attack was simple.

This is it.

This was our only chance for victory.

"My knight."

Teoritta reached into the empty air and moved her hands as if drawing a sword from an invisible scabbard. Radiant sparks shot into the air. A bolt of lightning ran over the palms of her hands, and in its wake appeared a sword.

It was a one-handed, double-edged blade of unclouded silver. It seemed to emit a glow of its own, but it was plain, like the weapon of a regular soldier fighting on the front lines. I was grateful for this touch. I hadn't forgotten all of my training.

Teoritta tossed me the sword, and I glared at Iblis as it descended. I caught the mysterious weapon, gripping it. The enemy's movement was simple—straightforward.

Direct.

I can counter this. I can do it. No problem.

I went on pumping myself up until Iblis was right above my head, heading straight for me from the front as expected. And then it did something that took me by surprise.

You've gotta be kidding me.

It was like watching a flower bloom. Iblis's body was transforming.

Cheating scumbag.

The demon lord's body tore open at the chest, and two more arms sprouted out of it, giving it a total of six sets of claws.

I blocked one arm with the knife in my left hand and twisted my body to dodge a second as it tore into my shoulder. A third arm dug into my stomach, but I wasn't going to let the pain bother me right now. It still had three more sets of claws. *Dammit.*

Arm number four and five were going for my neck, while the sixth was reaching out toward Teoritta. I had to protect her, even if it meant giving up my only chance to attack. To me, she was more important. It was a major tactical error, to put it lightly. Once I was killed, she would be next.

There was no way I could justify such a foolish mistake.

The only reason I didn't wind up ruining everything was because of a misunderstanding on my part. I'd forgotten that I was no longer a Holy Knight. There were more people than just Teoritta and I fighting this battle.

"Xylo!"

The first voice I heard was Dotta's. It didn't come from the sacred seal on my neck this time. It was his real voice, piercing and frantic, shaking my eardrums. I could see a man on horseback, his face twisted in desperation, riding this way. His lightning staff was already held out, and he was firing—four bolts in a row.

"What are you doing?!" he yelled. "Are you out of your mind?! Let's get out of here!"

Dotta couldn't tell the difference between Iblis and the other faeries. His staggering ignorance was the very reason he could do what he was doing. The idea of me engaged in one-on-one combat with the demon lord must have seemed so incredibly stupid to him that he couldn't even consider it. I kind of agreed with him there.

At any rate, while Dotta was a terrible shot, he still managed to hit Iblis's spread wings. With his skill, it was probably the only thing he could've hoped to hit. Even then, two of his four shots missed.

Nevertheless, Dotta managed to knock Iblis off-balance, causing its sixth arm to shake and miss Teoritta. Iblis might be able to quickly repair its wounds, but there was no way it could instantaneously attack and defend with holes in its wings. And apparently, Dotta's attacks were even visible from the fortress.

"Oh, I see it. This is my last shot, okay?"

Tsav's listless voice was immediately followed by a dry pop.

A bolt of lightning sped across the sky, far more powerful, piercing, and accurate than Dotta's, and that shot alone opened six holes in Iblis's wings, knocking it firmly sideways.

"*Did I really hit it?*" said Tsav. "*Wow. That's His Majesty's work for you…*"

He'd sniped the demon lord all the way from Mureed Fortress's keep.

In the middle of the night, with only the moon above, he'd utilized the flashes from Dotta's lightning staff to take aim and shoot Iblis's wings from a truly impressive distance. Tsav's skills were godlike. When I asked him about it later, he told me he had attached a scope to a sniper staff tuned by King Norgalle.

Whatever the case, Iblis's attack failed, and its extra arms got it nowhere.

I charged toward the demon lord as it fell. The part that most resembled a head was once again transforming. It opened a mouth, revealing rows of fangs. But it was acting out of desperation now, nothing more.

I couldn't completely dodge its attacks from this distance, but I didn't care. I held out my left arm and raised my sword. Iblis immediately clamped down on my left arm, and the intense pain from its fangs piercing my flesh only made me angrier. That was my driving force. Anger was my fuel.

There was no way I could miss now. I thrust the Holy Sword forward, piercing Iblis's body with its glittering silver blade. It sent out vivid sparks that lit up the area as if it were day.

I already knew what was going to happen. Teoritta had said that nothing in existence could survive a strike from this sword. And Iblis was a demon lord that could adapt to counter any attack and regenerate no matter how badly it was wounded. Only one thing could happen when the two of them collided. It was simple, really.

"There is nothing in existence that can survive a strike from the Holy Sword," murmured Teoritta, her voice weak with exhaustion. "…Nothing in existence."

"Yeah."

I pushed the sword in deeper until I felt the tip break something.

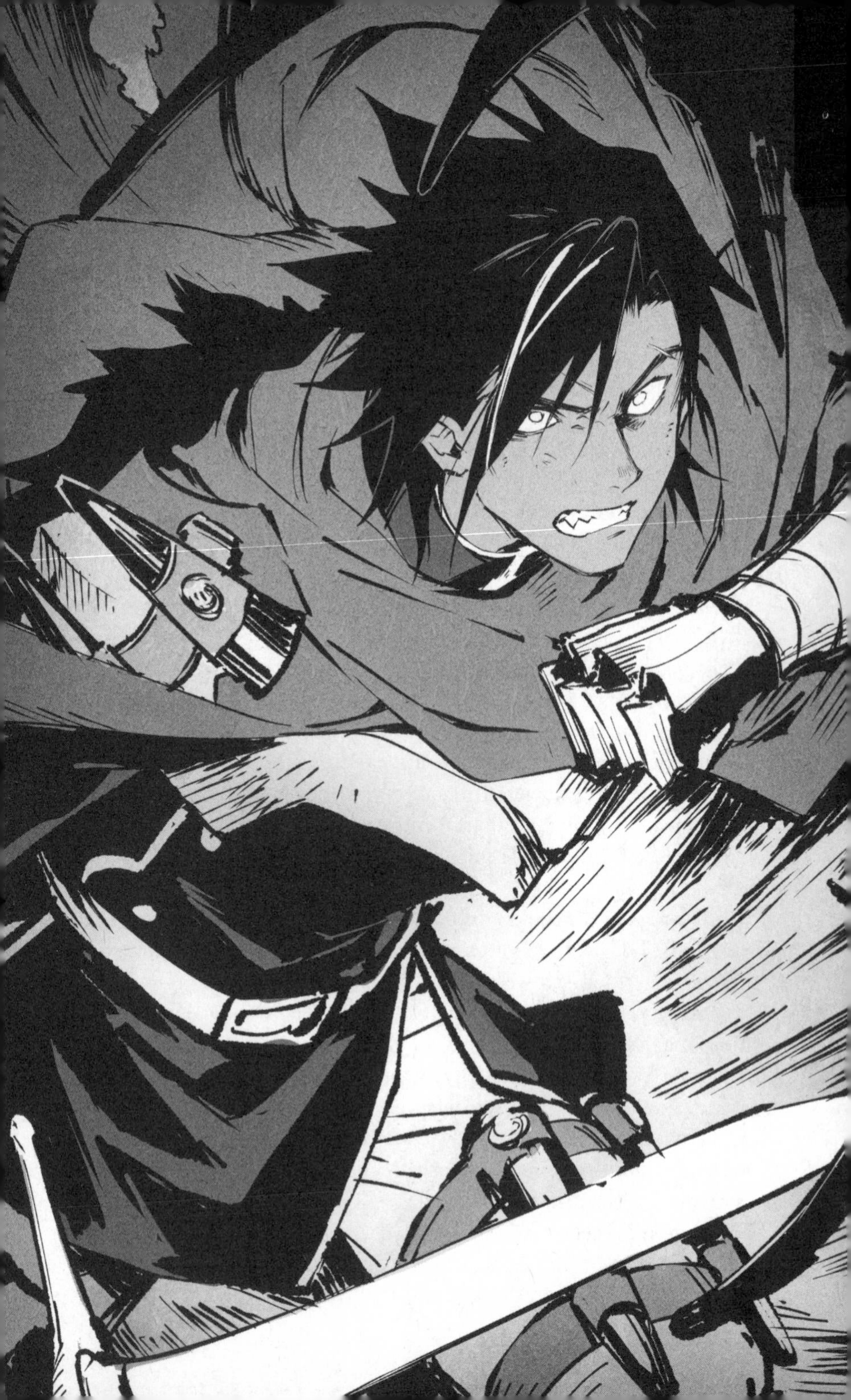

A sharp flash of light surged out from within Iblis's body as wind violently swirled around it. Sparks flew, so bright that I could feel the back of my eyes burning and my head starting to ache. And the very next moment, the enemy had disappeared without a trace.

It was no more.

All that was left was a swirling gust of wind. The instant I pierced it with Teoritta's sword, Demon Lord Iblis ceased to exist.

Incredible.

I looked down at the sword in my hand. Rust covered the blade in the blink of an eye, and before I knew it, the sword had crumbled into dust. There was nothing in existence that could survive its strike. In other words, the sword forbade the existence of any enemy it couldn't destroy.

Teoritta could even summon swords like that. To be honest, it was absurd.

She called it the Holy Sword.

I didn't know of any currently active goddesses who could do something like this. While there were goddesses who could summon weapons, those weapons were mere physical objects. But Teoritta was different, and I was starting to get the feeling that might be pretty dangerous.

"My knight." Teoritta could no longer stand. She was struggling just to hold herself up. "I accomplished something great, didn't I?"

"Yeah, you did."

I was at my limit as well. My shoulder, my back, the side of my stomach, my left arm—I was covered in wounds and had already lost too much blood. I couldn't remain conscious much longer. My vision was blurry, but I could faintly make out the stupid look on Dotta's face as he approached us on his horse.

"You did a great job," I said and rubbed Teoritta's head.

"Right? Which means you accomplished something great as well, my knight."

She grinned from ear to ear as if to say it had all been worth it.

Maybe, just maybe...

Maybe we really could rid the world of the Demon Blight, as long as we had Teoritta on our side. We could find the conspirators in the army and the royal castle, put an end to whatever scheme they were planning, and crush every last demon lord. How nice that would feel.

Hilarious. The delusions of a desperate man.

I laughed at myself. But before, I couldn't even imagine such a thing.

I guess you can't blame me. I won. The undefeated goddess and her knight killed Demon Lord Iblis.

But I couldn't allow myself to show weakness, regardless of how exhausted I was. I used every last bit of strength and stamina I had to lift my head, face Dotta, and say:

"You're late, dum-dum."

But that was all I managed before I passed out.

I woke up to find a man I didn't know standing before me.

He wore a shady smirk as he looked down at me.

Who the hell are you?

I desperately tried to gather my thoughts despite the fog in my brain.

An unfamiliar man, an unfamiliar location, a white ceiling, sheets, a blanket. I could tell I was lying down, but where? A hospital? That made the most sense.

This must be a hospital.

I'd been severely injured while fighting. I could still remember the agony I'd felt as my left arm was almost severed. I'd been on the battlefield. Yes, that's right. I'd fought the Demon Blight, and it seemed I'd been sent in for repairs.

"How do you feel, Xylo?" asked the unfamiliar man. He had a smile on his face, but his tone was insincere and affected. It didn't seem like he was trying to hide it, either. I even detected a note of sarcasm. But no matter how long I thought, I couldn't remember who he was.

"Who the hell are you?" I asked.

"All right, then. Everything seems to be working properly," he said, nodding slightly and turning around to face a woman behind him. I didn't know her, either. What was it about her? She seemed sleepy. She was a tall woman, and she wore a simple white robe with only one hole in it for her head. She must have been from the Temple.

"It's just as you said. He can talk, and he doesn't seem to have any issues with language."

The woman in white didn't say a word in response. She simply nodded slightly and stared into space like she wasn't interested.

Who are these people?

I considered my situation. I'd sustained grave injuries on the battlefield. I was probably sent straight out for repairs. It made sense, considering what I'd been through. So then had I been transferred to this hospital after that? The repair shop was a lot more depressing than this. Plus, this appeared to be a private room. *Look at me. Got my own room now. I must be famous,* I thought.

"There's no need to worry," said the man suddenly. His fake attitude seemed to me like a great reason to start worrying right away. "Fortunately for you, you didn't die. You were on the verge of death, but you made it. Of course, that isn't to say you'll suffer no aftereffects."

"Got it," I said blandly. I felt exhausted. Several parts of my body were numb.

"According to the doctor, you've lost a lot of your ability to feel pain. At least judging by your reactions during the operation. You'll have to be careful."

I figured something like that was possible. Tatsuya was a prime example.

"Soldiers like that die more easily, and we'd prefer you survive whenever possible."

He'd said "we." Something about that bugged me, but the more important question was, who was this guy? He wasn't a hero. I was almost certain of that. I thought back to every member of my unit: Venetim, Dotta, Norgalle, Tatsuya, Tsav, Jayce, Rhyno… I could remember everyone. There didn't seem to be any problem with my memories.

"That means nothing from a guy I don't even know." I glared at him. "I already asked you once. Who are you?"

"Consider me an ally." His laugh was more of a throaty grunt "…On second thought, you don't have to if you'd rather not. Either way, be careful. I'm just glad you're okay. The hero unit is our trump card, after all."

He was talking out of his ass. I didn't trust a word he said. The fact that he wouldn't tell me who he was annoyed me. I hated people who tried to act mysterious. There was only one way to treat guys like him.

"Get lost." I waved a hand in his direction. "I'm gonna be sick if I have to look at those shifty eyes of yours for one more second."

"Ouch. You know, I went through a lot of trouble to sneak over here to see you. It wasn't easy bringing you these presents, either."

The mysterious man held one hand out to the table by his side. I hadn't seen it there. On it were small packages, flowers, and even a big loaf of bread.

The hell is all this?

He must have read my thoughts from the look on my face.

"A token of gratitude to the penal hero unit."

"I don't remember doing anything deserving thanks."

"Oh? From what I've heard, the nearby settlements of Weigerla, Tafka Duha, and Khaosant; the miners of Couveunge Forest and Zewan Gan; and the traveling merchants of Western Riso are all very grateful for what you've done. Of course, you wouldn't know any of their names or faces. But you protected their livelihood when you defended Mureed Fortress. The military's not sure what to do with all this stuff... Oh, right."

The man burst into laughter, as if he couldn't hold it in any longer.

"A few little girls even brought you some flowers just yesterday."

"Whatever. I don't care."

I was lying. I did care. This meant that what I'd done had meaning.

In the face of the Demon Blight, these presents were nothing more than well-meaning trifles. But that was precisely why they had value. Of course I was happy about it, but I wasn't going to let this man tease me. The thought alone twisted up my insides.

"People are calling you the Lightning Bolt, and you're being treated like some mysterious warrior. Maybe because you aren't officially part of the military. But with mystique comes popularity."

"Is this all you wanted to talk about? Get outta here."

"Very well. My apologies. I will respect your wishes," said the man, still smirking. He raised his hands like he was trying to calm me. Or maybe it was a gesture of surrender.

"But there is something I want you to know," he continued. "It isn't just the general public who has their eye on you. There are people in the Temple and the military watching you heroes with—"

"Scram already."

I would have thrown something at him if I had anything nearby. It was probably a good thing I didn't have my knives. The shady man finally gave up, shook his head theatrically, and made his way to the door. The woman dressed like a priest followed him.

"One more thing before I go. Be careful not to violate your orders too often. There are forces out there who consider you heroes an eyesore. Especially you, Xylo."

"To hell with 'em."

Tell me something I don't know, I thought. Couveunge Forest, the Zewan Gan mines, Mureed Fortress—even before all that, since the time I became known as the goddess killer, there were people at the highest levels of the military and the Allied Administration Division who wanted me gone.

"I already know they exist. But who are they?"

"Coexisters," was the man's brief reply. "That is what people call them."

I knew about coexisters. They wanted to promote harmony between humans and the Demon Blight. They had been around ever since the demon lords started appearing but supposedly faded away as the war became more serious. They believed that if you could talk with its creatures, you could negotiate peace with them, even if that meant the enslavement of mankind. In their minds, that was a fair price to pay to secure a tiny sliver of land where they, the coexisters, would rule, managing the slaves and acting as negotiators with the creatures of the Demon Blight. They were scumbags—the worst of the worst, to put it lightly. But I had never expected such a group to gain enough traction and power to set me up and turn me into a criminal.

"Until we meet again." The smiling man opened the door while I was still lost in thought. Then he turned to speak with someone outside the room.

"We're finished, Goddess. You are free to go in now."

"Xylo!"

A small shadow rushed into the room. It was Senerva. A young girl with golden hair and fiery eyes— Wait. A young girl? No. Senerva wasn't this small. Which meant…

"Why are you looking at me like that, my knight?" The young girl stared at me critically…or perhaps her gaze was pleading. "Rejoice, for I came here myself to greet you."

My head hurt. I knew this girl. I traced my memories. She seemed so familiar.

"You are about to make me angry, Xylo." She looked like she wanted to cry. "I will not allow you to forget me—my greatness, my generosity, my compassion…"

I could tell tears were forming in her eyes. I felt like a bully. *Dammit.*

"Xylo, I shall not allow you to forget me…your goddess."

"I didn't forget." How could I say anything else? But my voice was panicked.

"Teoritta." I said her name. "I didn't forget you."

"Good."

"So stop crying."

"I am not crying."

"Really?"

"Really. I am far too dignified to cry."

I smiled as sparks flew from her hair.

"At any rate, I am impressed, Xylo. You deserve praise." She reached out and awkwardly rubbed my head. Sparks jumped off her body.

Eh. Fine.

I decided to allow it. I was so tired that I didn't have the energy to knock her hand away. A woman with a sharp gaze was glaring at me from behind Teoritta, but I ignored her.

"…Xylo Forbartz." The woman, Kivia, put on a grave expression. "Allow me to tell you what happened after you defeated Demon Lord Iblis."

"I'm not in the mood." I frowned.

"No, you need to hear this," Kivia insisted. She really couldn't tell when people were joking. "First, you and Goddess Teoritta are being temporarily lent to the Thirteenth Order of the Holy Knights."

We were being "lent" like pieces of equipment. So nothing had changed. We were still in the same position we started in. I didn't even have the strength to joke about it.

"Goddess Teoritta's situation is still concerning. The military and the Temple are currently debating the respect she is owed. There has been a large shift in opinion due to your overwhelming success at the fortress."

The fact that she was still using such respectful language said a lot about her personality. They were debating the "respect she was owed." In other words, they were discussing how to deal with her. Now that we'd proven how strategically valuable she was, the military was probably split down the middle between those who wanted to dissect her and those who wanted to continue actively using her.

What about the Temple, though?

That was a world I wasn't familiar with, so I could only guess. But if they were playing politics, they might let the military decide as a bargaining chip to pass some other measure, or they might have Teoritta placed in their custody at the Temple using some excuse.

Whatever the case, neither organization was a monolith, and the debate would probably drag on for some time.

"And so, Xylo, you are to continue protecting the goddess," said Kivia.

"If you want me to protect her"—I looked over at Teoritta, who had finally stopped rubbing my head—"then take us off the front line. I haven't gotten a single day of rest since I became a hero."

"Very well. You will not be stationed on the front line for the time being."

"Wait. What?"

I was genuinely surprised. I'd said it as a joke, but as usual, Kivia took me seriously.

"Your job will be to protect Goddess Teoritta while stationed at the port city of Ioff," she said.

"You make it sound like the city's more dangerous than the battlefield."

"It would be wise to assume so," Kivia said. Her face was so serious it was annoying. "There are forces within the Temple who are after the goddess."

I couldn't believe my ears. I thought people at the Temple worshipped the ground the goddesses walked on.

"There are various factions within the Temple," added Kivia. She'd probably picked up on my skepticism. "The most dangerous are those who wish to uphold the goddesses' purity over all else. They call themselves the Orthodox faction, and they refuse to even acknowledge the new goddess Teoritta."

"That doesn't make sense."

"They're purists who believe the goddesses are absolute. The addition or subtraction of goddesses challenges their beliefs. Their numbers are small, but they have been increasing their sphere of influence further and more quickly than expected."

Ridiculous, I thought. Goddesses could die. I knew that all too well. There were even records of a few goddesses dying during the Third War of Subjugation. Had they simply ignored all that?

"These extremists wish to harm Goddess Teoritta. We have uncovered their connection to an order of assassins as well."

"…All right, I've had enough. My head's starting to hurt. Fill me in on the rest later because—"

I looked back at Teoritta. Was this really a conversation Kivia wanted her to hear? But it appeared my concerns were misplaced.

"I expect you to protect me, Xylo. You and the other heroes."

Teoritta grinned from ear to ear as if she couldn't have been happier. Why was she so pleased? Thankfully, I had to wait only a few seconds for an answer.

"We are finally getting some time off, Xylo," she said. "You are to take me out into the city the moment you feel better. Got it?"

"Guess I don't have a choice."

I looked out the window. Winter was almost here. Lead-colored clouds covered the sky, the sign of a coming storm. It would probably snow that night.

My next mission is to protect the goddess.

Venetim would somehow talk his way into some comfy role. As for Dotta, we'd need to tie both his arms if they were going to let him loose in the city. Norgalle would take a leisurely stroll around the market, grabbing whatever he wanted to eat or drink without paying, just like a king. We'd have to prohibit Tsav from going into any casinos or shopping districts. And...

What am I doing?

I couldn't help but laugh. I was enjoying my situation far more than I ever had before—more even than when I was a Holy Knight. Ever since I'd met Teoritta, I'd begun to feel differently. I was genuinely having fun, and that terrified me. Things weren't so bad. I was surrounded by a bunch of numbskulls, and yet I wasn't angry.

"Xylo." Teoritta tugged at my sleeve. "You are my knight, and I order you to hold my hand when we are in town so that I do not get lost."

"Sure thing."

This had happened before.

I remembered a time like this. I tried to think back to the look on Senerva's face and the conversation we'd had—and I couldn't.

"What an honor."

I forced myself to smile.

Hello, everyone. Rocket Shokai here.

I like *kehyarists*. This is a made-up name given to those weak, tropey villains who hide in the attic with a poison-coated knife and leap down to attack the unsuspecting protagonist while yelling *Keh-hyaaa!* before promptly getting their butts kicked.

Personally, these are my favorite kind of villains, so I spend my days thinking about various iterations of them. Allow me to present you with some representative examples as reference, just in case you ever need to act like a disposable mook.

Type A: The Cave Cricket

These villains are cunning and quick. The moment their opponent lets their guard down, they rush out screaming, "Prepare to die!" and attack with poison claws or a poison knife. But they never use lethal poison. Instead, it's always a kind of poison that temporarily paralyzes their enemy. Why? Because there is nothing they like more than beating on the weak. This always ends with their opponent counterattacking and easily defeating them. Whenever you want to play the cave cricket, keep in mind that letting down your guard is key. You want to move like a snake. Make sure you look creepy and move way more than is necessary.

Type B: The Doctor

These guys have a superior intellect and excel in gathering data and analyzing their opponent. But they lack objectivity, and that is always their downfall. They calculate their chances of winning, and it's always something like 100 percent or 99.999 percent, which is highly unlikely. Then when things start going south, they inject themselves with some sort of nerd drug and transform into "the ultimate monster" (their words). Of course, their chances of winning after that are extremely low.

Type C: The Rich Man

These goons are always unrealistically rich, and since they've got an endless supply of money, they can hire countless bodyguards, assassins, ferocious pets, and the like. Unfortunately for them, the more skilled the person they've hired, the more likely they are to betray their employer once they realize how much the move will benefit them. If it's a pet, they'll bare their fangs as if the rich man was their next meal. Where this archetype really begins to shine is when they're about to die, and they're begging for their lives. They'll say something like "If it's money you want, I'll pay! Just name your price!"

This concludes my list of three common *kehyarists*. I really hope it will improve your lives as low-level grunts. Such henchmen still haven't made an appearance in this series. I get the itch to create mooks like this from time to time, but I was able to stop myself thanks to everyone's love and support, and in the end, I safely saw this story to print. I would like to thank you all for reading until the very last word and end the afterword here.